I0589406

A NOVEL
DARKDIARY
P. ANASTASIA

Other books by P. Anastasia:

Grave Burden
ISBN 978-0-9974485-9-7

Exile of the Sky God
ISBN 978-0-9974485-8-0

Fates Aflame
ISBN 978-0-9974485-3-5

The Fluorescence Series:

Fluorescence: The Complete Tetralogy
ISBN 978-0-9862567-7-6

Tell your stories as only you can.
Be brave.

"I will belong to no other." Muffled by the effects of recently ingested poison, my voice was nearly inaudible.

I clasped my hands together near my lips and closed my eyes to absolve myself. It is often said that you will find God when you are near death, but God was not who I sought.

Lingering on the thought, I glanced down at the icy water sweeping over my bare feet. The rocks were slippery and the darkness made it difficult to see anything besides the reflection of the vigilant moon.

With each step, my legs grew heavier—weaker—until I could stand no longer. I slipped and hit the water with a splash.

The current pushed and pulled at my limbs. Coils of seaweed and dead branches weaved themselves into the curls of my hair as my body swayed against the tide. My fingers glided across waterworn stone, indentations in the rocks catching my fingernails.

ോ

Then I felt nothingness.

Life and death battled for my soul, their claws tugging me violently from side to side. The score was easily settled as a wave crashed into my face, filling my mouth and lungs with seawater.

Numb, my limbs no longer responded to my will. As I was dragged deeper through the blackness, my consciousness drifted in and out—my sacrifice to the watery beast, voluntary.

Heavy. Weightless. Then falling forever. Death triumphantly possessed me, a ghostly hand wriggling down my throat to claim my soul. My heart surrendered to the trauma and control over my body faded from my grasp.

A final thought fluttered by and I opened my eyes. Through my blurry, distorted vision, I almost thought I could see him gazing down at me through the ripples of moonlight.

I almost thought I could see him reaching out to me.

ോ

KATHERA

I PRESSED my foot down onto the switch and a dense buzzing noise filled the air. The needle pierced the soft flesh of the inside of her wrist and she flinched.

I lifted my foot. The room went silent.

"Are you going to be alright?" I asked. She stared blankly ahead, preoccupied with something. Following my question, the girl swallowed hard and shifted her weight in the chair.

"Yeah. Y-Yeah," she stammered. "I'm fine. Keep goin'."

But she wasn't "fine."

I could smell fear on her breath. The tension in her blood was undeniable. She smothered her anxiety by biting her tongue and lying to me. Female intuition led me to believe something terrible had happened to this girl, and that she was concealing her memories with denial. And ink.

It never ceases to amaze me how quickly people succumb to decisions born of anger. She would have this mark on her always, and yet she was hesitant to imagine herself *ever* being in a different state of mind.

Pain fades with time, as all things do.

The buzzing resumed, and I carefully traced the arches of the shattered heart tattoo with black ink.

"S-So... where are yours?" she asked, motioning toward me with a nervous grin.

I had known the question would arise eventually. It *always* did.

"Sorry to disappoint, but I don't have any," I replied.

Her jaw dropped. "B-But... you're an artist. How can you *not* have any?" The sharp curve of skepticism in her eyebrows implied that she took me for an amateur, but I'd given the lecture dozens of times in the past. Tonight was like every other night.

I smiled politely. "Tattoos mean something to those who get them, just as this one means something to *you*. They're like a diary entry on a page of skin. That's how I see them." I strapped a smaller needle into the machine and then reached for the white ink. "There isn't a moment of my life I want to carry with me forever."

"Oh," was all she managed to utter. She seemed bewildered still, but acknowledged the legitimacy of my statement and looked back off into the distance.

I was an artist, not a psychiatrist, but the emotions of my clients affected me. Each of them told a story without words, and those stories gave reason to my craft. It *needed* to be done. My drawings yearned to come alive on human flesh and fill a void within their masters' souls.

I changed inks and began shading the heart with red. Ink oozed against the lines of the pattern and I wiped it off frequently as I colored. The popular dark red I used resembled blood and haunted me always, reminding me of my thirst.

"Looks good," I commented, wiping off the final patch of colored ink. She took a deep breath and seemed relieved to know it was finally over.

"Good luck with everything," I said softly to the girl, trying to mind my own business and be considerate, as well. She didn't seem to be listening as I rubbed a thin layer of ointment over the design and then taped a bandage over it. I peeled the gloves off my hands, tossed them into the trash, and watched the girl head off. There was nothing more I could do for her.

At that very same moment, another person walked in through the front door. I could easily hear the heavy patter of his clumsy feet in the other room. Then my nose twitched and wrinkled in disgust. I entered the lobby and wasn't even sure where to begin with the man waiting there.

"Can I help you?" I asked, glancing over his tattered clothing and abhorring the overwhelming stench of alcohol on his breath. The man stumbled closer to me and fiddled with his belt.

"I... uh... want a tattoo," he muttered, the rings on his lips chinking together as he spoke. His fluorescent yellow hair came to a spike atop his head and his body was already covered with tasteless tattoos—none of them my work, *obviously*. He wasn't my usual sort of customer, but I humored him.

"That's what I'm here for. Do you know what it is you want and where you want it?" In my gut, I knew the reply wouldn't be a simple "yes."

"Yeah..." He made a loud sniffing sound and dragged the back of his hand across his lips.

I couldn't smell whether or not there were drugs in his system, but that didn't stop me from thinking it.

"And... I want it on my stuff, here." He fidgeted his hands and jiggled his belt buckle like he was proud of what he was asking for. The stupid grin on his face made me scowl. He was drunk.

I had to remain professional.

"I'm sorry, but I won't do something like that." I pointed to the door. "You'll have to find another artist."

He took another heavy breath, wheezing as he exhaled.

"What's the big deal?" he groaned. "Nothing you haven't seen before, right?"

I clenched my teeth. "I already told you—I won't do it. Now leave, please."

The rising of my voice drew attention.

A figure came from out of the back room and approached

me from behind.

"Is there a problem?" Matthaya asked, his velvety voice remarkably menacing. He took another step and stood beside me.

The unwelcome man staggered backward with fear. Matthaya's piercing green gaze and stern tone could stiffen the hairs on one's neck. He insinuated so much, so subtly.

"Sh—I-I didn't wanna cause trouble." The man's pulse quickened, the fervent thumps resonating in my ears. "I'll leave."

He did, and I rolled my eyes as the repulsive creep slid out the door and back into the streets from which he had come.

"Are you alright?" Matthaya asked, his expression as concerned as always. His fingers brushed against my hand.

I nodded and smiled. "Yes, I'm fine. I was better before *he* came in, but that's business. Things don't bother me the way they used to."

"I know." He walked over to the front door, locked the deadbolt, and then switched off our sign and all the lights in the lobby.

"I'm worried about you," he added. "You aren't yourself tonight."

"It's nothing." I pulled the drawer from the cash register and carried it into the back room.

This was my shop now. We had purchased it a while back after the owner had died.

I had been there, too... when he'd died, I mean.

I had been there, watching it happen.

That's a part of my past I will never forget. That and...

"It was the dream again, wasn't it?" Matthaya walked closely beside me, his gait in sync with mine.

Yes, it was *the dream*, but I feared telling him the truth. It wasn't the first time I had dreamt it, after all.

"It doesn't make any sense." His voice became gruff, and his fingers formed a fist. "There's no reason for it to haunt you still."

Ghastly visions terrorized me as I slept and I could not bear the anguish and guilt each unwelcome visit brought. They had occurred for several days in a row and seemed all too abrupt to be a side effect of anything in particular.

Matthaya took the cash drawer from my hands and set it on the table behind us.

Money meant nothing.

"Sit down." He implored me to rest in a softly padded chair to which he had turned my attention. My head was weary with the endless horrors I endured each night, and he found little comfort in his inability to stop the nightmares. The depression of helplessness slowly crept into his veins and I could feel his sadness growing.

He didn't deserve this. My love for Matthaya was great— so great, in fact, that I had given up my life to be with him. The *least* I could do was be honest.

It was dark in the back room. Matthaya struck a match and lit a stout ivory candle for the sheer novelty of it. Gazing upon the warm flames tamed the beast in me.

He set it down in front of me on the table and a soft yellow glow filled the room, bouncing from wall to wall, playing tricks with our shadows.

My sensitive ears twitched from the clink of two wine glasses as he set them on the table and tipped a bottle over them, filling them with rich crimson liquid. The smell teased my senses with intrigue and delight, like a crisp spring breeze. I took a deep breath and filled my lungs with the aura of its purity and youth.

He took a seat beside me.

"Where did you get this?" I asked, swirling the precious drink around in my glass. Such an indulgence was uncommon for us.

His expression turned dark and defensive. "What difference does that make?" he replied firmly, implying that the source was no longer a concern.

I shrugged and relinquished my query.

My lips pressed against the rim of the glass and I poured the drink slowly into my mouth and swallowed. It left my lips painted with scarlet tint, which reflected back at me in the sheen of the glass. Matthaya mirrored my actions, and we shared a much-needed moment of peace in the darkness.

I still remember when a cup of hot milk could settle my tumultuous pangs, but those days are long gone. I set down my glass and ran the edge of my tongue across my lips, savoring the last trace of infant blood.

Many months had passed since we had tasted humans. We sought to keep it that way indefinitely, but the violent churning of nightmares left me susceptible and weak to its sensual charms. Matthaya knew our eternal hunger well, and he knew that a weakened state left me vulnerable to my lust for young blood.

Modern formalities aside, you could call Matthaya my husband. He rescued me from the mortality that plagues you now. Together we share our lives in the darkness. Together we face our fears... our limitations.

It was a choice that I made not long ago. A choice *we* were forced to make to preserve our feelings for one another. In exchange, we now face the monstrous truth that surrounds the myth that is *"forever."*

There is no morning, no dawn, and no dusk. Spring and summer mean nothing to us. There is only the bitterness of winter and the darkness of night.

And while the virile emotions of surrounding mortals infiltrate my mind, the fiery kiss of passionate love has grown cold to my anesthetized skin.

Matthaya and I share our strengths and our weaknesses. This is our world now and, together, we are damned to spend eternity trapped in the icy shadow of the moon's ghostly light.

My name is Kathera.

I was just like you once.

PALE CANDLELIGHT bounced from headstone to headstone. I closed my eyes to the whispering of the trees, and brisk air kissed my cheeks, making me sigh. Deep breaths of petrichor soothed my nerves with hints of rain and dampened earth. The quiet darkness was my lullaby, and I felt at peace amongst nature and the dead.

The hairs on the back of my neck rose and the sensation made me shiver. I rubbed my arms to chase away the chill, but then a sudden gust of air shook me with its thunderous beat—like the flap of a wing—and the candlelight died.

"What are you doing here?" a stranger asked, concealing himself in the shadows. The menacing tone of his voice sent a wave of goose bumps across my flesh and my pulse began to race. My hearing was very good and I wasn't easily caught off-guard, but he was as silent as a ghost.

"That's none of your business," I replied, squinting at him while my eyes adjusted to the moonlit overcast. His silhouette moved and I tried to follow but quickly lost sight of him in the darkness.

"You shouldn't be here." His breath tickled my ear and I jolted backward with a shriek, swerving around to find him no longer there.

"You shouldn't be here, either!" My voice trembled. He was nowhere to be seen.

No one was allowed on the cemetery grounds after dark. Not even me. I had once met the caretakers of the cemetery. They were two very *old* men. The man speaking had a youthful, silky voice. He had tried to make it unwelcoming, but it simply wasn't. "*You're* trespassing, too," I added, gaining a little more control over my shuddering breaths.

Silence.

I couldn't tell if he was listening anymore.

A hand neared my shoulder and I jerked away, turning to face him. Our gazes met and I gasped.

Phenomenal! His eyes were unnaturally green.

He immediately looked away, but I had already seen them. They were an extraordinarily rich hue—almost mythical. The color of his eyes had me so captivated, I'd forgotten how frightened I was.

"Go home," he commanded, his voice growing huskier,

which snapped me back to reality.

"No. You can't tell me what to do." I straightened up, holding my ground, though I probably shouldn't have.

"Perhaps not." He scoffed as he turned toward me again, his outline still too dark to see. "But I can *make* you go." Brilliant, chemical-green light flared in his eyes, piercing my soul and freezing a breath in my lungs. He reached out to me again with a slender, pale hand, and I recoiled.

"No," I cried, shielding my face with my arms. "I'm at peace here."

The air went quiet and I slowly looked up from behind my hands. He was just standing there, looking at me. He took a step back and a twig cracked beneath his shoe. In the open patch of soft, white light, I finally saw him. He was slightly taller than me and dressed in slacks and a knee-length trench coat. In the darkness, his skin was porcelain and gray. Details were few, but...

"Why?" he asked. "*How* do you find peace amongst the dead?"

I hadn't told anyone else before, but I didn't know the man, and his threats prompted me to be earnest. If he wanted to know the truth, I'd give it to him.

"Because coming to my mother's grave," I paused to compose myself, "is the only thing that keeps me from joining her here."

His dark, arched eyebrows twitched.

"Since I was a teenager, I've had dreams about my own death." My voice softened. "Sometimes the lines blur and there are days when I-I can't shake the visions."

"You shouldn't dwell on such things," he said sternly, as if he'd held a sliver of concern for me. "But you cannot return to this place again," he reiterated.

"I'll return whenever I want!" I clenched my teeth. "Coming here helps me let go of those images for a little while, so I'm not leaving forever just because you're asking me to. You can't stop me, whoever you are."

His dark presence approached my side, as if he were about to walk past, but instead his fingers came up to twirl a lock of my hair teasingly.

I should have backed away, but I was blinded by anger and I refused to budge.

"What makes you think you'll be safe here anymore?" The cool lick of his breath caressed my ear.

I'd probably risked my life every night, walking home from work in the dark—alone. His threats couldn't be more dangerous to me than my own recklessness. I wasn't afraid of him; I was going to stand up to him, and no amount of fear or instinct would sway me otherwise.

I lifted my chin. "You're not here to hurt me or you would have tried to already."

A deep, throaty growl escaped through his teeth and he bolted at me like an animal, the green of his eyes turning poisonously bright. He grasped my throat with one hand and tangled my hair around his other, jerking me backward until my feet slid forward on the slippery grass and my back arched.

"Leave!" The hideous roar nearly deafened me. I struggled to pry his hands away, but his grip was unyielding.

My heart raced and I could hardly swallow as he effortlessly lowered me to the ground. "I will *not* be so kind if you return," he hissed, baring his teeth while looking me straight in the eye.

His irises kept flickering with neon green light.

"Wh-what... are you?" My voice strained beneath his hands.

My feet came out from under me, and I fell.

I hit the ground hard and the thump knocked the air from my lungs. I coughed and quickly sat up in the grass to look around.

He was gone.

I brought my hands up to my neck and massaged my tender throat. He could have killed me if he had wanted to.

What was he?

I stood and swept flakes of dead leaves from my pants.

"I'm sorry you had to see that," I whispered toward the nearby headstone. My mother had encouraged me to avoid altercations at any cost, but I wasn't about to let a stranger push me away from my one and only haven. "I don't know who he is, Mom, but I promise to be more careful... next time."

I took a deep breath and smoothed my ruffled long hair down against my head and neck. The roots stung from his clutch, but the discomfort would pass eventually. My ego was more bruised than anything.

Thinking about how I had let the man get so close to me,

though, made me question my sanity. How could I have let my guard down that easily? What had possessed me to assume his intentions *weren't* lethal? He actually *could* have killed me.

What an idiot I was!

There was an obvious hint of darkness crawling beneath his skin. He wasn't normal. But I wasn't afraid of him. Even though he was threatening me, there was a gentleness in his voice that calmed the very fear he had tried to invoke. Once his icy fingers grasped my neck, the spell was broken and reality set in.

But then his eyes radiated light. Like fireflies in the night, they had glistened with a spark of unexplainable, almost chemical luminescence.

He had wanted me to be frightened. He had wanted me to recoil and retreat from that place *forever*.

It wouldn't happen. My mother's grave was a safer place than any other on a dark night in my city. I picked the locks, I called my own shots, and I knew my way around. It was *my city* and *my territory,* and he would never take that away from me.

I would return to her grave again, tomorrow, and any other day that I wanted to. As long as there was breath in my body.

3

A SECOND cup of coffee did nothing to help with my inability to concentrate. There were colored pens and incomplete sketches scattered to the left and right of me. They were terrible. Every one of them.

Damn. I couldn't focus. If I kept it up, Derek would surely notice and—

"You feelin' okay tonight?"

Too late.

"I'm sorry." I lifted my face up from my drawing and sat back in my chair, crossing my arms.

"Some days, things don't click," Derek said with an understanding smile. He rolled the chair next to me away from the table, spun it around, and straddled it, resting his forearms across the back of it.

For someone who *should* have been mostly concerned with productivity and revenues, he cared a lot about my feelings. Then again, you could say I had become the heart of *Restless Ink*—the shop he'd renamed for my popular artistry. The tattoos I designed often stemmed from the nightmares I'd had; people loved the vision of my works.

But tonight, I couldn't grasp that vision. The dark, quickly fading silhouette of the stranger from last night had dampened my creativity. All I could think about was how I wanted to see him in the light. I wanted to see the face of the man I should have been afraid of—the man with the vivid green eyes.

Derek stretched across the table to scoop together the loose pens. Then he picked up one of my drawings and raised an eyebrow.

"Uh..." He tilted the page before glancing over at me. "Don't push yourself, Kathera," he said, trying to sound unaffected. "Besides, there's someone here who's thinking about getting one of your older designs." He rolled several pens into a bunch in his hands and then tucked them away into a drawer below the desk. "You up for that?"

I chuckled. "I'm always up for that." I could tattoo one of my past pieces onto someone on even my worst day, without a noticeable drop in quality. "I'll make sure they love it. I promise."

Derek's patience in me was a virtue of his, and I was more than thankful for it. If I had lost my job, I don't know what I would have done with myself. Dad had been pushing me to go back to school for some time now, but I had refused. I had always felt like I wasn't cut out for the daily grind, that I was meant for something more.

You could say there's irony in what I do. Every day I make an impact—every day I make a *permanent* mark on someone's life. It makes me happy to draw, whether on paper or skin; it's a canvas all the same. And there's something about knowing that my image can last someone's entire life that makes my work so special to me.

"When you're finished with this client, you can head home." Derek stood from the table and shot me a kind glance with his warm, dark brown eyes. "You seem distracted today. You should get some rest."

That *wouldn't* happen, but I returned a nod of agreement anyway.

There were still so many things to do around the shop before I could go home.

As I sat, etching one of my own creations into someone's calf, my mind kept drifting away, and the outline of another creature occupied my thoughts.

It was just before dusk when I completed my work, and all I could do was hope for a glimpse of colorful twilight before true darkness came.

I gathered my things and headed off down the street, well prepared, with a handful of candles in my bag. Perhaps I would stay a bit longer... *if* he let me.

Nervous feelings whirled inside, but I kept walking, never letting my steps waver even as fear and anxiety tightened my throat and rattled me to the bone. I imagined the horrible things the stranger might try to do to me, but my heart pushed me onward with courage I couldn't explain. My gut feeling was that he was far more bark than bite.

A quick glance left and then right. There was no one in sight, so I climbed over the fence instead of picking the lock of the gate this time. I wondered if he would even come, now that the gate would be closed tightly. How legitimate were his threats?

I unzipped my bag and took out three small votive candles. I placed them along the top of my mother's gravestone, making sure they were aligned and set evenly a few inches apart. I struck a match on the side of the matchbox and lit the candles one by one. The soft, yellow-white glow came to life with a spark, and I took a few steps back to sit on a concrete bench close by and observe.

The skies were clear. The wind was still.

Maybe he won't come.

I watched night envelop the horizon, while the candles sank lower and lower.

Maybe I should have left the gate open.

Maybe...

The shades of gray in the distance changed and my eyes abruptly met his.

I gasped, clutching on to the cold, concrete bench with

both hands.

He was right in front of me, barely a few feet away.

I started breathing again.

"How long have you been standing there?" I asked, trying to downplay my surprise. His silhouette was difficult to make out amongst the shadows.

"You've returned?" The voice was *unmistakably* his.

Candlelight bounced off the sharp curves of his face as he stepped closer.

"Why do you not fear me?" he asked, stopping behind my mother's gravestone and dragging a hand slowly through the candle flames. "Did I not make my intentions quite clear yesterday?" He seemed unaffected by the fire dancing between his fingers.

"I don't know," I replied, sitting up straight, brushing a few locks of my hair behind me. I was strangely relieved to see him again and tried to hide the senseless smile drawing at my lips. "My life at home is a living hell, and I haven't had a good night's sleep in years. Maybe I'm an idiot for coming back, or maybe things just don't scare me as much as they should."

His eyes narrowed and he came out from behind the candles.

He appeared to be close to my age, but something was off. There were well-maintained pleats in his dark slacks and he held himself with great poise. The top button on the collar of his crisp, light-colored shirt was left undone, and the cuffs of his sleeves were fitted perfectly beneath those of his black duster jacket.

His arms somewhat stiffly hung at each side of his waist in military-like fashion. Exquisite posture. Refined hairstyle. For someone with nothing better to do than lurk in grave-yards at night, he was overdressed.

His eyes locked with mine and I struggled to restrain my curiosity and bite my tongue.

Where was he from and, most importantly, why had his eyes glowed the night before?

His appearance provoked many questions. He couldn't have been more than twenty-something, but he was dressed as if he had just stepped off a red carpet. There weren't a lot of wealthy neighborhoods in my city, and none of them were within walking distance.

All dressed up and nowhere to go? Or... no one *else* to... *murder*?

No. I didn't get that vibe from him at all, and I've always been a good judge of character.

I didn't fear him this time and he wasn't in a hurry to try to scare me away, either. It felt surreal.

We remained in excruciating silence for several mo-ments. Words were biding their time until they could get out of my mouth. I tried not to look him over too blatantly, but he was just so... different. I couldn't put a finger on ex-actly what it was that made him seem that way, either.

"How old are you?" I blurted. The question wouldn't stop burning.

He flinched and cocked his head the tiniest bit. If I hadn't known any better, I would've thought no one had *ever* asked him.

"Twenty-one," he whispered. "I think." His brow furrowed.

"You think?"

How did he not know?

"I lose track, sometimes," he added casually, his broad shoulders rising and falling in a shrug.

"I take it most of the parties you attend aren't for your birthday." I smiled, trying to lighten the mood. His expression hardly changed, but a tiny curl tugged at the edge of his lips. "No offense, but you're really composed for someone your age. It made me think you were a little older than that."

An old soul, perhaps. I think that's what people call it.

He could pass for a pretty-boy who had, no doubt, faced some serious hell in his past. His face was clean-shaven, fair, and youthful, but the faint, rusty shadows tracing his eyes told a different story.

"Genetics, maybe," he said, with an unconscious brush of his hand through his hair. The thick, subtle curls ended at the nape of his neck. Parted unevenly, some tumbled across his brow on one side. A few shorter locks rested just across the tops of his ears and framed his temples with a ripple of wispy, dark tresses. The onyx waves looked temptingly soft as I imagined my fingers combing through them.

"Maybe." I shrugged, shaking off the childish admiration manifesting from my curiosity. There was much more than "genetics" at work in him. Grandpa's well-aging good looks probably won't make your eyes give off supernatural light. Unless, of course, Grandpa had it, too.

I wanted to keep prodding him for answers, but I didn't want to push him away. His voice was soft and truthful, but also guarded. I had a feeling he spoke only in partial truths for his own protection. There may have been a great deal of pain and regret inside him, cloaked in indifference.

I wanted to learn all about it.

Maybe he'd tell me the answers, in time.

He sat down on a nearby, broken headstone and studied me, staring hard into my eyes. Being the center of attention made me nervous.

"Why do you *really* come here?" he asked. "Aren't there people out there who want to spend time with you?" He rested his hands, one in the other, in his lap and leaned closer.

"I don't make friends easily," I replied.

"What about your family?"

"I'm an only child. My father works dead shifts at the hospital ER. I hardly ever see him."

"And your mother is..." He glanced at the headstone in front of me.

"She died when I was twelve."

"I'm sorry to hear that." He looked at his hands.

"I got over it. My father remarried and my stepmother is horrible. He just doesn't know it." I sighed and adjusted myself on the bench. "And if she has it her way, he never will."

The stranger went silent. He was gathering his thoughts,

I figured. It seemed fitting for him to be in deep contemplation.

"So you've been coming out here for a while I take it," he said. "It's no wonder you put up such a fight. You *should* protect what is important to you." His eyes met mine, more intimately than they had all night, and he bowed his head slightly. "I apologize for my actions the other night." His voice softened considerably. "I had no right to touch you. No man should *ever* place his hands on a woman without her consent." He finished with a shake of his head and a guilt-ridden look away from me. He tangled his fingers together in his lap. "And certainly *never* the way I did."

His confession was refreshing.

"I don't regret my stubbornness," I said, stealing another glance from his exquisite emerald eyes. "It was worth it to see your face in a better light."

"Speaking of light." He motioned toward the candles, which were hardly aflame now that the wicks had burned down to nubs.

I shot up and pulled another one from my bag. "I have more." As I bent to tip the wick of a new candle into a dying one, the man stood.

"You shouldn't be out here alone at this hour," he said, looking sternly toward me.

"Stay, please." I lifted a hand, but he was already distancing himself.

"The night grows short and you should go home."

His face disappeared into the shadows as he turned

away from me and my heart sunk.

"You never told me your name," I said, eager to regain his attention.

The side of his face reemerged, as he turned halfway to reply.

"And neither did you."

"It's Kathera."

He turned away again and his silhouette vanished into the night.

I was left with silence and an intense urge to gaze into his remarkable eyes once more—the captivating green irises that must have concealed incredible secrets.

4

MATTHAYA

MY NEWFOUND weakness sickened me. It was difficult enough to go unnoticed along the streets of brightly lit cities after nightfall, but *she* was too close to my new residence.

This city would be no different than the last. Those who wandered into my territory would feel my wrath; the boundaries of my solitude would quickly be made known to trespassers large and small.

But the girl—Kathera—did not fear me as she *should* have. Surely a second fright should have sent her scurrying back to her mortal matters. Surely... I could have tightened my grip upon her throat the night before.

But, no.

Things were not easy anymore. My conscience was plagued by my past, feeding my ever-growing lust for solitude. It wasn't violence I sought. It was silence.

I had never been eager to gain friends, and enemies were few in my world, but peace and quiet never came without a price. And now, that price had become the strange girl who took refuge in a place too close to my own dwelling. It was something that could not be ignored, though finding an appropriate solution was perplexing.

It was the thought of her that kept me stirring long into the daylight hours—long past the hours I would have *normally* rested in the sanctity of my darkened room.

It wasn't safe for a young woman to be out in the streets past dusk. Perhaps she had done it dozens of times before I had come around, but it would only take one heartless individual to ruin her for life. If I had gotten that close to her without her noticing, who or *what* else may do the same?

Why did I care?

Why was she so unafraid of me?

She had told me herself that finding sanctuary in the cemetery made her resist my threats, but how she could live with constant nightmares was beyond comprehension.

Another thing... the night before, she had clearly seen my eyes—as I had made no attempt to hide their fire—and yet, she had not questioned me about what I was.

I sat wondering... and worrying about her intentions—disgusted by her fearlessness but curiously attracted to her story.

Those who do not change will die. Vampires cannot die as humans do but, instead, grow stagnate and weary when deprived of knowledge and learning. My restlessness that day left me hungry for more. I wanted to know why she made my spirit uneasy.

I had to confront her again. I had to learn the story behind the girl who did not fear the evil inside me.

As expected, she was there the next evening. Alone, accompanied by nothing more than dim candlelight and her dead mother's soul. I shouldn't have bothered. I *really* shouldn't have given a damn about her... but she was human. She was human, just as I had been and would never be again.

I wasn't sure how to approach her this time, or whether or not she would be pleased to see me again. I watched from the distance as she closed her eyes, took in a deep breath of midnight air, and exhaled slowly.

A sigh—a delicate expression renounced to my curse.

"I was hoping you'd come," she said softly, a reserved smile forming on her lips.

I had been utterly silent in the darkness, but she had still known I was there. There was no use remaining in the shadows any longer, so I took a few steps out into the flickering candlelight.

Kathera's skin was very fair—as if the sun had never touched it. Her unnaturally dark, burgundy-red hair fell in long, flat tresses across her back and shoulders, held out of her face only by tiny pins behind her ears. Fine bangs framed her eyes and forehead just above her auburn eye shadow.

"What is it?" She uncrossed her legs and rested her palms on the knees of her black jeans.

"I apologize." I broke my stare and took a seat slightly closer to her this time, on a small concrete bench a few feet from her. I couldn't help but study her; it wasn't often I stopped long enough to learn a person's name, let alone commit to a conversation.

There were questions I sought to ask, but the nerve to ask them escaped me. I was distracted by the pale flesh of her shoulders at the straps of her teal, sleeveless blouse. My intrigue alone was quite foreign. Attraction to human features was something I hadn't experienced for centuries, but the gentle color and *scent* of her skin enchanted my sensitive receptors.

"I need to ask you something," she said, tangling her fingers together in her lap.

I knew, already, what it was.

"Promise me you won't run from me if I ask this," she pleaded, leaning forward.

Her voice was soothing to my ears, but the question, regardless of how I answered it, was a dangerous one. Still, I tipped my head to her in agreement. Curiosity had bound us and I was willing to put aside my better judgment.

She seemed troubled by the inquiry and fidgeted nervously with her hands.

"What makes you believe I am so *extraordinary?*" I asked, forcing a reply from her. "That I haven't deceived you?"

"I've worked with hundreds of people—dozens of strangers and self-proclaimed freaks," she said. "You aren't anything like them. I saw your eyes glow and I know it wasn't some kind of contact lens trickery." Her fingers combed her bangs from her brow. "It was brief, but I saw it. You're not like me."

"I once was!" My voice rose unintentionally. I was more offended than I should have been.

"Then tell me your story," she whispered, remaining calm despite my outburst. "Please." Her eyes met mine with an honest, compassionate gaze and she scooted toward the edge of her bench. Her elbows rested on her knees and her palms came together below her chin.

My secrets had never been known by more than a few mortals, and they had all taken them to their graves. It was dangerous to share such history. The details of my *condition* seem poisonous to those who learn them. It is painful to keep such knowledge private, as the need to share it tends to form a deep burden in one's soul. It can eat at you for life and destroy you with delusions of immortality and power. I did not want the charms of my paradox to seduce yet another.

But, perhaps, there were some things I *could* tell her.

"What can you offer me in return?" I asked. "If you want answers, I want compensation for my time."

Kathera's eyes narrowed as she sat back and crossed her arms in a brief study of me.

There wasn't anything she could possibly—

"A friend," she said softly. A shy smile grew across her lips. "Maybe?"

A friend?

Did I look like I needed one?

"A... friend? That's your offer?"

She shrugged, her smile fading.

It seemed silly at first, but the more I considered it, the sweeter the suggestion became. She fascinated me for reasons I could not yet grasp. It was more than the scent of her innocent blood that drew me in—there was something far beyond that pulling me toward her company. Sitting near her had me briefly forgetting what I truly was, and that was more than I could have asked for from anyone.

Without further gesture, I stood. "Very well." I offered her my hand.

She got up from her bench and reached out to shake my hand. Just as her fingers met mine, she let out a small yelp of surprise. The soft blue of her eyes nearly vanished beneath the startled black of her swelling pupils. My skin was abnormally cold—a fact mortals found difficult to acclimate to.

The beat of her heart pulsed through her trembling hand and my head throbbed in unison with its sound. "Your heart is racing." There was a tinge of irritation in my words.

She cupped her other hand over mine and lowered her head.

"Please, tell me what you are," she said, her voice straining beneath her heaving breath. "So I can put my imagination to rest." She fell to her knees and clutched my fingers tightly. "I won't tell anyone—I swear it. I swear it on my mother's grave."

Astounding.

Kathera was a courageous young woman with a heart clearly burning with passion and inquisitiveness, but there was no need for her to beg of me so. I was no more impressive a creature than she, and possibly even less.

I knelt down on one knee to meet her and her eyes rose to mine. Her lip trembled and her deep, sapphire eyes begged for my honesty.

"Calm yourself," I whispered. "You are correct in believing that I am not like you, but you're not ready to learn the truth about what I am."

I stood and politely stretched my hands out to her. She grasped them and pulled herself to her feet.

I squeezed her warm fingers.

"You shall stick to your promise, Kathera."

"The same for you, I hope."

I released her.

"What do you want to know?" I asked.

"Your name." She lowered her hands to her sides. "May I please know your name?"

It had been a long time since anyone had asked.

"Matthaya."

Her smile broadened, exposing her teeth.

"Matthaya," she echoed, lovingly. I'd never heard it spoken so melodically before. "That's a beautiful name. Where does it come from?"

"I don't know," I replied with a partial shrug. "I never knew much about my family. As a child, I learned little of my heritage and, as an adult, I have never had the urge to do research."

Who I had been back then hadn't mattered after I had become the wretched thing I was now.

She bit her lip and looked off into the distance.

"What is it?" I asked.

She hesitated.

"Kathera?"

"I take it you're not *really* twenty-one. Are you?"

A faint chuckle flitted through my lips.

"Anatomically, yes, but chronologically, I am much older than you. In fact, I have been around for more years than this city has been in existence."

Kathera sat back down on her bench and gazed at her dying candles with a sullen glance. "It must be hard living so long... losing many friends."

It *was* very hard.

"I've learned that it is by far easier to *not* make friends than it is to lose them."

"Oh." She sighed as if she already feared that she, too,

would someday be lost to me. "Are there others like you?"

"There are few," I replied. "I've rarely run into a pair or two in my travels, but they are not the best companions."

I hated what I was, but I hated what *they* were even more.

"We choose our own paths. We make our own decisions about how we treat mortals and... immortals. Some prey on humans and some do not."

Kathera's eyes widened and the word "prey" formed silently on her lips. She shuffled an inch closer—nearly on the edge of the bench.

"What do *you* see them as?" she asked.

I scanned her face. In comparison to her peers, she was quite pretty. There was uniqueness in the rounded curves of her ivory features that made her beautiful in her own way. Her full lips were colored with deep brown stain and her cheeks were barely pinker than the rest of her skin.

Going back to her question, I recalled my limitations and formed a response.

"Frozen visions of the life I cannot have... the things I cannot do, and the friendship I shall never possess."

5
KATHERA

LISTENING TO his words made my heart ache. They were full of passion and disdain. I wanted to reach out and touch him—to comfort him somehow—but he'd likely recoil if I tried.

His head fell and his hands dangled haplessly in his lap. A few fine locks of hair tickled the front of his ears, but he pushed them away from his face a moment later.

"You have my friendship now," I said, in an attempt to ease his pain. "I hope I can prove to you that it is worth having."

He looked away stoically, a master at hiding his feelings even when it was probably healthier for him not to.

"Life is not worth living when you have no one to share it with," he spoke. "A friendship, no matter how long it lasts, shapes you and makes you who you are." Matthaya's eyes met mine again; they had been doing that a lot tonight. Their beautiful green color put me at ease.

"So," he began, softly, "why do you hate your life so much?"

I had never hated life.

I had only hated *her*.

"I *don't* hate life. I hate my stepmother. Everything was fine until she came along and made every day hell."

There was a subtle movement of his feet and I noticed him fighting the urge to move slightly closer.

I ignored the hope that he would do so, just in time for him to ask me another question.

"What has she done that has made you so miserable?"

Opening old wounds made my chest tighten. I swallowed the pain in an attempt to be strong in front of Matthaya.

"When I was fourteen, my father gave me an adorable little collie puppy to keep me company. I named her Reverie—*Dream*. She would sleep beside me on my bed every night and help chase away my sorrow. Then, my father remarried when I turned sixteen and Aldréa, my stepmother, told me the dog had to go because of her so-called allergies."

"Did you give her up?"

"No." I gritted my teeth. "But I should have. She might still be alive today."

Matthaya's brow wrinkled and his lips curled with

disgust.

"She killed Reverie. Aldréa did." My fingers curled around the edge of my bench and tightened even as the concrete dug painfully into my palms.

"Why?"

"I refused to give her away. So she poisoned her and told my father it was an accident. 'She got into some rat poison,' she told him. It was a lie. Ever since that day, I've been tormented by nightmares. All of my good dreams died with that dog."

The memory of seeing poor Reverie's dead body sprawled across the backyard was painful, and as much as I sucked in my tears, a few still escaped my eyes.

I just *had* to be strong in front of him.

I *had* to be brave.

I took a deep breath. "It was just a dog, I know, but..." I cleared my throat and wiped my face quickly, hoping he wouldn't notice.

A cold sensation swept over my knuckles and I turned. Matthaya's mystic green eyes penetrated mine and his outstretched arm rested a set of fingers atop my hand.

"A friend is a friend... no matter what kind." His soothing voice was assuring. "She had no right to take her away from you."

His touch, however cold and unusual, *was* comforting. He looked into my eyes and I could almost feel the softness of the face I'd never touched. One sincere look from his hauntingly beautiful eyes left me feeling like I had known him forever... like I could trust him with my life.

What the hell was I thinking?

I'd known Matthaya for only a few days, but my inherent fascination with him was obvious. Too obvious.

The smoothness of his voice enchanted me and his glances sent me reeling into the majestic green sorcery that was his gaze.

This wasn't a crush.

I had a dozen logical reasons to fear him and yet I didn't. I refused to. He was a shy creature, indeed, but my courage had rewarded me with his trust. And now... his touch.

He pulled back and took a broader look at my face. An unsettled expression washed across his face; his fingers slipped from mine and he stood.

"I have to go." He withdrew several feet from me in an instant.

"What? Why?" I stood. "What have I done?"

I could barely make out the shaking of his head in the fading light of my candles as he moved further and further into the shadows.

"Matthaya, please!" I strained. "Where are you going? What did I say?"

"Goodbye," he said, his voice nearly inaudible from within the darkness.

He was gone.

In the blink of an eye, he was gone.

I couldn't get used to it—the way he'd come and go like the wind. Frightening one moment and concerned the next, but so wary of his presence that he wouldn't stay long. He was nervous, reserved... whatever you want to call it.

Had I said something? Had I looked at him the wrong way?

There was no telling.

I took a deep breath and exhaled. My heart was racing.

I wanted to understand him. I wanted to know what secrets and treasures he clung so tightly to. Somehow, I knew he had told me them before. I knew his eyes had once put their trust in me—and that he would learn to trust me again.

I struggled with this thought. How I could know him and he not know me? How could I feel so right by his side and so unnerved by my inability to recall why? When I looked into his eyes—those electric green irises—I felt something: a closeness I couldn't explain. They were familiar somehow.

Why?

The candles burned out and I poured off the excess wax before tucking them back into my bag.

How had I upset him so quickly?

My stomach churned with nausea as I contemplated what I could have done and what had driven him away. I was angry with myself.

It felt so empty in the graveyard without him there and it wasn't something I had felt before we had met. I had always felt soothed and comforted by the dead of night and the memories of my mother, but now...

I felt so empty...

6

MATTHAYA

IT WAS warm, powerful, and spiced with the richness of her pheromones. I had smelled similar essences before but never with such potency. Kathera *was radiating attraction,* suddenly and without the slightest forewarning.

A few words... a glance and... it hit me. She drew toward me with instant passion, and I was caught completely off guard. Stunned by her subconscious motion, I had no choice but to leave and to do it with haste.

Attraction was a fatal game to play with creatures like myself. The scent of her fear was soft and well-hidden, but the intense desire welling up inside her breast was utterly unnerving.

I don't think she even recognized it—most people can't. But it was impossible to misinterpret with my uncanny ability to detect variations in mortal scents. What mortals may observe in a glance or an expression, took only a sniff for me to decipher.

Something had changed in her, and the soothing peace of her company had become dangerous territory.

The rest of my night was spent pacing, lost in thought within my quarters. The thick piled carpet beneath my feet began to show a dashed trail from my footsteps.

It was too soon.

I had scarcely grown accustomed to this new city and I already found myself entangled in a mess of emotions with a mortal girl. I'd felt the air of delicate crushes before, yes, but this was powerful.

The last time I'd dealt seriously with something of this magnitude had been before—back when I had still been human.

I had never had more than a few possessions with me at any one time, but my most prized and coveted piece of all was suspended gracefully at the center of the wall above the fireplace.

Misplaced for many years but finally acquired, it was a very old oil painting of a girl I had once known. The thick curls of her glorious copper-red hair fell delicately across her shoulders and her restrained smile was hardly what I had known her for. There was such innocence in the gentle curve of her fair-skinned face and faintly blushing cheeks. Her mischievous sky-blue eyes concealed a dark secret from the artist who had painted them that day.

Faded and weathered from centuries of travel and mistreatment—not by me—I still remembered what it had looked like the day it was made. The colors had been radiant. The detail had been superb and the model... uncooperative *at best*.

I could still almost feel the fiery touch of her fingers drawing across my skin even as her image loomed above me. In all her grace and beauty, Kathryn had been the *only* girl I would ever love.

It was the year 1606. I was only about six years of age in a large, unfriendly land known as Ireland. At least, it began as such.

Four centuries later, I can vividly recall the day I was separated from my mother. My father had recently passed away and she had been forced to give me up to a life of indentured servitude right before she fell victim to the same fate. I was luckier than most; the family who took me owned a large plantation near the shore. The owner was of English descent, his wife was Irish, and together they had a tiny little girl whom I mirrored in age.

On the first day of the traumatic beginning of my new life, my mother knelt down to the ground, cupped my face in her warm, weathered hands, and smiled hard to keep herself from sobbing. Her fingers drove through my hair and then she pulled me to her chest in a tight embrace.

"You are meant for great things, my son," she whispered, the warmth and love of her words distracting me from the reality of what was happening. "I hope God will forgive you for my sin."

With those words drifting hazily through my young mind, I was taken away by the strong hand of the man who was Kathryn's father.

The first night was hell for me in that place. Not one man or woman in the household glanced at me a second time. Curled up on the hard floor of the pantry alcove inside the massive servants' hall, I did not sleep at all. My mother would return for me. I was sure of it. But the vacant darkness suggested otherwise.

Morning came, and amongst the bustle of servants doing their chores, I saw a glimmer of blue color beaming my way—a tiny red-haired girl in a frilly, white dress was watching me from the hall.

I ignored her stares and sat in a corner up against a cupboard door where I rested my face in my lap... and cried.

Not long after, she approached me. She did it carefully— tip-toeing closer so as not to startle me. I lifted my damp face from my knees and looked toward her shyly, embarrassed to let a girl see me disheveled.

At first, little happened between us, but I felt a comforting warmth in her tender smile. And then she knelt down onto the dirty floor at my feet, cupped my cold, shaking hand between hers, looked me straight in the eye and said, simply, "Let us be friends."

6.1

1616

IT WAS rumored that Kathryn Shallon carried the blood of an ancient king in her veins. Though she may have had royalty in her genes, her father cared very little for his mixed-breed Irish mutt and often disregarded his daughter. Despite the intentions of her mother to segregate us in light of his negligence, Kathryn and I became very close friends, growing up in the same, majestic household.

I spoke little at first, though I knew very well how to. It was not long before our lives united and both English and Gaelic words were common between us. She spoke with an elegance acquired from her noble lineage and I was quick to learn the differences in the languages spoken by the separate classes to which we belonged. I used each dialect only where it would be considered acceptable by those around me.

It was overlooked by Kathryn's parents in the beginning—our closeness. Like a brother, I was both cohort and confidant in every scheme she plotted. I grew with her and she passed her knowledge of reading and writing on to me so that I would not be ignorant in the eyes of others.

She may have been born of higher status, but the years of time spent at each other's sides and the hours of teaching she shared with me made us much more than servant and master. And though I always had work to do, there were brief hours of fading light and early dawn where we found the time to speak to one another.

It was an age when a man's life was worth only as much as the change in his pockets, and I had none. Still, I was determined to arm myself with what currency I could. It was uncommon for a servant to be educated in the higher arts of calligraphy and inflection, but I took pride in my decision to secretly master them both. And I will always be grateful to Kathryn for lending me her patience as my teacher.

Things were fine with my quiet new life. I spoke to few, complained of nothing, and kept to myself during the day as I worked around the manor. Everything was as it should have been.

Until we changed...

When our eyes met, Kathryn would return a shy glance. Her breath quickened whenever I approached. Her fingers often brushed against mine, inadvertently, or so she wanted me to believe. I, too, felt a disturbance in the air between us.

The angelic curves of her face and the subtle blush of her cheeks became apparent to me. Her eyes bluer than the sky. Her lips the color of frosted rose petals.

Words were harder to find, and the scent of her presence filled me with new thoughts and desires—desires I cursed myself for conceiving at all. And so, I ignored them. With all of my might I pushed my feelings aside in order to preserve the friendship we had. In her world, it was not within my rights to feel the way I did.

Kathryn called for me one evening, just before the sun had begun to sink below the horizon. I hesitantly obeyed and went up to her room. It wasn't the childish snickers from the young servant girls that discouraged me from going, but the unsettling and increasingly frequent glances of suspicion I'd recently begun to receive from Kathryn's mother. Her father, on the other hand, took little notice of our meetings and sometimes ignored my presence altogether.

When I approached, she sat on the edge of her bed and motioned for me to partially close the door for privacy. As always, I did as I was told, but the creaking of the iron hinge planted a seed of guilt in me this time.

She held out her hand and curled her fingers inward, drawing me closer. Reluctantly, I neared her bedside and watched as she pulled a white handkerchief from a plate, uncovering a sumptuous array of baked sweets.

"For you, Matthaya." Her voice was pleasant as her hand

gestured to a space beside her on the bed.

She had always done this for me—saved bits from dinner. *"You deserve more than you are given,"* she'd always say. Her kindness comforted me on my darkest days.

Some of my duties were pleasurable—working with the family horses was a secret escape I treasured—but beyond that I'd often find my hands calloused and aching, my skin burnt red by the sun's rays. Working with the animals. Repairing the things I knew how to repair and learning to fix those I did not.

I had been worked very hard with burdens no man should have had to endure, but I had no other choice, and I was not the only one. It was the world I had been given into and the life I had been forced to live. One my mother likely endured, as well, but I would never know.

"Sit with me," Kathryn requested, a sweet smile curling at her lips.

I hesitated, looking down at my tattered clothes. The sweat was still moist on my brow, my hands not their cleanest, and I feared the dirt might tarnish her rare silken coverlet.

"It's alright, Matthaya," she assured with a sweep of her auburn lashes, patting her hand on the bed near her hip and grinning to soften the command. "Sit."

I did as she had asked and sat beside her. She put the plate onto my lap and took one of the sweets for herself.

Kathryn's manner of eating was anything but dainty, and I chuckled at the way she quickly munched down the small treat.

"It's not polite to stare," she sneered jokingly, wiping a crumb from her lower lip.

My eyes returned to the biscuit in my own hand and I brought it up to my mouth.

A small bite of it was all it took for me to relish the elegant texture and sweetness. It may have been a small thing for her to share, but it was a piece of heaven to my taste buds, just as staying within Kathryn's company was a moment of paradise in my otherwise chaotic day.

"Your eyes are beautiful," she said, as if she had just noticed them.

"What?" I looked up, half of a biscuit still pinched between my fingers.

"Matthaya, you have magnificent eyes," she continued, reaching out to graze my cheek with her fingertips. My brows twitched from the contact. "Like the emeralds of a Celtic crown, they shine—strong and brilliant. I'll never forget them…" Her voice trailed off as she lovingly fixated on me.

I wanted to retort, but heard a soft patter of footsteps in the hall and realized our conversation was now over.

"I must go." I stood and tucked the leftover sweets into a pocket in my tunic.

"Wait," she said, tugging at my sleeve as I turned. Her romantic blue eyes glistened with concern. "I want to help you," she whispered, her gaze intensifying. "Please, Matthaya, return to me on the morn tomorrow. There's something I wish to do for you."

Kathryn's mother paced the halls just outside her room.

I had already long outstayed my welcome in the house. I *had* to leave.

I nodded in agreement and flashed a gentle smile along with it.

"Yes, Milady."

She chuckled.

"To you, I am only Kathryn," she corrected. "And I am *always* your friend."

Her eyes embraced me with their compassionate gaze and an unfamiliar layer of maturity garnished her voice.

I left the room and spotted her mother, Lady Maria, a few doors down. To avoid a confrontation, I bowed and swiftly dismissed myself from her presence.

Kathryn's mother had her suspicions about our relationship, so I had to be watchful of my actions. I could not escape Kathryn's heightened feelings for me, or my own constant thoughts about her, but we had to keep them hidden from everyone—including each other.

6.II

1616

I COULD not act against Kathryn's will. Per her request, I met with her the next morning at dawn.

Her father was out on business for the day, so that was at least one less stress on my mind. I feared him more than any other, as he was less forgiving and more foreboding than Kathryn's mother. I had heard—and seen—horrible things happen while Lord Shallon was intoxicated, but he was even worse sober. Impatient. Provocative. He would strike someone down over a rumor before confirming its validity, and I cringed at the idea of what would happen should he misinterpret my situation with his daughter.

I swallowed my fears and entered Kathryn's room. She

motioned for me to shut the door, completely this time, and then pulled open her window curtains. Sunlight burst through, washing across her skin like heaven's light. Morning glow poured over her, embellishing the gentle folds in her shimmering, green satin dress and setting the long curls of her red hair aflame with copper sheen.

Kathryn stepped closer, pulled a chair up behind me, and then took a seat directly across from me in another chair. She plopped down and a porcelain bowl of water swished around in her lap. There was a washcloth already fully saturated and resting at the bottom.

She withdrew the cloth, wrung out most of the water by making a tight fist, and then opened her fingers and brought the rag up to my brow. I wanted to squirm and pull away, but my body refused to budge once the cool moisture wicked my forehead. The fresh water soothed my face and I closed my eyes as her fingers guided it over my skin.

It was surely a sin for a lady to tend to a servant the way she did, and I wanted to tell her that. But her attention was so heartening, I couldn't resist letting my shoulders relax and allowing my weight to sink deeper into the chair.

She swept a stray lock behind my ear. My lashes rose and I looked her in the eye. Her breath stopped and the cloth fell from her hand, splashing into the water bowl.

"What? What is it, Kathryn?" I asked, startled by her silence.

Her hands grasped my face and a thumb slid across my cheek.

"Matthaya." She paused to look me over. "Behind all that dirt and hair, you are very beautiful."

What!?

"No!" I pulled my face from her grasp and hissed. "If your father were to hear you, he would kill us both." Her honesty was kind to my ears but painful to my heart—we were not at liberty to think such things and the struggle to ignore them grew more difficult with age.

"I'm not finished with you!" She pulled on my arm hard as I attempted to stand.

"You cannot change who I am," I growled, flopping reluctantly back down onto the chair. "This will not alter the way *they* feel about our friendship." I crossed my arms and tucked my hands into the bends of my elbows.

Metal clinked as she took a small pair of shears into her hand.

I didn't like being touched, but...

"You *do* know how to use those? Don't you?" I asked, a hint of sarcasm in my voice.

She said nothing in reply and wrinkled her lips angrily to one side. I looked away.

Lock by lock, unkempt pieces of my hair drifted to the floor. A frightening amount of hair was coming off.

She took a small comb from her dresser and ran it through my hair, brushing more to one side than the other, some back behind my ears and then the rest down against the nape of my neck. I rubbed the base of my neck with my fingertips and looked back toward Kathryn, who was now holding a dainty mirror in her hands. It was odd, indeed, feeling nothing where hair had once been.

A groan slipped from my lips involuntarily as my reflection was revealed. "It's too... plain." I raked both hands through my hair and ruffled it between my fingers to give it more life. "Otherwise, it's wonderful," I noted with a grin. "Much better. Thank you."

Kathryn sighed in relief.

She didn't argue with my adjustments and turned to gather a pile of fabric from atop her dresser. She handed the stack of clothes to me and I stiffened.

They were her father's.

"He disposed of them years ago, Matthaya," she said. "And I assure you they have long since been forgotten."

The jacket was made of fine linen, deep ruby-colored and looked to be my size. I pulled my arms through the sleeves, shrugged it over my shoulders, and marveled at its near-perfect fit. Both the color and texture were exquisite— something the likes of which I had rarely seen and certainly never possessed.

Though it sorely matched my dingy off-white tunic, the jacket felt good—wonderful against my skin—and I couldn't help but smile at the way it fit me.

But as I turned my wrist over to study the details, a fine pair of silver cufflinks snagged my attention.

"Are you *certain* your father does not want these?" My thumb massaged the soft fabric again.

"Yes." Kathryn nodded. "I am certain of it."

My stomach churned anxiously. Her father was a horrible person and I wanted no part of him—even if it meant giving up the one piece of finery I could have called my own. What I would have given to wear something as fine as it in Kathryn's presence. But it wouldn't change me or my place in society. Nothing could.

I slid the jacket from my arms, folded it neatly, and then stood and handed it back to her. "You can dress me however you wish, Kathryn, but it will not alter the reflection I cast."

"I am not trying to change you." Kathryn's voice broke and she hugged the folded jacket close to her chest. "I swear it, my love."

"Your *love*?" I echoed bitterly. "I am no one to your family. I am nothing to those above me, and despite how you may disregard the fact, that *does* include you." I turned to leave. "Regardless of what you believe, Kathryn, I will never have permission to love you."

She gasped and I immediately made the regrettable mistake of looking back at her. Her pupils were enlarged and her eyes were pink around the edges—the whiteness in them shining with the threat of tears.

Everything she had done for me had been out of the love and kindness of her heart. She had been my friend for as long as I could remember and I could not stand to see her cry.

"I appreciate your good intentions," I said in a quieter tone, approaching her. "But I cannot help but fear that others will misinterpret them."

Her frown radiated with sorrow dark enough to shake the heavens. Her smile had always been uplifting and angelic, but her sadness hollowed out my body like death seizing a victim.

"Please!" I took a step closer and cupped her warm, reddened cheek with my palm. "You do not understand how painful it is for me to see you like this. You mustn't cry when I am with you."

"But, Matthaya, I…" Her breaths were short and sporadic as she gathered the strength to look me in the eye again. "The feelings of others may never change," she said, choking on tears, "but my feelings for you have grown stronger with each passing day."

As had mine…

"I cannot approve your confession, Kathryn." I bent down onto one knee and grasped one of her hands between my own. "God knows what your father would do to me if he suspected anything other than child's play. Our friendship means little to him." My hands tightened over hers and I hardened my gaze. "Do you want to lose me forever?"

"No!" She shook her head violently. "No!"

"If you wish to keep me near, you must tell no one else of your feelings."

She trembled within my grasp as I spoke. I didn't want to scare her, but I had little choice. I would have given anything to be by her side—and everything to remain there. As friends or… more.

Our differences were facts we had to face. Sooner or later,

she would be forced to marry some other man and would be lost to me forever. Until that day, I could not bear to be parted from her and, until that day, I would not ignore the tears she shed for me.

I awoke the next morning, the crowing roosters rousing me from my sleep. The servants' quarters where I stayed were small and plain, but they suited the very basic needs of living. I was lucky enough to have my own room, though I was hardly there at all. With Kathryn's frequent invitations to join her elsewhere, one might assume I was an average member of the household.

There was a bowl of mostly-clean water placed atop the dingy table near my bedside. I dipped my cupped hands into it and splashed the water onto my face. The air was already hot and sticky—a sign the day was going to be long and the sun unforgiving.

I reached across the table for my tunic and paused at the sound of footsteps outside my door. Muffled voices followed. I pried open the door to investigate and was startled by a swift lunge at my throat.

I choked and gasped as two large, heavily-built men grabbed ahold of my arms and jerked me outside and into the nearby field. I had barely caught my breath before the stench of their foul body odor wrinkled my nose. I didn't recognize their faces, but the scent of alcohol lacing their skin had me assuming they were friends of Lord Shallon.

"Where are you taking me!?" I called out, fighting to

free myself. "What have I done?" Neither man answered.

I trusted Kathryn to keep silent, but our secret was beginning to wear heavily on my conscience.

Had she told him something about us?

I couldn't keep my footing as I was dragged forcefully across the property, over a rocky stretch of dirt and fallen branches. Mounds of stones and twigs grazed my bare feet, leaving them scraped and bloodied from the treacherous journey.

We paused. I brought my head up and stopped breathing.

My... God...

They released me and I fell to my knees upon a dusty pile of sand and rocks. On each side of me stood a tall wooden pole. There was about six feet between them and brown traces of old blood stained the ropes that dangled ominously from each side. I had imagined some of the torturous things Lord Shallon had done to those who had discredited him, but this petrified me.

"Please! Tell me what I have done wrong!" I flinched as dry, crusty threads dug into my flesh. They wrapped the ends of the rope in tight knots around my wrists. My arms rose up and out to the sides as they pulled the ropes tautly around the poles until I was unable to move in either in direction. My arms burned from the pressure of my shoulders being tempted from their sockets and I clenched my jaw.

A hearty laugh came from the distance.

"Well, well, well..." Kathryn's father croaked. "I knew

someday you would be trouble, boy." His deep, sadistic voice sent shivers up my spine, numbing the sting of the shredded ropes around my wrists.

"What have I done, my Lord?" If I was to be punished, I at least wanted to know the reason. "Tell me. Please!"

The piercing crack of a leather whip shocked my ears and I craned my neck in the direction of the sound.

Lord Shallon came out from behind me, his hands drawn out to the sides with thick straps of a whip stretched tight between them.

"So... you think you can pick up anything you want and take it with you," he growled. "Not in *my* place. Not on *my* land. Here... my servants *obey* me." He snapped the whip.

"I took nothing!" I cried hoarsely. Sweat drizzled from my forehead into my eyes and fear strangled the air from my lungs as panic set in.

He disappeared from sight and I braced myself.

CRACK!

The strike rattled my spine and sent me reeling forward. I gritted my teeth, but it did nothing to dull the pain of the rigid strap slicing into my bare back.

"Please, my Lord, I swear it!"

CRACK!

The breath was knocked from me. I coughed hard. My entire body shook from the deep ache ripping across my skin.

CRACK!

Again... and again. Each successive strike intensified the hellish heat of the leather tearing into my flesh; each blow was stronger than the previous one.

CRACK!

I howled in pain and lunged forward, my body hanging by bloodied, tattered ropes as my eyes watered. My mouth became dry and I could barely swallow. Fresh blood drizzled from the wounds and my surroundings blurred, shifting in and out of focus. The searing fire pumped through me like poison, flooding and stinging every inch of me.

He snapped the whip back and I was tempted to bite my tongue to prevent myself from crying out again.

"Father, stop!" Kathryn yowled, her sharp voice quaking with fear. She was not far from where I was. "Stop! He has stolen nothing from you!"

Kathryn came tumbling down to her knees at my side and I felt the weight of her arms across my shoulders. My vision was fuzzy, but I could make out the pale blue fringe of her skirt fanned out near my legs. I didn't have the strength to lift my head.

"How do you know this?" Lord Shallon growled. I could not see his face, but he sounded disappointed about having to halt the abuse.

Kathryn's trembling hands held tightly to my bloody shoulders, but it was a pain I welcomed.

"I know this, F-Father, because... I..." She stumbled over her words. "Because..."

"I gave them to him," Lady Maria, Kathryn's mother, interrupted. "Let the boy be. He has done nothing to scorn you. I gave him those clothes. You had no use for them!"

She motioned for her daughter to untie the ropes binding my hands, but Kathryn had already begun to do so, her precious fingers painted red with my blood.

"And you two should be ashamed of yourselves for hurting this innocent lad." Lady Shallon sent a piercing gaze toward her husband's accomplices. "Get out of here." With the show now over, they obeyed, slithering reluctantly out from view.

Lord Shallon scoffed angrily at his wife. "You cannot treat the servants so well or they'll assume they are privileged."

"He is human like the rest of us." Maria's voice rose and one of her hands came to grace my shoulder. "I will treat him as one." She leaned over and helped pull me to my feet. "I will tend your wounds back at the manor, Matthaya."

"No!" Kathryn wrapped her hands tightly around my arm. "I will tend to him, Mother." She pulled me in her direction and lifted my arm across her shoulder to help me balance.

Each step sent a shockwave of pain through my ribs, but Kathryn's presence gave me the courage to bear it.

"I am sorry," she said, frowning. She returned to where I sat at her bedside and brought a bowl of water. "I did not mean for any of this to happen." Kathryn squeezed the excess water from a white cloth and patted it gently against my back. I stifled the urge to cough.

"You did not want them to begin with and I should not

have left them for you," she said, dipping the bloody cloth back into the bowl and then wringing it out again. "I had no idea my father was capable of such cruelty."

I had.

I hadn't even had the time to notice that she had left the clothes for me outside my room during the night.

"I made a mistake, Matthaya." Her voice shuddered as she wrung out another handful of blood into the bowl. "I did not think he would assume what he did." She shook her head and exhaled a sigh. "I am such a fool."

The ache dulled for a moment and I turned toward her. A tear rolled down her face and she used her forearm to wipe it away, hoping I wouldn't notice.

I hated to see Kathryn cry because I could do very little to ease her suffering. With each fresh tear, I yearned to take her into my arms and comfort her—feel her breath on my skin.

But... I could not, because if ever I did wrap my arms around her... I would never let her go.

"It's not your fault, Kathryn," I assured her with a gentle nudge. "I am grateful for your bravery." I trailed the back of my fingers down her cheek and smiled. "Thank you."

She scooted closer to me and rested her face lightly against my chest.

I inhaled slowly.

The smell of her hair was intoxicating. Wonderful. The essence of rose oil drifted from her skin and she felt warm and real against me.

For a brief moment my pain subsided. Not the pain of my wounds, but the one in my heart—the eternal longing I had for her. I wanted to take her into an embrace, but stopped myself from doing so.

"Are you alright?" I tucked a curl of her soft hair behind her ear as she lifted her face from my chest.

"I will be." She sniffled and twisted around to take up a stack of cloth bandages from her dresser.

The greasy, dark yellow ointment she applied stung like hellfire, but she assured me it would keep the wounds from becoming infected. She then wrapped a cloth across each line of broken flesh and secured them around my ribs for support. The work was intricate but done with a gentle and skilled hand. I had no idea she had such good bedside manner.

"You can remove them in a day or two, once the bleeding has stopped and the wounds have dried," she said. Her fingers followed the lines of her handiwork. "I..." she began, a stutter catching at her tongue. She cleared her throat and rolled her shoulders back. "I know that what you said to me yesterday was a lie, Matthaya."

"What?" I turned to her.

"I know it within my soul," she continued, her voice breaking with emotion. "You cannot deny it."

Kathryn's silky fingertips traced my brow and slid down the side of my cheek to my chin where she brushed her thumb across my lower lip. My body gravitated toward her involuntarily.

"Can you?" she whispered, leaning closer to me as the words slid off her tongue. Her rose oil perfume teased my nose again and I fell silent.

Her eyes devoured me and, without letting me answer, she slid her other hand to the back of my neck and brought her lips to mine.

There was a knock on her door and before I had even tasted her breath, Kathryn pulled away.

"Kathryn," her mother called. "May I come in?"

Kathryn's cheeks flushed and her eyes sheepishly avoided me. She reached for the clean tunic she had brought and placed it in my lap, still avoiding my gaze.

"Yes, Mother," she replied, shifting a few inches away from me on the bed.

Maria entered, scanned the bowl of bloody water on the dresser, then the bandages across my chest.

"How are you?" She tilted her head.

She *seemed* concerned.

"I am better, Milady," I answered with a bow of my head. "Thank you." I shrugged the shirt over my shoulders as quickly as I could without hurting myself, and then laced up the leather strings at my collar.

"Kathryn." Her mother approached. "I would like a word with the boy. Alone."

Her daughter seemed shocked to hear such a thing, but doing as requested, stood and made her way to her door.

"I will be in the hall if you need me," Kathryn said with a curtsey toward her mother.

"Shut the door, please," Maria added sharply, before Kathryn had fully left the room.

The door clicking shut gave me goose bumps.

Lady Shallon shook her head, took a seat in a chair just across from me, and crossed her legs beneath her dress.

"Matthaya, there is something you must understand about my daughter," she began, licking her lips as she gathered her thoughts. "She is young... impulsive and impressionable. She does not comprehend the consequences of her actions."

My eyes narrowed.

"I know how she feels about you," she said, intertwining her fingers to hide her frustration. "You must not let it be."

"But we have been friends since we were small children," I defended. "I have done nothing to make her think any differently of me."

"You don't have to!" Her hands flinched. She tried to keep her composure. "You are merely a novelty to her. The fire of her naivety will fade in time."

"Is that what you want?" I sneered, speaking a dangerous tone to my superior. "For the precious fire within her to wither and die?"

"We have to do what we must to preserve our name. She will be married off soon and you cannot be a temptation to her in the meantime. You *must* push her away."

A temptation? How could she refer to me as such? I had made absolutely no effort to *tempt* Kathryn and I never would. I recognized the boundaries of servitude all too well to dare cross them.

"It's not just that," she added. "If my husband suspects something, he'll surely—"

"Beat me?" A flare of rage roiled within me. My fingers drifted over the bandage across my ribs. "I'd sooner wish for death than go through this again."

"Matthaya..."

"No!" I stood from Kathryn's bed and glared at Maria, my hands curling into fists. "All of these years we have been friends and you have done nothing to discourage that. Now, you want me to send her away like *she* is a servant to be dismissed." I unclenched my fists and took a deep breath. "I will do it if you ask. But, I will do it *my* way. Kathryn is a delicate creature, and if you force her against her will, there will be more blood on your hands than merely my own."

Her eyes grew wide. "Matthaya!?"

I knew Kathryn well enough to know that I spoke the truth.

"I will do it soon," I added. "But you will leave us be until then."

I bowed only halfway this time. My head lowered and we locked cold stares.

"Good day, Milady."

6.III

1616

SEVERAL DAYS had passed, and Kathryn and I did not discuss what had happened between us. And, despite my warnings, it seemed Maria was keeping a close eye on my every move.

She *would* leave us be.

I slipped Raven's bridle down over his ears and tightened the straps beneath his chin and throat. I gave his neck a gentle stroke and spoke softly to the incredible beast.

He was a beautiful, strong Friesian horse, midnight black with a glossy sheen in the sunlight, and Kathryn's prize since he had been broken to ride several years ago. Lord Shallon often used his horses for hunting, but Raven was reserved only for his daughter's pleasure.

A muffled snort pressed into my shoulder as his head rubbed against me eagerly. The long tufts of fur at his hooves flickered in the straw as he twitched with anticipation.

"Calm down, boy." I patted him on his neck. He pulled and tugged excitedly at his bridle as I opened the stable door to lead him out.

He had been left in my care—as all the horses had been—and I could read his movements better than anyone in the manor. I'd been working with him since he was a colt. Raven was a magnificently powerful creature and we had grown close throughout the years.

I took hold of his mane in one hand and vaulted up onto his back.

"Kathryn!"

She pulled her window drapes aside and glanced down at me from her window.

The shutters flung open and she rushed out onto her balcony.

"What are you doing, Matthaya?" she asked, resting her hands on the patio banister and peering over the edge at me. Excitement sparkled in her eyes.

Raven's reins were tight in my other hand, but he would hardly stand still. I stretched out an arm toward her and called out again.

"Kathryn, come!"

She disappeared from the banister and reappeared around the back of the manor, trotting toward me with the skirt of her dress hiked up to her ankles and the pleats bunched in her hands.

"Where are you taking Raven?" she asked, teasing the end of his snout with her fingers. He flapped his lips happily at her.

"The same place I am taking you," I replied flatly. "We must speak—in private."

Her eyes narrowed. "In private?" Her words echoed mine and her voice became hushed. "Do *they* know you're doing this?"

I didn't have to look up to know Maria was watching us from her bedroom window as we spoke.

"They know enough, yes." I slid back on Raven just enough to make room for her.

I bent down and stretched my arm out to help pull Kathryn up and in front of me. She grabbed his mane and tossed her other leg over. Her dress draped across Raven's withers and her bare ankles dangled in front of mine. She passionately hated to ride like a *lady*—sidesaddle. This way made the trip much easier, though, since I wouldn't have to hold so tightly to her when we picked up pace.

"Where are we going?" Kathryn asked, twisting around and leaning back just enough to meet my eyes.

I tightened my grip on the reins and pressed my forearms closer to her waist as I squeezed my heels inward, asking Raven to speed up into a swift trot. His body was strong as a wolf's, but his fluid gait was smooth and pleasant.

Past a few acres of grass and fence line, we came upon a clearing just behind a row of trees that bordered the back of the property. By the look of the tall underbrush, the land had not been touched for some time. I guided Raven through the forest maze and into a shallow clearing not far in. There, I dismounted and helped Kathryn down.

In every direction, there were trees and leaves blocking most of the view, and I finally felt secure enough to tell Kathryn what I had to say.

She smoothed her dress down her knees, knelt down onto the ground, and picked a small bunch of wildflowers from the grass. She tucked one into the crease behind her ear and turned back toward me with a smile.

Enchanting as a forest sprite.

The colorful accent brought out her innocence... and beauty.

We had *almost* kissed the other day, and now the mere thought of her sent quivers of agony through my veins. What restraint I had to maintain around her! She was the first thought in my mind each time I awoke, and catching a glimpse of her devilish smile left my lips moist with the memory of hers so fatefully close to mine. Kathryn didn't deserve the sinful visions I had recently begun having of her.

And yet, she teased me again and again with her charm. She feared nothing and I feared *everything*.

She remained blind to the impossible nature of our

relationship and I despised that.

"What did you want to tell me, Matthaya?" She came closer and brought a hand to my face. I took a step back to avoid her touch.

She pursued.

"You can run from me all you like," she said with a sly grin, making a quick and careful move closer. "But it will not change the way I now feel about you."

The sting of my wounds reminded me of the consequences of our relationship and the last thread of my nerves collapsed in the wake of her fantasies.

"Kathryn, no!" I grabbed her forearms and shook her. She gasped and I had to assure myself that my violent intentions were noble.

"Matthaya? Wh-what are you doing?" Her eyes widened, the blue irises swallowed up by frightened, black pupils.

"You cannot say such things!" I tried to make my voice gruffer and my grasp on her firmer. "You don't know how hard it is. What a struggle it is to contain the horrible things my body craves. What sins I imagine against my will—things I have no right to consider."

"God would not have given us hearts if he did not want them to love," she said, trying to smile through her discomfort. My grasp on her weakened. "And he would not have sparked a fire inside you without a purpose for its warmth."

She was right, no less, but I doubted she fathomed the heat of that fire.

"Kathryn... I am no longer a child," I said, unable to keep

my voice harsh as I faded into the depths of her azure eyes. "I am becoming a man." The delicate and soft lace of her dress tickled my fingertips. "And with that progression... the needs and desires of my body have become... undeniable." My hand slid down her arm and to the side of her waist. "I fear that I will gain no further satisfaction from a childish friendship alone, and the thought of it blackens my soul. This must end, for your own good."

Kathryn's eyes closed. She heaved a sigh and slowly re-opened them. She brought her hands to my neck and walked her fingers along the brims of my shoulders. I released her completely.

She pressed her body against mine, and an airy kiss against my throat paralyzed me. She combed her nails through my hair and I became breathless in her hands—a slave to the angelic touch of her slender fingers.

"I, too, am no longer a child, Matthaya." There was an edge of rebellion in her voice. "I have felt the very same desires you speak of." Her hands trailed the ridge of my collar as she spoke.

I swallowed hard.

"I know what it is you want, and if you are so eager to consummate this... *childish friendship*... then let us do so."

"No." I veered away, trying to shake the overwhelming sensations raging through me.

It was wrong in a thousand ways and I could not stand the thought. I would not tarnish the innocence of a woman I could never rightfully call my wife.

"You cannot ask me to come and take you for myself, when I've not even the very basic right of a man to court you properly."

"Perhaps not." She walked in front of me and pressed an open hand over her heart. "But you do have the right as a man to love me. And if you feel the way I do then let us banish this fear you have." Her eyes scanned the ground and returned to me. "Now."

My lips curled with disgust.

"And your God will watch us burn for our sins." I scoffed. "After your father is through with us both. You are not ready for this."

"Neither are you."

She was right. Still, I could not disregard the purpose of our meeting.

"You're changing the subject," I said, resorting to a huskier tone. "I cannot have you and, therefore, I-I..." I cleared my throat. "And, therefore, I do not want you."

Kathryn tipped her head and shadows cast by the trees overhead darkened her eyes. "Then no one will have me," she said, bending over to reach a hand down to her ankle. She pulled a small silver dagger out from under her dress and held out her other wrist.

"Kathryn!?"

"You will not reject me, Matthaya," she seethed. "You will not reject me because of fear, and if you wish to pretend there is some other reason, then I insist you hold your tongue."

The dagger shook in her grasp. She then pressed it into the milky flesh of her wrist and cried out a muffled groan as the tip of the blade pierced her skin.

"Kathryn, no!" I dashed to her side as her knees hit the ground. She hadn't the nerve to go any further and released the dagger.

That single drop of blood was all it took to break my heart.

A heaving sigh pooled in her breast and she wept.

I picked up the dagger and tossed it behind us, out of her reach.

Her body shook and she gasped small breaths, as tears poured from her eyes.

I gently lifted her wrist and pressed my thumb against the incision, applying slight pressure to stop the bleeding.

"Can we not be together?" Her weakened voice was nearly inaudible.

"Even if your father does not kill both of us, we will still lose everything. We are not at liberty to choose our own paths. And you... you should not do these things because of me." I caressed her palm and kissed the inside of her wrist before letting go of her hand. The bleeding had ceased.

"To say that I do not feel the same passion for you as you feel for me would be a lie." I wrapped my arms around her shoulders and pulled her trembling body close to my chest. "But to say that I do not fear the consequences would also be false." I kissed the top of her head. "I have known for so long that it would someday come to this. That someday, we would have to confront the curse of our friendship."

Her eyes came up toward mine and her shimmering red curls parted to the sides of her face.

"I would give up everything for you," she uttered.

"You... would?"

She took a deep, congested breath and cleared her throat. "I know you can do many things I cannot, and you may think I am naive, but I *want* to learn from you. I *want* to be part of you and I am willing to share the hardships that you face each day in order to do that." She wiped the remaining tears from her cheeks and swept her hair behind her shoulder. "I *must* be with you. We can lie to ourselves and to others, but the connection between you and I will never fade. It is irreplaceable, and it is as sacred today as it was the day you arrived here."

Her words were beyond her years.

"You would renounce the life you have now, just to be with me?"

She brought her fingers to my face and forked them lovingly through my hair.

"Matthaya, I would give up my entire world to be with you," she said with an earnest smile.

I wanted to believe her.

"They will never accept us," I said, sighing. At that point, I realized that I could no longer deny myself the touch I longed for. I did want Kathryn. I needed her and she needed me, too.

I hugged her again and savored the warm, rosy scent of

her. She pressed her palms to my chest and rested her head against me. I moved a tousle of her hair to the side and kissed her neck.

She gasped.

That tiny breath of surprise from her lips intrigued me and seduced my senses in an instant. The sweet, delicate taste of her skin filled me with impulses I had never before experienced. There was newfound strength in the quickening of her heartbeat and my body pulsed with the thrill of finally having Kathryn in my arms—alone and utterly mine. A second kiss to the base of her neck made her fingers twitch and move to the sides of my body, searching for a place to rest.

I brought my hand up to cup Kathryn's cheek and noticed a striking peacefulness fill her eyes. There was a flutter in my stomach and my heart raced as I gravitated closer to her. It was want, need, instinct—whatever you want to call it—and it drew me into the beauty and softness of Kathryn's lips.

Her lashes lowered and I kissed her.

My fingers wove into the back of her hair, pulling her closer and deeper into me. A warm, contented breath escaped her mouth and caressed my lips. To breathe in and taste that yearning sigh of hers was heaven.

It was as if I knew exactly how to kiss her and she knew exactly how to be kissed by me. I'd fantasized about it for so long that it was strangely natural between us. Our lips moved in a unique and distinct rhythm that was anything but awkward.

Her arm quivered slightly, growing weaker from the weight she had been resting on it. The flowerbed of the clearing beneath us was soft, so I carefully drew her hand up and let her lie back onto the grass. With both of her hands on my neck and her nails still combing through my hair, my mind grew cloudy and overwhelmed, and I leaned down to kiss her again.

I wanted to stay there forever—to feel her breath mingle with mine and share with her a kiss that would atone for all that I had withheld. Kathryn's restless fingers wandered to the middle of my collar where she untangled the leather threads so she could slide her hand between them and touch my skin. She tried to grasp my shoulder, but released me as a quiet grunt of pain welled in my throat. The wounds were healing, but still tender.

She pulled her hand away, but I took it into my own and entwined my fingers with hers as I pressed her arm back down into the grass. The fingers of my other hand traced her collarbone and she closed her eyes beneath me.

The sun's rays sprinkled through the trees and reflected off the small gold cross that hung on a fine chain around her neck. Rose blush colored her cheeks and tinted the skin across her chest at the brim of her dress. Her beauty was breathtaking. Captivating.

"It is nice to see you smile," she said, opening her eyes and letting her fingers tighten around mine. "I had once thought you couldn't because you never did."

"You have always made me happy, Kathryn," I said, kissing her forehead. "It was the fear of that happiness that made it appear otherwise."

I rolled over to the side and then lay back. She followed, curling up close to my ribs while my arm closed around her and pulled her in even nearer. It was uncomfortable to be on my back, but holding her made me happily endure the pain.

We shared a peaceful sigh and watched as the branches overhead rustled in the wind. Every breath filled me with a force that left me comforted, whole, and never wanting to leave that splendid place.

Raven was a few meters away, munching happily at a patch of clover, completely ignorant of our secret.

Kathryn was motionless in my arms for some time. The minutes ticked by and evening threatened us. I nudged her gently and helped her to her feet.

As I laced up my shirt, she remained steadfast in thought and fell very quiet. I approached her from behind and rested my arms around her shoulders.

"This love can only flourish if kept secret." My lips touched the edge of her ear. "Until the time comes, it must be this way. The world is not yet ready for us."

"I understand," she replied, her eyes fixated on the nothingness in the distance.

6.IV

1616

I BRUSHED her hair to the side and kissed the nape of her neck. She flinched, just as I had predicted she would, and my hands slid across her back until my fingers could take gentle hold of her shoulders. Pressed close to me, I felt her chest rise and fall with a contented sigh, and I couldn't help but smile.

"It's beautiful," she said, placing her palms onto the banister and leaning forward. "Isn't it?" I imagined the morning light reflecting in the ocean of her eyes as they glistened in awe at the sunrise.

"Never as beautiful as you," I replied, walking my fingertips across her shoulders and down to the hollow of her throat.

From Kathryn's bedroom balcony, we could watch the day awaken in peace. The rest of the manor did not stir until just after light and we secretly found time together in the very early hours of morning. We kept our distance and spoke little to one another during the day. This is how it had been for many months, and it would remain so until we could find another way.

My fingers tangled in her necklace chain and I caught the cross charm between my thumb and index finger. She'd had it since I had known her and I knew she had devout faith in it, as I had never seen her without it. Recalling little conviction from childhood, I'd harbored my own doubts about God. With no other defense to support my decision to love Kathryn, I eventually gave in to her beliefs. I needed to believe that someone or something could help us.

"You are my sun, Kathryn," I continued in a quiet voice, my fingers tracing the thin chain around her neck.

These simple moments were worth the world to us, and I cherished every second of her presence. She had selflessly spoken to me of love many times over the past weeks, but I could do no more than listen. I loved her with all my heart and soul. I would have died for her, and no doubt killed for her, as well. All she had to do was ask and I would obey. Yet, I could not release myself from my final inhibition. I would not seal her fate with my words. She knew this but did not enforce the same restraint upon her own lips. I struggled to bite my tongue when all I desired was to fill her with promises of devotion and happiness.

The future was so very uncertain.

We had discussed many ideas, conjured up a dozen plots and possibilities, but none of them seemed feasible in the end. There was one option—in the very back of my mind—that begged for my attention, but I could not yet bring myself to make the sacrifice it required. Kathryn knew nothing of it, and I would keep it that way until the time was right.

Kathryn had even inquired about marriage, which I knew she longed for more than anything. All I could do was promise and swear myself to remain bound to her regardless of when (and *if*) the church would sanctify such a thing. I, too, wanted nothing more than to lawfully call her my wife.

℘ ℘

Whatever she wanted with me at this hour, her request that I come to her was beyond reason—and meant nothing good, *I was certain*. Still, I went to her. I went to her as I *always* did and *always* would.

It was deathly quiet and the lanterns outside had been extinguished hours ago, leaving the pathway to the manor pitch black. There was soft golden light resonating from Kathryn's room. I looked around before reaching a hand up to latch onto a balcony post. I climbed several feet, and then stretched out my other arm to grab a hold of the top of the banister railing. I pulled myself up and over and took a third glance in both directions. It was silent. Empty. Everyone had gone to sleep by now—everyone but Kathryn.

She pushed the balcony doors open quietly and welcomed me with a smile, taking me by the hand and pulling me into her room. She shut the doors behind me and closed the drapes. As a final precaution, she went to her bedroom door and turned the lock, holding her hand tightly over the keyhole to dampen the click.

"Is that a good idea?" I motioned toward the door she had just locked.

"You are here after dark, my dear Matthaya. Is *this* a good idea?" she replied, challenging my question and proving my suspicions were correct.

Of course not...

She returned to me and snuffed out one of the two candles atop her dresser. The room became dim and the remaining glow was... intimate. The dress she wore tonight was much lighter and softer than her usual ones. The fine white satin flowed down her body, hugging the curves of her waist and hips. There were two lines of indigo lace ties hanging gracefully down each side of her ribs. Each one was intertwined with a row of grommets used to fit the dress more tightly around her. The delicate bows at the end of each looked *painstakingly* perfect.

It was not the kind of dress she would ever be seen wearing in public.

She looked me in the eye with a deep and determined

gaze, and then licked her lips in preparation to speak. "I cannot stand this anymore, Matthaya," she said, moving toward me and backing me against the patio doors. I had to brace myself to keep from rattling the frames behind me. "I cannot take this distance—this... agony coursing through me. How long must we wait?" She pressed into me and twisted a lock of my hair between her fingers. "Matthaya, please. You say that we should be married, but how far away is that day? When will I legitimately be yours?"

There was a sparkle in her eyes I hadn't seen before, and though I pretended to be unaffected by it, the subtle change made my thoughts run wild. My mindset was in such a delicate balance, teetering between rationality and impulsiveness— threatening the sanctity of our friendship. And her dress... how it accentuated the sumptuous curves of her body, leaving so little to my imagination.

Her nails traced the collar of my shirt down to my throat and then to the leather threading along the center of my tunic. One of her ankles trailed up and hooked behind my leg, where she pressed her foot seductively against my calf. The slit in her dress made the fabric pour over her thigh, revealing porcelain skin. Thoughtlessly, I lowered my hand to caress the firm, warm flesh of her naked leg.

"I am sixteen years old now and my father is trying to sell me into marriage as quickly as he can." Her delicate fingers worked apart the overlapping ties of leather as she spoke. "I will not let another man have me. I refuse to let a stranger who can simply buy my father's favor *conquer* me."

The heat of her words crushed against me. The urgency in her voice and the overpowering needs of our bodies bewitched me, draining me of all reason. The little nymph's inherit ability to torture me had never faltered before, and tonight was no exception. This confrontation was potent and dangerous. A fire sparked within me and she kindled it further with a sensual stroke of her palm down my inner thigh. It was as if she was mocking my inability to hide the desires of my body—daring me to confront them.

Her touch enchanted me, and she somehow knew my body much more intimately than I knew hers—a fact proven by the way she manipulated the powerful sensations coursing through my veins.

A cunning girl and a cleverly plotted ambush.

No. A brilliant, irresistible... *woman.*

She wanted to feel my lips against her neck... along her shoulders... soft kisses across her chest.

She wanted my skin pressed against hers... our breath in unison.

She wanted to feel my hands holding her tightly at the waist... my fingers dragging over her thighs.

The shortness of breath left me vulnerable. Hardwired, primitive instincts yearned to test the limits of my will. Her desire for me burned inside her trembling body and vivid thoughts of her flesh mingling with mine flashed through my mind. Her fingers tightened on my hands, which had unconsciously migrated to her hips.

She wanted me with every beat of her fervent heart...

And this time... she would have me.

I pressed my fingertips against her thighs and let her leg slip back down to the floor. I took a step toward her, forcing her back.

And another.

And then another.

Her calves met the heavy wood frame of her bed and she stumbled, flopping down onto her sheets and pulling her legs onto the bed as I knelt down beside her. There was curiosity in her eyes and she bit her lip in anticipation.

As I approached, she parted the sides of my open tunic and exposed my skin to her touch. Fluid and unreserved, she stroked a gentle path down the center of my chest.

I crawled up beside her and leaned over her body, bringing a slow, steady hand up along her ribs, feeling every tiny rise and fall of the lace ties along her dress.

She was so willing—so eager to give me *anything* I wanted from her.

And right then and there, I wanted everything from her.

A nervous shudder escaped her lips and I silenced her with a deep kiss. My hand moved across her shoulder and down her arm toward her wrist. I lingered there, tracing the edge of her palm with a graceful touch and teasing the tips of her fingers as my other arm stabilized my body above hers.

As we kissed, she quaked beneath me, electrifying my senses. Thrilling me. God, how I wanted her, and how the warmth of her skin made my body throb with the anticipation of having her.

The powerful thumping of my heartbeat sent a flutter up my throat and my breath quickened. Part of me feared for our secret, but only part of me. I was too submerged in animalistic needs to rationalize. My fingers entwined with hers and I brought my lips to her throat and left a trail of kisses down her neck. I exhaled a hot breath behind her ear and her lips parted to release a groan of pleasure. Every heartbeat seduced me further until I was consumed by the vision of an endless night of us making love.

A gentle tug on the cap of one of Kathryn's sleeves sent it sliding off her shoulder and made her fingers tighten against my ribs. I lowered myself down to lay a firm kiss onto the base of her neck and yet another soft groan emerged as the ridge of my tongue trailed across her collarbone, tasting the salt on her glittering skin.

Sweet-sounding whispers. Painfully eager tremors flowing through her hips. I couldn't ignore how distracted I was by her incredible curves. For a moment, I had forgotten to breathe.

The tips of her fingernails teased the jut of my hipbones as her palms pressed into my belt, forcing it lower. An involuntary shiver made my teeth clench. I wanted so much from her—so much of her, but I hesitated still.

"I don't want to hurt you," I strained to speak. My hand traveled up to her wrist and I sat back on my heels so I could meet her gaze.

"I'll be fine. It would hurt no less if we waited," she said reassuringly, desperation evident in her tone. "I know it will be worth the cost. I will be yours and only yours." Her fingers tucked a lock of hair back behind my ear and then traced my cheek. "I know that there is no gentler a man on Earth than you."

She trusted me.

She loved me.

Still...

She took my face between her hands and smiled. "It was *meant* to be you."

My blood tingled with the romance in her words.

She was right... and I knew it.

I shifted my position until I was nearly on top of her and slipped my free hand beneath the lace ribbon at the rib of her dress. The velvety ties loosened and I pulled them free, making her dress loose enough for her to wriggle the other sleeve down and off her shoulder. It was a painfully conscious decision to delay the intense urges pulsing through me, but I wanted to grant her the satisfaction of every second possible. It became even more difficult as my fingers traversed the bare skin of her thigh. There was no turning back.

"*Matthaya...*" the word escaped her in a heated exhalation as her knees pressed into my sides.

My heart raced. Her hands drove through my hair and she pulled me down to her lips again. I was lost in her sensual breath... her sweet scent...

I took a breath from her kiss and balanced my weight upon my palm to reach down and unbuckle the clasp of my belt. The subtle clinking noise was interrupted by another.

My ears caught the quiet sound of a door opening and

closing down the hall.

"What was that?" I asked, quickly sliding the tip of the belt back into the loop atop the buckle.

"I heard nothing," Kathryn replied with a frustrated scoff. She curled her fingers around the hem of my shirt and tugged me closer.

The tiny hairs on the back of my neck stiffened.

Someone was awake.

"Forgive me, Kathryn," I said, kissing her briefly. I lifted my leg over hers and got off her bed. "I heard someone stirring," I continued, searching frantically nearby for the ties to my tunic. "I am sure of it."

She rolled onto her side to face me. Anger creased her brow. "It is surely nothing to be concerned with, Matthaya." Her voice rose. "Matthaya?"

"*Shhh...*" I raised my fingers in a gesture to silence her and then listened.

A clicking noise?

My head turned.

The lock!

I couldn't make the patio doors in time to escape the sound of her bedroom door unlocking from the *outside*. Kathryn rushed toward it and thrust her weight against the door.

"Let me in, Kathryn!" Lord Shallon's voice boomed.

I snatched the chair from her writing desk and wedged it under the handle of her door. It would buy us some time, but not much.

Kathryn turned to me. "Take Raven and get out of here," she said. "You can return for me later."

"I know that boy is with you," Lord Shallon roared, bashing his fists against the door. "Let me in!"

"I won't go without you." I took her hands. "I can't lose you."

"You'll be faster without me and no good to me dead." She unhooked her necklace. "Take this," she whispered, quickly placing it in my hand and closing my fingers around it. "May God protect you always," she added, hesitating to take her hands from me. "Return it to me. Please."

I heard wood splitting; the door wouldn't hold much longer.

We hurried to the balcony and I leapt over the banister to climb down.

"Do not look back! I will wait for you," she said, stretching her hand out to me as I dropped from her reach. "I love you, Matthaya!"

My feet had just hit the ground when the words slipped from her lips, more faithful than ever. I turned my back to head to the stable, but my heavy heart stopped me.

There was no time!

I shook my head and gritted my teeth at myself for hesitating, but I had no choice. I flung a hand back up onto the balcony post and climbed back to where Kathryn was. She was holding her breath and fearfully watching the door.

"Kathryn," I said, pulling myself up to her level.

She turned and gasped. I didn't give her a chance to

speak.

"I will always love you, Kathryn. I will return for you. I swear it." I tightened my grip on the banister with one hand and reached out to pull her back to me and kiss her good-bye.

Her bedroom door burst open.

I climbed halfway down to the first floor and then braced myself for the remaining drop.

Raven awoke with a startled jolt and came to his feet as quickly as I had flung open the stall door. I tangled my fingers into the base of his mane, leapt onto his back, and held tightly to him as he bolted out of the barn and onto the dirt road.

I had no idea where I would go, but going anywhere was better than staying to face Shallon's wrath.

I had to get away long enough to devise a plan. Long enough to—

A thunderous clap rang through the air and I reeled forward onto Raven's neck. Pain blasted through my shoulder and I grunted. Raven instinctively paused to look back at me. Beneath the moonlight, I could see blood covering my hand and felt it saturating my shirt.

Damn it! I had been shot!

The sky was cloudy, the moon dim, and I was riding a black horse—it had been a lucky shot, *indeed*. I ignored the pain and used what little strength I had in my other arm to rebalance myself as I kicked a heel into Raven's ribs, asking him to gallop. I clung to his mane as he raced blindly through the darkness.

What would happen to her?

How could I return?

So many questions and no time to consider them.

Raven followed the moonlit path of the road and trusted in my will and sense of direction. His pace eventually slowed to a trot and I bent over in pain, my blood dampening his coat.

The night was filled with silence and solitude and the road ahead was empty and bare. The trees along the pathway had already lost most of their leaves in preparation for winter and their thin skeletons made poor company in the night.

Raven stopped abruptly and stamped his hooves into the dirt with a heavy snort.

"Easy." I rubbed my hand across his neck and patted him.

There was a strange presence in the air and it had been following us for several minutes. Perhaps the scent of blood was drawing attention to us.

I spotted a dim yellow light in the distance and squinted. From out of the shadows, came a thin, sickly-pale woman who looked about twice my age. With each of her steps, a thick stack of bangles on her arm jingled against one another.

"Hello, young one," she said in a scratchy voice as she approached; her thick accent was distinctly English.

Raven pulled back and twitched nervously beneath me,

making the pain in my arm unbearable.

"I-I am in a hurry. Leave me be," I said.

Ornate golden earrings shimmered on her ears and a heavy necklace hung at her collar. Her black cloak made me suspicious of her occupation. Though my manners taught me never to assume things, she had the aura of an untrustworthy soul.

I tugged on Raven's mane and sent him darting past the stranger. No sooner had I avoided her than she reappeared before me in the road.

"Where are you headed with such haste?" Her head cocked and her eyes flickered with eerie amber fire. "You're injured." She pointed, though she didn't sound concerned.

"I must get away from here," I snapped, enraged by the pain and her stubbornness. I kicked my heels in and braced myself for the charge.

There was a sudden shuffle of dirt and leaves and Raven reared up, sending me flying to the ground. The wind was knocked out of me and my consciousness faltered. I took a moment to catch my breath before coming to my feet.

Raven let out a deafening neigh and my heart skipped a beat. The ground shook as his body came crashing down before my feet. His legs twitched violently and then froze dead in an instant. From what I could see in the shadows, it looked as though his throat had been torn clear of his neck. I quickly stepped away from the pooling blood.

What had she done?

"Show yourself, witch." I looked frantically in every

direction but saw and heard nothing more.

"You had to be difficult, didn't you?" the creature hissed from within the shadows. The direction of her voice was indiscernible. "You're lucky you're a pretty one, or I would kill you where you stand."

I gasped. She was behind me, but I was too slow to react. Her arms came up beneath mine and she clasped me tightly around my shoulders, pressing me into her chest and against the heavy necklaces around her throat. She took a deep whiff of my hair.

"Your blood is powerful," she said. "You will make a good companion."

I tugged and pulled to get away, but her thin arms were unnaturally strong. The cold touch of her skin frightened me and I fought with every ounce of my strength to break free.

And then... then the pain of my shoulder vanished— replaced by the crushing sensation of fangs sinking into my neck. I cried out to deaf ears and my body shook with the blinding ache of what felt like the remainder of my blood oozing down my chest. My hands grew weak and numb and my eyes heavy and dark.

I fell into nothingness.

Dizzy, paralyzed, dying at the hands of the beast, I collapsed and my world turned black.

With my mind clouded by the curse, I had little comprehension of the events taking place around me over the coming days. In the darkness I waited, watching in ignorance as Kathryn stumbled along the ocean shore. The tides were wild with the night, crashing and rising over the sand and rocks with tremendous force. All the while, I was trapped inside myself, forced to watch a nightmare unfold through the eyes of an animal I had not yet learned to control.

Her words were inaudible and quiet as she stepped out into the tide, and I could do no more than stare as Kathryn toppled over into the water. There was no struggle and no cry for help as her body was dragged deeper and deeper into the rift.

I approached the shore, but the eerie glow of my eyes met only the moon's reflection.

She was gone.

It was not until later on that I learned Kathryn had poisoned herself that night just before running away from home. There were too many rumors about my death and Ve'tani, my Sire, had helped to spread them. This woman had pulled me into her abyss, making me a pawn in her hunt for blood and power. She had torn me away from my life—from my Kathryn—and buried me in her tomb of eternal darkness, making me the creature I am today.

I **TOOK** my eyes off Kathryn's portrait and turned away. Her necklace still hung at my neck, treasured above all my possessions—one of the only other things sacred to me still. I gazed up at the ceiling and ran my hands over the plush velvet arms of my seat.

It was rather early in the morning and not exactly a fair time to be awake. Not that I had a choice. Like humans, we don't always tire when we should, and my mind was racing far too much to even consider rest.

No number of days could make me forget.

A million years could not steal from my mind the visions of her beautiful face. The warmth of her blazing fingertips across my skin had vanished when I had changed, but the vivid imagery of her smile would not fade from my memory.

Damn myself for even trying, but there were days I did want to forget her. There were times I longed to be free of her love. It was a curse less bearable than the one I had endured for hundreds of years.

Relief was far from my grasp. Heavy blood consumption barely dampened my conscience. I could never drink enough to cloud reality. There was no escape.

Though I admit...

Kathera had granted me the closest thing to friendship I had experienced in years. Moments spent in her presence quieted some of the pain, but new wounds took shape with each flutter of her crimson lashes and each arc of her smile.

Our friendship was self-sabotage and I could not tolerate another century of pain. It was a harsh truth, but one that I had to acknowledge soon... before the desire for her blood became too great for me to ignore.

7

KATHERA

IT WAS stupid of me to dwell on thoughts of him. I was old enough and smart enough to know better than to brood over a man. Especially one as strange as Matthaya. A vision of him had visited me in my dreams last night, and even then, he was detached and distant.

But despite what his body language conveyed, his eyes seduced me with unspoken promises of security and compassion. His brilliant green irises drew me in as if I were a moth to a flame.

Too close and I would burn.

"How's it coming over there?" Derek's soft steps into the room had gone unnoticed, and the ink line from my pen thickened from my surprise.

"It's going great. I think I've really got something here." I put down my black pen and took a dark-red marker into my fingers. "I'm almost done. Would you like to see it?"

"Yes!" Derek shuffled into the next room and his voice became muffled by the walls. "Let me get some papers filed and I'll be right over."

With small circular motions, I colored in the eyes of my drawing and it instantly came to life. I sat back in my chair and sighed.

She was beautiful.

My newest creation—a thin, seductively posed demon-like goddess with ice-platinum skin, waves of thick black curls, and a triple set of powerful flame wings.

Derek poked his head over my shoulder.

"Do you think they'll like it?" I asked, my brows raised hopefully and my grin half-cocked.

"Are you kidding? It's incredible!" He bent over beside me and rested his forearm on the table, taking a closer look at my drawing. "I'm just a little awestruck at the amount of detail work you were able to accomplish. It's a lot more than usual."

"You could say I was in the zone, I guess."

"It's very nice." His eyes traced my line work and he grinned in approval. "When are they coming back in to get it inked?"

"Later tonight."

His brow furrowed. "Cutting it a little close, aren't we?"

I exaggerated the batting of my eyes and smirked. "You said it was great, didn't you?"

"Yeah. I suppose I did." He shrugged off my humor. "You're good at your job."

He stood and took a step back.

I picked up my black pen and cleaned up part of the outline.

Derek was still standing behind me. I could hear him breathing softly.

The room became awkwardly quiet.

I started to turn my head.

"Hey, Kathera." Derek returned to my side and sat on the edge of the table. He took up one of my markers and began twiddling it between his fingers.

"Is... everything okay?" I asked, watching him tap the cap of the marker against his knee. His uneasy smile made my heart jump into my throat. I'd known him for several years and it was unlike him to hesitate.

Had I screwed up something?

"Speaking of tonight." He looked away and chewed his lip. "Uh... Would you care to get out of here for a little while? After work, I mean... just for a cup of coffee or a drink or something?" A nervous smile twisted his lips.

Derek was a really sweet guy and probably only five or six years older than I was. We'd known each other for several years as coworkers—even before his father had passed down ownership of the place to him.

Despite the ferocious dragon tattoos that decorated the

length of his left arm and the many scars across his skin, he had a very docile nature. He had been polite to me from day one, and never judged me because I didn't have or want a tattoo. Derek was always willing to help me learn new techniques and grow as an artist.

It had begun as a business relationship, but now here he was asking me to go out with him. *Awkward.* He *was* my boss, after all, and I didn't know what to say.

"It's okay if you want to say 'no,' Kathera," he assured. "But please don't let this get between us being partners here. If I'm overstepping my boundaries, I—"

"No. It's fine." I grinned. "I wouldn't mind getting to know you better off the clock."

I suppose Derek and I had a lot in common, but he had always just been the man I worked for and... I'd never thought about *dating* him before. Truthfully, I kind of considered him to be a little out of my league.

"If tonight is too late for you, we can meet up during the day sometime."

"Tonight is fine."

Derek beamed. His smile was honest and enthusiastic.

I wanted to see my mother and... Matthaya, too, but apparently they would have to wait.

The motion sensor at the front door chimed.

"Oh, that might be them." I smiled and snatched my drawing from the table. "Wish me luck."

He winked. "They'll love it."

Derek may have had more years of experience under his

belt than me, but my artistry captivated even the most stubborn clients.

The client getting the female demon tattoo was paying a high price for it, so we made the exception of staying open late to accommodate his needs. It was going to take several visits to fully flesh her colors and wing patterns out, but it would be worth it in the end—for both of us. My commission rate was decent. Derek made sure I wasn't going to take my talents elsewhere anytime soon.

He was right. The client loved the design, and I started work immediately after the initial approval. A few hours into the outlines, I wrapped up and we scheduled the next visit for further detailing. It was never a good idea to tattoo for more than several hours in one place, on one person, and with one artist. People tend to get fatigued. The vibration and buzzing of the needles had even gotten on my nerves when I spent too much time on one piece. Some artists can endure it, but it wasn't a preference of mine. That, and my customers needed to be comfortable, too.

We said goodbye for the night and I watched as my beautiful demon goddess sashayed out the door on the arm of a husky, middle-aged man with more than enough tattoos to keep her company. His clean-shaven head and thick sunglasses reminded me of the biker type, but the mud splatters that dirtied the edges of his heavy red work truck indicated another profession.

I glanced at the wall clock. It was past midnight and we

hadn't even cleaned out the money drawer. I sighed and headed into the next room.

Derek shut off the store lights and flipped open the plate covering the alarm box.

"Come on, Kathera," he said, his tone soft and encouraging. "You've been here long enough. Get your stuff and let's get out of here."

"But..." I stuck my head out of the back room. "What about the money and—"

"I took care of it," he continued. I could tell he was trying to sound concerned and not anxious about our "date." He was known by those of us at the shop to do nice things on the fly, but it still surprised me a little.

"Thank you, Derek," I said with a grateful smile, coming back into the main room to meet him. "I appreciate you doing all of that for me." I gathered my things and he set the alarm system as we stepped out the door.

The smell of coffee and the sweet aroma of pastries tantalized my nostrils at the only place still open after midnight— *Café Au Late*. It was a two-story, 24-hour café that had some of the most unique blends of coffee and tea in the city. Five at night or five in the morning, there were late-nighters and coffee enthusiasts alike trickling in and out of the place non-stop. The padded, bar-style seating, mood lighting, and free Wi-Fi made it an obvious choice for anyone looking to finish a thesis or sip away their woes.

Warm air comforted my weary body and I took a seat on

a bench in the corner of the shop overlooking a quaint shopping strip outside. All I wanted was quiet, and the soft lights of the café invited me to curl up in the corner and rest my mind for the day. Jazz played from the speakers around the room, but it was kept to a minimum volume so people could converse unhindered. *Café Au Late* was no sports bar, and I liked it that way.

I took a deep breath and sunk into the soft, cushiony seat of the corner booth I had chosen.

"Comfortable?" Derek asked, his voice subtle with a hint of jest. He set his drink down onto the table in front of me.

I had almost forgotten he was there.

"Sorry!" I straightened myself up from the cushions and shuffled through my bag for my wallet.

"Can you just get me a decaf latte, please? Extra sweetener and whip cream?" I plucked a five from my purse and presented it to Derek.

He lifted his fingers and flattened his hand, rejecting my money.

"Let me get it tonight, okay?" He flashed a modest smile my way and returned to the counter to order my coffee.

"Thank you..." my voice trailed into silence.

Derek's eyes were softly lit by the colorful lanterns around us and he seemed more relaxed than usual while he spoke. I was too tired to talk about much, so I was an intent listener for most of the night. It seemed to me that he really needed a kind ear to take in his thoughts.

He kept to himself mostly, doing bookkeeping in between tattoos for his own clients. His artwork had been very popular back when I had started working there, and demand was higher than supply. But he'd become introverted since the death of his father, and took on less tattoo work nowadays. I could relate.

Some of my grief had faded a few years after the loss of my mother, but fresh sorrow crept up on me as my stepmother, Aldréa, drove her thorns deeper into my skin with each wicked accusation.

I wished my father were as involved in my life as Derek's had been. Fighting with your parents during your angsty teen years is one thing, but not having them around to argue with can leave an even deeper hole in you.

Not that I regret it, but I had learned everything the hard way. I'd learned things the quickest and most unforgiving way possible—through experience. I was proud of my street smarts and had taken care of myself well enough, considering the odds, but a tinge of jealousy bloomed in me as I listened to Derek's heartfelt recollections of his father.

"I'm boring you already, aren't I?" Derek shrugged guiltily. "You can tell me the truth."

I took the last sip of my sweetened coffee and set the cup down with a hollow plop.

He hadn't even touched his drink yet.

"No, of course not, Derek. I'm just a little tired, that's all." I gestured for him to continue, but a single glance at his untouched drink sent him reeling into hesitation.

He brought the rim of the cup to his lips and took a drink.

"Lukewarm coffee. Yay."

His sarcasm made me chuckle.

"Do you want me to have them warm it up for you?" I asked, about to stand.

"Don't worry about it." His hand rose.

Nothing bothered him.

I only wished I could say the same about myself.

Even as I tried to forget about Matthaya for just one night, his verdant, unnatural green gaze snaked in and out of my thoughts. I glanced out the window beside our booth at the rain sprinkling the sidewalk and wondered where he was tonight.

"Are you still living with your father?" Derek asked. He was aware of my situation for the most part, but really had no idea how vicious my stepmother was.

I looked back at him. "Yes. I am," I replied, unable to mask the regret in my voice. I could have moved out if I had wanted to, but it had never seemed like the right thing to do. I wanted to run away from my life in that old house... from Aldréa and her cruelty, but I loved my father too much to leave him completely alone with her.

At least, that was the excuse I made for myself.

"Need help looking for a place?" he questioned. "I know some nice houses that are probably within your budget. If you're interested, I—"

"Thank you, Derek. I'll be alright for now."

"Oh. Alright." His fingers grasped the edge of his coffee

cup and he shook it in small circles to stir the contents before taking another sip. "You're always welcome to ask for help if you need it, Kathera. With *anything,* I mean."

I opened my mouth to reply but nothing came out. So I smiled instead.

Derek's generosity and kindness stemmed directly from his father's good nature. This wasn't the first time he had offered to help me and it surely wouldn't be the last. It was nice to know he cared enough to offer it.

BUZZ.

The whir of my phone vibrating in my pocket caught me off guard.

I pardoned myself to check what it was. It was a text message from my dad.

"Sorry I missed you tonight. Hope we can catch up again soon."

"Soon" was probably days away.

I checked the time.

It was almost two in the morning. I didn't feel like leaving yet, but for the sake of my clients I needed to call it a night. There in the warm café, sitting across from Derek, I felt safe for a change.

Safety couldn't last forever.

"I should be getting home." I scooped my purse up from the seat and stood. "It's really late and I told that client with the demon goddess to come in early tomorrow."

"I can reschedule it for you, if you'd like," he suggested. "It's not a big deal. Not like I didn't know where you were tonight."

"I'll be fine." I could deal with a lack of sleep.

Derek stood and shrugged his red leather jacket on over his shoulders. His expression changed into an awkward grimace as he looked to the windows. "Would you mind if I drove you home tonight?"

I could have walked to my house from this part of town, but my eyes followed his to the window and to the sudden downpour. It rushed through the city and took the building by storm with a patter of heavy droplets on the roof.

"Sure. Thanks." A second glance toward the parking lot confirmed where he had parked.

Derek was a fan of boxy-looking, vintage cars and had spent years fixing up a '70s Firebird with his dad. The metallic, neon green sports car wasn't my type of ride—not to mention I couldn't afford one—but the elaborate dragon decals spread across both sides of it made it look incredible.

He held open the door for me and I got in, tucking my wet bag behind my calves.

"Seatbelt?" he asked, turning on the car.

CLICK.

He shifted the gear stick and we pulled out of the parking lot.

The trip back was short and I remained quiet, intently watching the empty sidewalks and blurry streetlamps buzz past. For an older car, it had a smooth ride. He and his dad had fixed it up quite well.

I glanced across at Derek, whose eyes were locked on

the road. His tanned olive skin was soft but imperfect—the edge of his right eyebrow was marked with a naked dash of skin that formed a scar from a knife wound he had gotten in his teen years. He had told me before that his early life had been rough and that he had picked his share of fights, which he regretted with age. It had taken him many years, but he had finally settled down to the responsibilities of his life and taken up work at his dad's place.

From the corner of my eye, I could see him contemplating whether or not to say anything else to me. He drove his free hand through his short, ruddy golden hair and rubbed the back of his neck. Then his elbow came to rest on the inside of the window frame and he exhaled loudly.

I didn't know what to say either. Derek was nice, and I was willing to give him a shot, but deep down, I wasn't ready for a relationship with him... Maybe I *never* would be. He wasn't really what I was looking for. Not that I had *ANY* idea what—or who—it was I was looking for.

I wasn't ready to tell him that. Silence seemed like the only sure way to remain subjective about our relationship.

Derek pulled up to the sidewalk just outside my house and stopped the car. He switched off the engine and sat there quietly.

The rain wouldn't let up.

Hopefully Aldréa would be asleep by now.

Derek popped out of his side of the car and jogged over to mine, where he offered me his jacket in lieu of an umbrella. I declined and quickly made a short jaunt to the overhang at my doorstep. He followed.

I shook water off my shoes and wiped my palms across my face. As nasty as the weather may have been, I wasn't in a hurry to get out of it. Maybe it was just the fear building inside me for what lay ahead. Anything was better than *her*...

"Thanks for the ride." I wiped my feet on the doormat and smiled at Derek. "And the coffee."

"No problem," he replied without hesitating. He slicked his bristly, wet hair back against his head and swiped water from his brow with his fingers. "Don't worry about tomorrow. Whatever you decide to do, I'll take care of it."

"Thanks, but I'll come in either way."

"Good night, Kathera," he said with a tender touch of his hand against mine; he couldn't hide the admiration in his gaze.

Derek took a step off the porch and tracked halfway to his car before turning again to face me. He was already drenched from the pouring rain.

"Take care of yourself," he added. His lips formed a small, sympathetic smile as he waved goodbye for the night.

I returned a small gesture with my fingers.

"I'll try," I uttered, too softly for him to hear.

8

I THREW the lock and spun around, startled by the hallway light switching on behind me.

The barrel of a black handgun stared back at me, the trigger tickled by the fingers of my stepmother.

"Where have you been?" she spoke through gritted teeth. The roughness of her voice made me cringe.

I backed myself up against the door in an attempt to gain a bare inch between us, just to catch my breath.

"I-I was out. What the hell is wrong with you?"

"With who? Where? Why are you back so late?" The gun trembled in her grasp.

My thoughts scattered as fear took over. No amount of

distance could settle my nerves with a gun pointed at my face.

"My boss... we... we were out getting coffee. Damn it, Aldréa, get that thing out of my face!" I shimmied my way past and toward the nearby staircase, her sight never breaking from me.

"I have worked far too hard to get where I am today." Aldréa followed me, her nose wrinkled and her lips flared. "I will not have it ruined by a worthless little whore like you."

My jaw tightened and my face grew hot.

Damn her.

"I am not a—"

"Don't lie to me." Aldréa's eyes narrowed.

She was so damn sure of her accusations. It made me sick.

I took one step backward up the staircase. And then another.

I had to get to my room.

"I won't share my home with a tramp who thinks she can come and go whenever she pleases." She waved her hand as she spoke, her finger slipping on and off the trigger of the gun.

Fear made my legs heavy and a tingling sensation started in my hands. I tried to stay focused and grasped the handrail with my sweaty fingers.

"I had to stay late for a special client tonight," I defended, realizing how wrong that must have sounded to her presumptuous mind. "I've worked at the tattoo shop downtown for years."

"It's a front. You disappear every single night. And just now, some stranger drops you off at the house and—"

"That was my boss, damn it!"

"You're a whore, and you can't hide it from me anymore." She raised her free hand to point a craggy finger at my nose. "Your father would be disgusted to hear about this."

"Leave my father out of this!" I lunged at her in an attempt to tear the gun from her wavering grip.

It was a stupid mistake.

She switched hands and jerked the gun from my reach, so her stiff fingers were free to come down across my face.

A yelp of pain burst from my lips and I plunged down against the staircase, banging my knees hard against the steps.

"I'll bring my *husband* into this if I want to!"

I held my face in my hands and cowered beneath her.

"If you know what's good for *him*, you'll keep this to yourself." She bent over me and nudged my thigh with the tip of her shoe. "Get out of my face. *Whore.*"

I wiped my fingers across my cheek and they turned bright red. A trail of blood oozed from my cheek. I wanted to scream. I wanted to strike back, but there was no use. She could kill me or, worse, my dad. I conceded and rushed upstairs to my room, slamming the door behind me. I locked the door tightly for good measure as my stomach churned with rage.

"Damn it!" I smashed my fists onto the marble countertop of my bathroom sink. The bathroom mirror eventually lured my eyes up and I whined at the sight of my reflection.

My face!

She'd narrowly missed my eye, but her nails had grazed my left cheek, leaving a gruesome gash.

I dug around in the bathroom cabinet until I found a bottle of peroxide. It stung like hell as it fizzed and bubbled up in the wound, but I wouldn't risk infection from her filthy nails.

I crumpled a blood-soaked tissue into a ball and tossed it into the toilet. The blood began to seep from the edges and cloud the toilet bowl with crimson. A second glance at the mirror left me fuming. The mark would leave a scar. There was no doubt about that. Right there on my face—a nasty, blatant scar.

I couldn't let anyone know the truth about how I had gotten the wound. I wouldn't risk letting anything happen to my father. Aldréa was vile. I didn't know what she was capable of—or how violently she would react if I were to go to someone for help. Figuring out how I would hide the mark from my father, who was *conveniently* attending a medical meeting out of the state for the next week, was one thing, but hiding it from Derek... or Matthaya... would be impossible.

I quickly made up my mind not to go to work tomorrow.

My eyes were bloodshot now, and I was beginning to feel lightheaded anyway. I patted another tissue against my face to dab up the blood that was still weeping from the cut. I spread some ointment over my cheek, removed some bandages from my medicine drawer, and placed them strategically over the wound to prevent it from rubbing against anything overnight.

The bathroom door unlocked with a click and I took a few shaky steps to get to my bed. I collapsed and saturated my pillow with more than just one night's worth of pain and tears.

Matthaya...

I wanted him—whoever he was. *Whatever* he was. Only God knows why, but I wanted him. And I soon drifted into a delusion that he could somehow help me, that he was there sitting beside me, his cool touch massaging a trail down the back of my neck.

I had slept for much longer than I had thought I would and awoke sometime mid-afternoon. I checked my phone and read a text from Derek confirming that my tardiness would be excused and telling me to take it easy for the rest of the day.

If only he knew the truth.

A brief trip to the bathroom confirmed my nightmare was, in fact, real, and I still had the wound to show for it, though it was now scabbed over with an unsightly layer of crusted blood. I took a few moments to reapply a fresh bandage and put a game plan together in my head for the day. I needed to get out of the house.

My stomach grumbled. There was no way in hell I was going downstairs for something to eat.

I changed out of my bloodstained shirt and put on a light jacket before prying open my window and climbing out onto the roof. I braced myself and dropped down to the ground. The overgrown grass in the backyard softened the fall. There was a high picket fence surrounding our property that, if I were careful enough, I could vault over to reach the neighbors' open yard and then the sidewalk. My fingers stretched warily over the tips of the fence posts and I pulled myself up and over, careful to avoid scuffing my arms as I landed.

I'd overslept by so many hours that by the time I had gotten myself something to eat dusk was already on my heels. My heart was set on seeing my mother that night. Only she could help me let go of the hatred and anxiety pulsing through me. I would have given anything to see my mother again—to feel her arms wrapping around me as gently and sweetly as any mother could ever embrace her child.

I would have given the world to have her in my life and to rid myself of that she-devil, Aldréa. I would even risk confronting Matthaya just to feel the presence of the sleeping soul beneath her weathered headstone. Even *he* couldn't stop me.

"What are you doing here?" a stern voice prompted me from behind.

"Leave me alone." My face was cupped in my hands and my reply nearly inaudible.

"Where were you last night?" He sounded disappointed. Soft footsteps made their way closer and closer to me, followed by a faint scoff and then a snarl. "What happened to you?" He remained behind me to avoid my gaze. "Why are you bleeding?"

He couldn't have seen the bandage yet...

"It was an accident," I lied. The quiver in my voice probably gave me away.

His steps were silent and he soon stood looming over me with an open hand near my face.

"Let me see it."

His request was more of a demand than a plea; he lifted his other hand toward me, threatening to pry my hands away if I didn't remove them from my face voluntarily. "Please," he added, looking me in the eye. I was surprised to hear that part.

The bandage tugged at my skin as I peeled it back. Without meeting his eyes, I could sense his shock and disgust. His fingers came to my chin and he tipped my face toward his.

"Who did this to you, Kathera?" he asked, kneeling beside me. Matthaya's usual coldness faded as his thumb pressed firmly against my chin and he further investigated the scratch on my face.

His eyes narrowed. "Your stepmother..."

9

MATTHAYA

KATHERA DID not verbally confirm the accuracy of my assessment, but her expression twisted with intrigue.

It was more obvious than she knew.

"Human nail marks," I divulged. "The essence of aged skin... *clearly* not yours. A trace of the oils of dark hair radiates from it. She was very angry with you at the time. The sweat of rage still lingers around the wound."

"You can tell all of that by—"

"Scent." I touched the peels of skin edging the scratch and she pulled away with a sharp breath. I had forgotten what pain felt like.

I had previously picked up the smell of her stepmother

in a foul mood, but tonight it was stronger than ever. There had also been a more potent human aura present on her. *He* didn't seem to be a threat, however.

"There was another," I added, and her eyes met mine as my fingers released her chin. "The owner of the shop."

I could sense him all over her; there was a deep, musky richness in the male pheromones saturating her skin. You've heard the expression "I can smell your fear." It's true. And I can smell your happiness, your anger, and... your desire.

"He is *very* attracted to you."

"I kind of figured that out already." She crossed her arms. "Did your supernatural nose tell you that?"

Her words brought the slightest grin to my lips.

"The pheromones of attraction infuse every breath that flows from your body. I can sense every bit of lust and fear that courses through your veins. You cannot hide your feelings from me... *Any of them.*"

Scattered shadows between patches of moonlight masked the brief flush of color in her cheeks, but I noticed it nonetheless. The rosy pink hue complimented her porcelain skin.

I stood and turned away from her. It was possible for me to help rid her of the wound, but it would require a great deal of trust in me—trust I had likely shattered with my seemingly weak understanding of courtesy.

Pity hadn't come easily to me in the past few centuries, and I shouldn't have cared enough to offer her my help, but I had believed she was too beautiful a young woman to be tarnished by such cruelty. Fear lingered within her for the life of her father and this kept her from standing up against the torture she endured at home.

"I can help you," I said. "If you allow me to."

"Help me what?" She rolled her eyes and huffed. "Kill Aldréa and bring my mother back to life?"

"Yes or no?" I asked firmly, gazing into her eyes.

She straightened up. "I'm sorry. I'm just angry and..." She sighed. "Yes," she said, shifting in place.

I lowered myself onto one knee again and leaned closer to her.

"What are you going to do?" Her eyes widened.

Vampires have little interest in old blood—the stale wound and dirty blood that traced her cheek was rather tasteless in comparison to blood that comes directly from the heart. I had no desire for it whatsoever.

"Close your eyes," I ordered, hoping she would squirm less. I really didn't know how she would react.

My lips parted and I brought my index and middle finger to my mouth, saturating them with a thin layer of saliva from my tongue. I wiped the fluid across her cheek, painting the wound. Kathera's breath fluttered and I pulled my hand away.

Her eyes opened. "What did you do to me?" she asked, her pulse racing. She came to her feet. "What... did you do to me... Matthaya?" Her breath quickened.

"Kathera, calm down. It will help—"

"Oh, God!" She doubled over. "What's happening?" Her voice rose fiercely and she cupped her face with her hands.

The flesh of the wound sizzled, reacting to the enzymes in my saliva. "It's burning!"

She brought her face up and glared at me spitefully. "There's so... much... pain! First Aldréa and then you! What did I ever do to you!?"

I reached out a hand to touch her shoulder, but she pulled away with a quick shrug backward.

"Don't touch me, you-you *monster*!"

"Kathera, please."

"Leave me alone." She turned away and took off running in the other direction.

"Be careful!"

I would have followed, but I knew such a pursuit would be in vain. She would understand soon, and then, surely she would forgive me.

If only things had been easier for her at home. Aldréa was an increasing threat and who knew what she was capable of?

It was inevitable my saliva would make the wound heal, but the exact time frame in which that would occur was unclear. I wished she had given me a moment to clarify what I had done, but it was too late for that.

I shouldn't have treated her the way I had and I felt like a fool for starting the conversation with such malice. Kathera had promised me her friendship in exchange for a companion. It was a promise I had accepted with questionable judgment and I suddenly found myself missing her company—even regretting the way I had neglected her fragile heart.

She was gone now and I had nothing to do but feel sorry for myself for being so inconsiderate. The most I could do was wish Kathera the best through the night and hope her stepmother kept her distance while the wound healed.

10

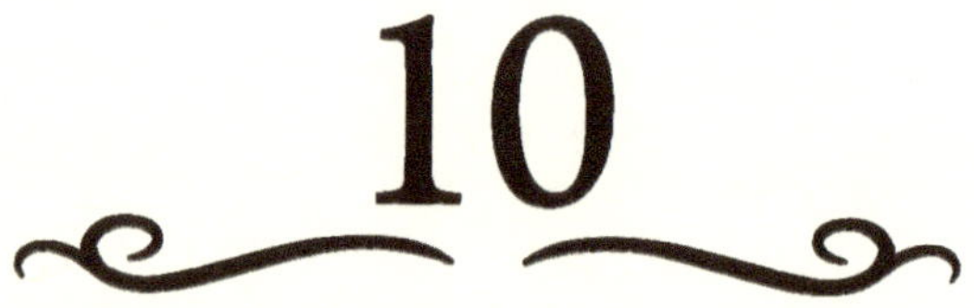

I MASSAGED the tips of my fingers against my temples and tried to remember what a headache felt like. It had been decades since I had befriended anyone and centuries since I had been called something so condescending. In the darkness of my solitude, I had escaped that wicked title by keeping to myself and drinking only the blood of animals. I had stopped killing and intended never to harm again.

I had not attacked her, but had I harmed Kathera by trying to help her?

As I sat pondering my actions, the gaze of another drew my attention. The painting above my fireplace mantel haunted me every day of my immortal life—but I would never have dared to take it down. Kathryn was a part of my past that would stay with me forever. The melody of her sweet voice had become distorted over the years and the scent of her body even less familiar. The feminine curves of her face and the supple ivory skin of her neck and throat could not escape my memory… as long as I kept her painting near.

A new voice was creeping into my ears—penetrating my restless sleep with new tragedy and need.

Kathera.

I refused to believe that she could invade my thoughts against my will, but it was happening. Slowly, my brain took what little memory I had left of my Kathryn and assimilated it with my newest acquaintance.

Perhaps it was the bright auburn fire peeking out from the roots of her rich, burgundy colored hair that lured my subconscious into such comparisons. Maybe it was her fair skin or her blue eyes that provoked it. Regardless of the external similarities, there was a dark maturity in Kathera, and the heavy burdens on her soul showed whether she knew it or not.

I had done what I could for her, but I could not save her from her fate—whatever it was—and that was part of the reason I could not bring myself to be patient with her.

My eyes met the terrace window and moonlight shimmered across the balcony. It was a gentle reminder of the hour and I felt compelled to see if Kathera would return to her mother's grave… or to see me at all.

I pushed my body up off the armchair I had been sitting in and decided to humor my concerns with some fresh air. I locked the door behind me and tossed the keys into my pocket. I wasn't very concerned about the possibility of thievery, but I took minimum measures to safeguard the sanctity of Kathryn's painting. No thief would get within yards of the place without leaving a strong scent in their wake. Evasion of my wrath would not be an option.

The rain had finally stopped and the ground had dried up enough to leave my shoes clean of mud. It was still soft under my steps and I searched the ground for signs of recent activity as I walked through the night. I had been around town many times, taking in the sights and sounds of the nightlife in the area.

I had seen Kathera's shop and even watched her as she walked home from work once. It was a quiet town with law-abiding citizens who kept to themselves during daylight hours, but even the sweetest city has its sins. The darkness brings forth prowlers and demons, and I have witnessed their deeds too often to forfeit trust to the night.

It surprised me how brave Kathera was to make the perilous journey home every evening—alone. A young woman of her sense should have recognized the danger of it, but perhaps the fate that awaited her at home made the risk seem trivial.

My shoes clicked against the sidewalk as I strode, and I witnessed the city shutting down. Shop signs turned off, buildings went dark, and the parking lots emptied. People had places to be and families to tend to. People had lives to live.

Faint sounds of a female voice echoed in the distance and my ears immediately tuned into it.

Kathera?

The breathing was heavy and distressed and not too far off.

I picked up the pace and jogged ahead to the location of the voice. Instinct told me to stay away, but my conscience begged otherwise.

As I opened the cemetery gate, the squeal of a creaky hinge pierced my ears and I flinched. In a gesture of invitation, the lock had been left open and lay neatly atop a nearby pile of chains.

She was there; I felt it.

A split second and I lost her scent to a gust of frigid air.

"I'm sorry." A small voice came from nearby. I turned and saw Kathera standing a few feet away from me, her hands at her sides and a frown tugging heavily at the edges of her quivering lip.

"I'm sorry, Matthaya, for what I said to you." She stepped closer and brought her hands together to her chest.

Relief filled me. She was not only out of harm's way, but the mark on her face had healed without a trace.

A red hue saturated the edges of her eyes and I could taste the tears she had yet to cry. Her agony captivated me. An advantage of my *condition* was that I hadn't many weaknesses, but the tears of a girl in pain could still enslave me. I was miserably at her mercy now.

"I was scared," she said, taking another step toward me. "And angry." And another. "I've been hurt so many times that I didn't know what to think. I shouldn't have said those things to you, Matthaya. I'm sorry." Her face fell and her eyes met the ground. Her burgundy tresses tumbled over her shoulders. "Can you ever forgive me?"

There was nothing to forgive. I *was* a monster and no amount of denial could change that fact, which I would live with for the rest of my days. It had hurt to hear it from her after what I had done to help, but what did she know? She didn't know what I really was.

Her courage crumbled. She let out a muffled moan and then burst into tears.

In a final step, I closed the gap between us. I opened my arms and offered a hand sympathetically out to her. I did not know how to soothe the pains beyond those I had caused.

Kathera leaned in cautiously, glancing at my hands and then back at me. I forced a grin in an attempt to assure her I had accepted her apology. She shuffled an inch closer and looked me in the eye, then she looked down and thrust herself into me, knocking me back a half step. She buried her face against my chest and her forearms close to my body and cried.

It wasn't what I had planned, but I couldn't push her away. She needed someone to comfort her—to hold her close and tell her what she wanted to hear. Heeding the obligations of a "friend," I closed an arm around her and my other hand came up behind her head, where I lightly stroked my fingers through her hair.

"You're safe. You're safe with me, Kathera." Her silky strands tickled my fingertips. "I forgive you."

Like a puppet with her strings freshly cut, she sunk into me, losing every thread of apprehension. She melted into my embrace as if she had believed my words to be true.

Surely, it wasn't a lie, but...

The scent of her tears filled my nostrils with a unique, salty odor as they saturated a patch of my shirt. Her breathing was erratic and her body reverberated against me as she cried heavily in my arms. It was painful, in a way, to hold her close and know that she was depending on only my affections to ease her heart.

My fingers combed down through her locks and caressed the back of her neck as I waited for her to regain her composure. She was alone in her fight with her stepmother and the quarrels between them were something she would disclose to no one else.

Without an outlet for her frustrations, she risked isolation and depression. She found her release in *me* just then, and I found a small amount of relief in knowing that I was able to ease at least some part of her mortal pain.

In the minutes that passed, her breathing relaxed and her fingers loosened their grasp on the folds of my shirt.

"Thank you," she murmured, her face still pressed against the damp fabric on my chest.

My fingers cupped the side of her neck. She felt

overwhelmingly warm, flushed with the delicate heat that often accompanied human sorrow.

Kathera's reddened eyes glanced up at me and she sniffled before clearing her throat. My eyes traced hers. Mahogany colored eye shadow had been smudged toward her hairline on both sides.

"I needed this," she said with a congested cough. A small smile emerged.

I had forgotten what a delicate balance existed between the emotions of joy and sadness. Something as simple as an embrace had rescued her from her misery, filling her fervent heart with a moment of sanctuary.

"I cannot keep you safe forever," I said, my fingers unconsciously brushing against her chin.

"Could you?" Her azure eyes glittered. "If you wanted to?"

No. I simply couldn't. She knew nothing of how the disease worked, or what I was for that matter. The sheer thought of taking her away from mortality and into the hell that was vampirism left me sickened. Even if it *were* possible.

"No." I shook my head. "I can—"

Her hands clasped my face and I froze. The pulse of her heart vibrated through her fingers. A skip in its beat diverted my senses, and before I could stop her, she lifted herself the inch necessary to press a kiss against my lips.

It was brief, and she soon sunk back down to her feet, taking a moment to savor the prize she had stolen from me.

There was a flutter in her chest as she anticipated a reply, but I said nothing.

The kiss had had no effect on me.

But, as I lingered a moment in thought, a remarkable sensation penetrated my lips from the minute trace of saliva that remained. I moistened them with the ridge of my tongue... and...

Kathryn's fair ivory skirt danced in the wind as she twirled about in the grass. A scent of fresh breeze teased my nostrils with hints of orchid and honeysuckle. Her face turned toward mine and the sunlight brought to life the radiance of her skin, accentuating the roundness of her cheeks and the stunning blue sparkle of her eyes. She hiked up her dress and jaunted toward me...

"Matthaya?" Kathera swallowed hard and a somber expression swept across her face. She tangled her hands together and took a step back, embarrassed. "That was stupid. I'm sorry, Matthaya. I-I shouldn't have..."

The urge to taste her again possessed me and our eyes locked. The scent of her soft, anxious breaths drew me in.

"Matthaya?"

I grasped her shoulders, cleared my head of discretions, and pulled her to me. The careful tug knocked a faint gasp from her lungs, but her heartbeat raced excitedly. My face tilted and Kathera closed her eyes, relaxing into my hands as I took back what she had stolen from my lips.

Curls of copper fire shimmered beneath the sun.

I closed my eyes to the darkness and let the kiss take

over.

Kathryn?

I caressed gentle folds of mossy-green satin. Morning light warmed my skin, and the lush fragrance of grassy Irish hills roused me.

Her delicate hands inched up my chest where they grazed the buttons of my shirt and then grasped firmly onto my collar.

A restrained grunt of pain escaped her lips and she flinched, withdrawing partially and then kissing me again without hesitation. I disregarded it, too, as she weaved her fingers affectionately through my hair and sent another wave of Kathryn's essence crashing through me.

"Matthaya?" She took a breath and slid her cheek to mine, her lips resting just at my jaw line. Her fingers slipped toward the gap of exposed flesh at the opening of my shirt collar and she traced over the thin gold chain that hung from my neck. "What is this?"

"Wh-what?" Sunlight stung my eyes a moment longer before reality returned and the shadows enveloped us once more.

Kathera tried to decipher the tiny cross.

Kathryn's necklace.

I backed away and covered it protectively with my hand.

"It's nothing. I-I..." I stammered, at a loss for words.

"It's alright." She took up my hand and smiled assuredly. "It doesn't matter right now."

But it did.

Kathera had put her trust in me and, as a friend, I was

obligated to share the truth with her. But... I wasn't ready to share the long, painful memory of Kathryn's story with her yet.

The heat and light pressure from her hands clutching mine convinced me she was willing to wait for it.

We took a walk away from the cemetery and through the sleeping streets of the city. I kept pace with Kathera and she lingered beside me close enough to latch her arm around mine. It was nostalgic—having her there. She had put so much faith in me even when I had told her so little about myself. Walking with her made me feel at ease and... human. Feeling her warm fingers cupped affectionately around my arm lifted my spirits and made me want to tell her so much more.

"Matthaya?" Kathera stopped abruptly and grabbed the cuff of my sleeve. "What do you see in me?" she asked, peering deeply into my eyes. There was hunger in them that I knew would only be satisfied by, well, by *me*.

"Answer me, Matthaya." She tugged again, more firmly. It was a question I couldn't answer with the truth.

An artificial cough grazed my throat. "I don't know," I lied.

She was a smart girl, as cunning as Kathryn, but with the insatiable darkness of the new century coursing through her spirited veins.

"You don't know," she repeated, "or you don't want to tell me?" Kathera stared hard into my eyes in search of one of the *real* answers. "You act like you don't care about me, but you came to me tonight when you thought I needed you. What does *that* mean?"

"Whatever you want it to," I replied in a sorry attempt to fend off her inquiry. I wanted to tell her the truth. Everything. I wanted to pretend she was Kathryn and free myself from the burdens of my secret past.

"Whatever I want it to, huh?" She stopped in front of me, wrapped her fingers around my shoulders, and pressed gently. "I want it to mean *something* to you." My eyes closed against my will at the feel of her fingertips sweeping down my neck. "And... I want you to trust me and stop holding back your feelings."

My eyes reeled opened. "Trust you?" I forced her fingers away. "Surely you don't believe there *is* something between us."

"Yes. I do."

She cupped both hands around the sides of my face. "You felt something when you kissed me tonight," she whispered. "I know you did. You let go—if only for an instant. And I want to know what it is that's keeping you from admitting it. I want to know why you wear a cross around your neck, and hide it so defensively. Believing in God is not a crime. I want to know why you keep telling me to leave, and then returning to see if I am still here." Her gaze hardened. "I only have one life, Matthaya. I'd really like you to be part of it."

She pressed her lips against my cheek.

"Thanks for walking me home. Goodnight." Her fingers

slipped from my face and she backed away gracefully and smiled.

I watched her unlock the door to her house and go inside with less caution than usual. Her stepmother was out and I felt confident that Kathera would be safe for the night.

The door closed and I was alone in the darkness. I sighed and stared off into the distance. I wanted to tell her that I could not be part of her life because I would have to witness the end of it. Immortality does not allow us to love for long, and so I have always chosen not to love at all.

But the lingering taste of Kathryn I had found on Kathera's lips allured me. Surely she would want me to love her for more than the apparitions her kisses induced.

Part of me wanted to believe I could possibly love a human, if even only for a short time. But that wasn't an option. Derek's scent was overwhelmingly strong in her hair and on her skin, and it was inevitable that I would lose her to his mortality if he pressed forward with his courtship.

She could love him... *if* she let me go. My uniqueness attracted her, but the harsh truth of our incompatibility would sink in eventually and then she would be gone.

Rain dripped into my eyes and I shook my head. Water droplets began hitting the ground much harder than they had earlier and the clouds thickened. Darker and darker they became until all but a faint glow of the moon had been swallowed up by their heavy gray cloaks. I felt what little humanity remained within me clawing at my skin.

Deep within my pale shell, there resided a shard of

humility and grief. That splinter of my former self was enough to pierce my still heart every so often. That heart had fallen and risen in the wake of only one.

Every scent of Kathera made my blood stiffen as I recalled the sight of Kathryn. They were too much alike and I was beginning to long for her. To feel... something for her I could not justify.

Just as quickly and surely as I had sworn myself to my childhood love, I was suddenly weaving a story with another, daring to bind myself once more to an inevitable tragedy.

Humans, like vampires, forget. After many years, we forget our mistakes. And so we are doomed to repeat them.

Memories are fragile things.

And someday Kathera would forget me...

11

KATHERA

MY HOUSE was empty. The silence was peaceful. With Aldréa gone, the night was less frightening. Maybe it was the crazy lovesickness fluttering around in my stomach, or the fantasy that, somehow, Matthaya would watch over me when Aldréa returned.

He had said it himself—I was safe with him. Though he had probably said it only to make me feel better, I wanted to believe him. I *needed* to believe him.

I felt no remorse over the fact that I had kissed him. But then he had kissed me back and a flurry of emotions made my heart race. At first, his kiss felt incredibly new and different— exhilarating and triumphant. But then I had the realization that I'd kissed him before.

Only I hadn't...

That was until the sensual pinch of one of his teeth had nicked me unintentionally and that sensation of familiarity evaporated.

I bunched a section of my pillow into my fist and clutched it tightly, retreating into the warm sheets of my bed. I could still feel Matthaya's cool skin. His soft fingers combing through my hair as he held me close and promised me safety.

I could still taste him, though our encounter had ended less passionately than I had hoped. No matter how much of myself I offered him, a thick veil of secrets came between us. I wanted him to trust me. I wanted him to tell me those secrets.

Where did he go each night?

Where did he go each day?

What was he?

So many questions riddled my brain, but my tired body could humor them no more.

Raindrops hit the roof hard, each one of them part of an unbearable symphony of clattering roof tiles. An annoying leak in the gutter outside my window woke me during times like these.

TAP... TAP... TAP. The water hit the sill of my window and ran off down the side of the house.

My father was still away at his meeting and Aldréa was probably out spending time—and money—with her rich friends.

Hopefully Derek was holding up well without me at the shop. I was way behind on my demon goddess tattoo and there was just no way in hell Derek would have been able to fill in for me as far as that went.

I sat up on my bed. My mouth felt dry and I rubbed my eyes with my palms. It was difficult to get up when the light seeping in through my window blinds was dull and gray each day.

Was it too much to ask for a little sunlight?

The rain refused to cease and I was feeling the saddening effects of constant gloominess. I was tired of walking to work in the rain and I hated taking the bus.

My feet touched the fluffy rug beneath my bed and wrinkled the familiar softness between my toes.

The awful weather did me no favors on my way to work and the heavy wind showed no mercy to my umbrella.

I smoothed a hand over the back of my hair and patted down the frizz. I pushed open the door and avoided Derek's eye contact by watching my shoes as I scuffed my feet on the entrance mat.

"How was your break?" he asked, coming out from behind the front desk. "You feeling okay?" He bent over to try to meet my lowered face. "Kathera?"

"I'm fine." I averted my eyes, feeling guilty about the man in my life Derek didn't know about.

I hung my wet coat up on a hanger in the back room and

shook the excess water from the hem of my jeans. My shoes were soaked. The wind had trashed my umbrella.

I wanted the rain to go away. I wanted to feel the sun on my face and—

"Sucks out there, huh?" Derek motioned to the window.

"Yes!" I tossed my umbrella to the floor. "I hate this weather!"

I popped open a small compact and dabbed the dark mascara smudges from the edges of my eyes.

Derek chuckled softly.

"What's so funny, Derek?" I took off my shoes and set them on top of the heater before turning to confront him.

"You're kind of..." he paused to tailor his words, "*entertaining* when you're upset."

"What is it with you guys? You were going to say cute, weren't you?" I laughed, even though I had tried not to.

"Maybe. Trying to avoid a lawsuit, that's all." He smirked. "But, hey. You said it. I didn't."

A rumble of thunder shook through the floor and I gasped, bracing myself. I looked out the front windows and up at the massive army of storm clouds marching across the sky. It was getting darker by the minute.

Derek came to stand by me and we watched a white-hot flash of lighting illuminate the city. The building lights flickered on and off.

"You know what? Screw it," Derek said, gruffly. He threw the lock on the front door and flipped the outside sign off. "Let's finish up what we can in here and call it a day." He turned to face me and shrugged. "No one's gonna show up in this weather anyway. The forecast doesn't look any better for tonight."

"What about Stephanie?" I asked. Our other artist was scheduled to come in right after me.

"I've already asked her not to come in," he replied. "I meant to tell you, too, but I wasn't sure how bad it was going to get out there so I waited. I'm sorry." He smiled at me and then gestured to the window again. "I think you brought the storm with you, Kathera."

"I doubt that," I sneered, closing the blinds and pulling the security grate down over the window. "The weather has been terrible for a while now. It's just a coincidence that I'm here."

"I was kidding," he muttered from behind the counter.

We cleaned up the shop, did some inventory, and checked over some books before Derek picked my shoes up off the heater and delivered them to me.

"You think your dad's home?" he asked. "You don't normally leave this early."

My dad was almost never home and this week was no exception.

"No," I replied. "He's at a conference out of state and won't be back for a week or so."

"Oh?" Derek handed me my shoes. "Sorry to hear that. What about your *incredibly pleasant* stepmother?"

I slid my jacket off the hanger. "Don't know and don't care."

Damn it. It was soaked with water and my umbrella was useless in its current state. Some metal wires had snapped at the joints.

"Kathera?" Derek cleared his throat.

"Yes?" I looked up.

"I'm not the best cook in the world, but... if you want to come over, I'd be happy to make you dinner."

"Oh." I squeezed my soggy jacket, unintentionally dripping water onto the floor. "Well, um..."

Derek grabbed a paper towel and bent down to wipe up the puddle.

"Sorry," I whispered.

"It doesn't have to be a date or anything like that. Really." He tossed the wet towel into the trash can beside me.

The last time I had had a real homemade dinner was back before my mother died. And that was a long, *long* time ago. Dinner with someone else—anyone else for a change— would be nice.

Besides, it *wouldn't* be a date this time, right? We were just closing early and he was being nice. Derek being Derek.

It wasn't like I had much else to do.

Matthaya was probably home keeping dry. Wherever *home* was.

Derek pulled his red leather jacket off a hanger and started to put it on. "Don't feel like you have to."

"Thank you for offering. I'd love to join you."

A second glance at my crumpled, soggy mess of a coat had him removing his own from the one arm he had barely gotten into it.

"If you're coming over for dinner, I'm not letting you get sick from being wet in the cold." He offered me his jacket, and the look in his eyes gently indicated I couldn't refuse. "You're the best I've got, Kathera," he said. "*Artist,* I mean."

I tossed on his jacket and rolled the sleeves up to my wrists. It fit loosely, but kept me dry as we made a break for his car in the downpour.

I hadn't been to his house before, but I had an idea of where he lived. Though he had the entire place to himself now, he had once lived with his late father. We went inside the single-story brick house and the massive living room filled me with awe. Hardwood floors at the entrance and pristine maroon carpeting from wall to wall. Warm and inviting off-white stucco walls. A large, flat-screen television on the other side of the room in front of his couch. It was a beautiful place and he had *really* good taste.

"I'm tired of this weather, myself." Derek shut the door behind me and trudged into his living room. He shook the rain from his hair. "Hey, do you mind if I change?"

"It's your house." I shrugged and smiled. "Sorry you got drenched, by the way, but thank you for letting me borrow your jacket." I slipped it off and handed it to him.

"Make yourself at home," he said, motioning toward the couch. "I'm going to hang this up and grab a new shirt."

"Thanks."

I plopped down on the soft chenille-covered couch in

front of his television and made myself comfortable as he stepped out of the room. Wearing his jacket had left traces of his scent on my skin. Sandalwood or patchouli. I couldn't tell what was blended together in his subtle cologne, exactly, but it reminded me of a cozy campfire in the woods with a splash of exotic heat.

There were shelves of old books and meticulously placed dragon sculptures around his house, along with a stack of DVDs in front of his TV. Classics. Action movies. A few thrillers. Exactly what I had expected to find. A stack of free weights and an exercise bike were tucked into the far corner of the living room.

The coffee table in front of me had a mirrored surface and Derek's reflection caught my attention as he returned to the kitchen with a fresh shirt draped over his arm.

I wondered if I should have been watching, but it was hard not to notice him walk in shirtless. I'd seen him a thousand times with fitted t-shirts and button-ups, but I had never really dwelled on his physical appearance before. Compared to Matthaya, Derek was muscular, but then again, he had always been a fitness geek when he hadn't been drawing tattoos. He was lean and toned, though, not ripped and intimidating like some gym rats.

As he tugged his shirt over his head, a thick ridge of scar tissue caught my eye. It trailed down his left side near his ribs and disappeared beneath his belt.

What the hell could have caused such a violent wound? My stomach turned at the sight. I knew he had gotten into a lot of fights as a teenager, but...

"You can watch something if you want, while I cook," Derek said, tugging the hem of his shirt down. He poked his head through the kitchen cutout and pointed behind me. "Bathroom is behind you and the remote for the TV is under the table there."

"Thanks," I replied.

"Let me know if you need anything."

I flipped on his TV and channel surfed for several minutes, trying to shake the image of his massive scar from my memory.

Water was boiling on the stove, something yummy-smelling was in the oven, and it wasn't long before tantalizing smells filled the air.

Later that evening, after dinner, Derek brought two cups of coffee to the couch and set them down on the mirrored table, sliding a small marble coaster beneath each of them first.

"Thank you," I said, taking the glossy, dark green mug on my end into my hands and polishing the handle with my thumb. "Do you mind if I ask you something?" The question had been whirling inside me for several minutes while I had waited for the coffee to brew.

He took a sip from his cup. "Fire away."

I felt awkward for taking advantage of his kindness but...

"I don't know if this is too personal, but I... noticed the scar... on your side. Where did you get it?"

"Oh." He cleared his throat and tapped his fingers against the side of his mug. "That."

Maybe I shouldn't have asked.

"I'm sorry, Derek, I—"

"I wasn't always this way," he said, placing his cup back onto its coaster. A frown stole the joy from his face. "I used to be a very different person. I was involved in bad stuff as a kid. A gang—*a lot* of fights. And my mom threatened my dad that if I didn't straighten out, she'd leave him."

He took a deep breath and pressed his fingers to his forehead.

"The night I ended up in the hospital with a knife wound that... *should* have killed me, she didn't come see me. When I came home, she had already left. All I had was my dad. That's when I realized how damn ignorant I had been." He wrinkled the fabric of the armrest with his fingers and bit his lip.

"I didn't mean to open old wounds," I said, scooting closer so I could put a hand onto his shoulder. "Really."

"I ruined my whole family and lost almost everything," he continued, looking off to the side. "All because I picked a fight with the wrong guy... over the wrong girl."

"Derek." I set my mug on the coffee table and rested my free hand over one of his. "Your mother would be proud to know what you've done with yourself. You've changed. You helped your father have a good life."

"And I haven't seen my mom since." He scowled and then cleared his throat again in an obvious attempt to change the subject. "So, what's your story?" He resituated himself on the couch and leaned back into the cushions.

"My story?" I asked, releasing my hand from his shoulder. "What do you mean?"

"Well, pardon my bluntness here, but you've been acting a little detached lately. It's like your mind's somewhere else or something." He paused. "Are you... seeing someone? You could have just told me, you know? Instead of—"

"He's no one you need to worry about." I should have lied, but he deserved an honest answer. "He's a little strange."

"But you really like him, don't you?"

"What makes you think that?" I knew I was blushing.

"I can see it in you. You've changed recently." His eyebrows rose slightly. "Why are you making excuses for this guy, anyway? Either you like him or you don't. Right? Is he worth protecting?"

Yes?

"Well, I-I care about him." I crossed my arms and sat back. "But, I don't think he trusts me."

"I trust you," he blurted, then swallowed hard and looked at his hands in his lap. "I mean... how do you know that? How do you know he *doesn't* trust you?"

"I..." I leaned forward and lifted my coffee cup up from the coaster, cupping it in my hands. It was cold now. "I doubt you want to hear this, but I kissed him."

Derek straightened up in his seat, his brow furrowed. "Did he kiss you back?"

"Yeah, but—"

"There shouldn't be a 'but.'" He tried to hide his disgusted expression. "What's wrong with him? Can he not decide if he wants you? Or is he just paranoid?"

"I don't know. I haven't known him for that long, but it feels like I have and maybe that's why he's scared. Maybe I'm trying too hard, or moving too fast, and—"

"He sounds like a fool. Sorry." He scoffed.

I laughed nervously. "Maybe I'm just blinded by love."

Derek smiled sheepishly and looked me in the eye. "That makes two of us."

My face was on fire.

"Damn it. I'm sorry, Kathera." He exhaled loudly and groaned beneath his breath. "I didn't want it to happen this way. I just wanted to have a nice, quiet dinner with you away from the rest of the world. Then you mentioned *him*..." He turned toward me. "I know I asked you to tell me, but still. I had expected to hear something about how great this guy was, or how happy he makes you feel, but... that's not what happened."

I remained silent and his dark brown eyes searched mine.

"I don't know what this guy has said or done to make you want him so badly, but whatever he *hasn't said*..." His voice trailed off. I could hear his breaths becoming heavier.

I'd never seen him so flustered before and I wasn't worth getting worked up over.

"Kathera, I..." He licked his lips and sighed. "I don't even know how to say this to you, but..." He stood and offered me his hands, which I took and leveraged myself against to pull myself up from the couch.

"Give me a chance," he said, his voice shaking. "Please." His warm hands cupped mine with the utmost care.

I watched discomfort twist his face as he fought to get out the words that were on the tip of his tongue.

I forced a smile.

"You deserve better," he said, looking me in the eye. "You deserve to live in a house where you'll never be scared or feel alone. And you deserve to have someone there who cares about you. Someone who *isn't* afraid to trust you."

His fingers tightened over my own and I felt a rise in his pulse as it throbbed through my hands.

"Kathera, you deserve to love someone and be loved by them in return." He swallowed hard. "I-I would like to try to offer you those things. If you give me a chance. But I can't if..."

I froze and a breath caught in my lungs. Even as my body trembled with surprise, the warmth of Derek's hands holding mine eased my nerves. He looked right into my eyes and I was sure he had meant every single word that had come from his mouth.

But... Matthaya? I thought I wanted *him*. When he had kissed me back, I lost myself in it—in him.

Was it wrong of me to fall in love with Matthaya? Was *he* a... mistake?

I gasped at the painful thought and pulled my hands away from Derek.

"Kathera?" He reached out to rest a palm at the base of

my neck, lightly stroking the side of my throat with his thumb.

"Derek, I-I..."

I couldn't even take in a breath.

He was real. Warm and... present. All I had wanted was for Matthaya to look into my eyes the same way—to *want* *me.*

He took a step closer and a rush of body heat made my pulse quicken. His arm came up and hooked me around the waist as he leaned down and kissed me.

A dizzying rush of emotion bolted through my veins, electrifying my heart like a lightning strike. My eyes closed and I unconsciously went for his hips. I tucked my hands underneath the hem of his shirt, sliding my fingertips over smooth, hot skin. Accidentally, I grazed the scar along his ribs and felt a crushing wave of sympathy.

It must have been devastating. And all because of some girl?

Derek massaged the sensitive skin near my throat, taking my breath away with the incredible tenderness of his lips against mine. His other hand slid from my neck and I gasped as it came up underneath my blouse to tease the side of my ribs. He embraced me tightly, igniting new, carnal sensations. There was a firm plane of skin and muscle running across his torso and I felt his arms flex when my ecstatic lightheadedness made me lean more weight against him.

The softness of his lips weaved a spell and the fingers that caressed my hips gained power over the rest of my body. I clasped my hands onto his face, my fingertips tickled by the stubble. He pressed a hand against the small of my back and I couldn't suppress a groan of pleasure that resonated through me. Every inhalation thrilled me. Every exhalation made my grasp on him tighten.

I didn't want it to end.

In a carefully executed movement, he coaxed me to move and I was released from his kiss just long enough to resituate myself down against the couch. Derek propped himself up against the back and I drew seamlessly back into his kiss and welcoming embrace.

So much heat between us. Sweat beading on our skin. His taste on my lips. The taste I couldn't get enough of just then.

He was willing to sacrifice a friendship and risk a broken heart for an uninvited kiss with a girl who was in love with another man.

And it had worked.

My hands cupped over his shoulders, my nails grazing his neck, and my own pounding heart burning with some new-found desire. He held me close, his breaths growing longer and deeper as the satisfaction of our kiss settled. I was tired, but it was a good sort of tired—content and whole. The feeling of finally being protected... of finally being found and wanted.

Had I betrayed him? Had I betrayed Matthaya?

But... Derek was so real. So very, very real.

12

MATTHAYA

"YOU REEK of *him*." I tried to keep quiet but couldn't ignore the overpowering essence of Derek she exuded.

"Wh—?" Kathera looked surprised to see me. "What are you doing here?"

She had barely taken a few steps out of the shop door before she saw me standing at the corner of the building.

Heavy cloud cover kept most of the UV light from bothering me at dusk, though it *was* uncomfortable. Sunlight can cause a lengthy and intolerable death if we are exposed to it for long. I wouldn't smoke or burst into flames, though both of those options might have been more pleasant in the end. Festering from the inside out is an experience not soon forgotten.

"I take it you slept well last night?" I asked, noticing how much more at peace she seemed in general. Perhaps the company had staved off her nightmares for a change.

"Excuse me?" She glared at me.

The comment wasn't meant to be malicious.

"My, my... aren't we touchy?" I replied. "I came here early to walk you home and I don't even get so much as a simple 'Nice to see you.'" I leaned against the side of the building and propped one foot up on the wall behind me, crossing my arms.

She straightened the strap of her purse along the crest of her shoulder and frowned. "I'm sorry, Matthaya. I thought you were... trying to insinuate something."

Guilty conscience?

I didn't have to pry to know what had happened last night after Derek had invited her into his home. The potent eccentricities of their mingling pheromones had stained her skin. He had finally won her over.

I also did not have turn around to know Derek was behind me, ready to defend his prize.

"Hey, can I talk to you?" He came up beside us. "Kathera, can you give me a minute with your friend?"

There was rivalry bubbling up in his blood and the fire in his eyes to prove it. It was nothing to worry about. There wasn't a mortal alive with the strength to intimidate me, though the rigid tone of Derek's voice was an effective start.

Kathera shrugged and glanced at me with concern.

"It's alright, Kathera." I motioned to the overhang just behind us. "Why don't you wait there for a moment while we talk?"

She backed off and took a few steps away until she was out of earshot.

Derek looked me over quickly. "You don't get out much, do you?" he asked, his brows furrowing at the unnatural grayness of my skin.

"My... *condition* won't allow it," I replied in a tone just as slated as his had been.

I'd had over 400 years experience in back talk and I knew exactly how to answer even the most undermining questions with poise.

He quieted himself in preparation for a second blow.

"I don't know much about you," he started, "but she told me about how you've been treating her."

"In what way have I *treated* her, exactly?" I sneered, letting him do most of the talking. I remained calm but could sense his frustration building.

"She's told me about you. About what you are." Derek's gaze became dark and serious.

"Has she now?" I shot a glance past his shoulder at Kathera who was still in the distance behind us. Our eyes met briefly.

Derek's breath was hot with anger and it filled the air with tension. "Why don't you do us all a favor and stop leading her on?" he growled. I noticed one of his hands forming a fist as his heartbeat quickened.

"I haven't led her anywhere," I corrected. "Her assumptions did all the leading for her."

Even from a distance, I could taste the scent on her skin, her hair, and in the wisp of her breath. I smelled passion in the blood flowing through Derek's veins with every thump of his jealous heart.

He had kissed her that night... and she had let him. She had even enjoyed it behind her delirious cravings for me.

But the truth was we did not belong together. Despite my temporary fixation on the hallucinations she granted me, I needed to end the charade.

For her sake and mine.

"If you want her, you can have her," I said, simply. I took what was likely my last clear look at Kathera. "She was never mine to begin with."

And she could never be mine.

I turned and started walking off on my own. Derek watched, unsure of how to react.

"What did you say to him, Derek!?" Kathera rushed over to him. "Damn it!" She pushed past him and came after me.

My steps hastened.

"Matthaya! Wait! Where are you going?"

"You don't need me anymore," I said, my eyes not meeting hers.

"Matthaya!" She lunged for my hand, but I pulled it from her reach and she stumbled. I didn't want to hurt her, but it had to be done.

"Derek loves you." I paused and glanced off into the

distance. "I... do not."

"But... you said I was safe with you... that..."

I fought back the thread of mortal emotion tangling up my tongue and I finally forced the words from my mouth. "I said what needed to be said because you needed to hear it." It took all of my strength to lie to her face. "This fantasy you have cannot be. No matter what you believe, Kathera, I will *never* love you."

I thought her newfound love for Derek would keep her composed through my dismissal.

It didn't.

The sun was setting behind us, but a violent fire sparked in her eyes and it terrified me. The rage brewing within her made her shaky and weak. She toppled to her knees and her eyes glistened at me.

"Do not walk away from me, Matthaya!" she screamed with a chillingly familiar inflection.

Derek darted to her side and she shoved him away with all her might. A painful cry escaped her throat and I couldn't stop myself from locking eyes with her. Torment and agony surfaced on her face and her pupils lightened behind a soft, white haze.

"You will not reject me, Matthaya!"

Her words. I'd heard them before. They pierced my heart with a violent echo from my past.

"You will not reject me," she repeated in the same cold, threatening tone.

My body stiffened.

The pale color in her eyes disappeared beneath her eyelids and she fell. Derek caught her in his arms just before she could hit the concrete. I grimaced but swiftly mustered the courage to vanish from the scene.

She would be safe with him...

℘　℘

I had to let go of my mistake.

As darkness fell, I disappeared from her life, leaving Derek to fend against whatever beasts she fought in her delirious state. Though I wondered if it was a delusional state at all, considering how her words were eroding a savage grain into my soul—haunting me throughout the night as I walked the streets. Alone.

"You will not reject me," she had said. I had heard it before.

A jingle of metal caught my attention and I veered around.

"You can't have it all, Matthaya," a rough voice crackled. A skinny, pale-skinned woman of middle age crept out from the shadows behind me, wearing a wide, wild-eyed grin beneath her hooded cloak.

"Hello, love," she piped, a thick British accent coloring her voice. The tone was hoarse and menacing even when she wasn't trying. "You can't have the best of both worlds. That's why we are given a choice."

"I was never given a choice, Ve'tani!" I roared. My maker

was not a welcome face and her advice was the last thing I needed.

"Kill the girl." Her vibrant amber eyes, flecked with browns and reds, gleamed with evil.

"I would never." My lips curled angrily. "How dare you ask me to commit such an atrocity! I am no longer under your control."

Her lanky legs were hidden beneath a long flowing cloak of black velvet. Fastened at her waist with an elegant brooch, a black sash fell from her hips down to her ankles and flapped and twisted as the wind came and went.

"But you are, whether you believe it or not. You *always* are." She pulled the hood down off her head. A pile of curly blond tresses framed her face and tumbled down past her shoulders. The heavy gold bangles at her wrists clinked together as her hands came back down to her sides.

"Humidity does such wonders to one's complexion." She grinned sarcastically, dragging her thin, craggy fingers through her hair. She paced as she spoke. "It's been many years, and you are still as naive as you have ever been."

"I have learned many things," I muttered through my teeth. "And I have grown in many ways." My fingers twitched and pulsed in anticipation of a fight. She had always hated me for my physical advantages because I was much stronger than her.

The DNA in my blood allowed mutations to occur in only a few decades, mutations beyond what some vampires achieve only after a dozen centuries. Ve'tani's jealousy seethed through her every pore, but she knew better than to anger me. She knew I was a powerful ally. I tried to distance myself from her, but she challenged me periodically in hopes that I would someday, again, take her side.

"Why are you here?" I snarled, baring my fangs to her. She never came around without some foul purpose.

"Your heartstrings have been resounding as of late," she answered. "The ambience of your dilemma has left me with little peace and quiet."

Our souls were forever entwined by an unbreakable chain of psychic energy. Thousands of miles apart—even whole countries away—she could feel my agony... my frustration. It was a treacherous bond I had endured because it was impossible to escape without one of us dying, or my maker severing the tie. Neither choice was a viable option for Ve'tani, as she would rather have me suffer in her wake than choose another companion in my place.

This unshakable side effect of vampirism allowed each pair of blood-linked hunters to keep tabs on the status and territory of one another. It was meant to help companions survive eternity. Ve'tani—driven by little more than vanity and greed—exploited the link between us to stalk me wherever I went.

When she had decided to take me, Ve'tani had sought a companion, and instead found herself an adversary. We were still connected, but she had lost full control over me centuries ago, a fact she refused to acknowledge.

"Do something with the girl, Matthaya. I am tired of this

woeful brooding you carry. I will not allow you to jeopardize our existence by allowing such knowledge to roam amongst mortals."

If I had been able to take Kathera as my own, I would have lost all connection with Ve'tani and become telepathically bound to Kathera instead, but this scenario clashed with the reality of my condition. Only the oldest vampires are able to sire. Changing her had never been an option.

"She is no threat to us," I replied, raising my voice. "She doesn't know what we are and, even if she did, she wouldn't tell anyone."

"Kill her, or I will do it for you. Those are your choices." Her head cocked to the side and she brought a finger to her lip in thought. "Although," she began, "her scent is impressive. She would make a powerful addition to our kind. It would seem a waste to kill one with such great potential." Her eyes met mine fiercely and she shrugged. "It's a shame you don't have the siring gift, but I like you too much to choose another in your place. Then again, fewer Sires means cleaner bloodlines." She took another step toward me and stretched out her fingers to touch my shoulder. I shrugged away from her touch and my jaw clamped down tightly in a snarl.

"What? Do you think you're in love with her?" She laughed dryly through her teeth. "Vampires cannot love. The only sense of attachment we have is for the sake and preservation of our kind. The weaknesses of your mortality haunt you with the illusion of emotion, but you cannot love another."

If we were truly unable to love, then we were surely as unable to hate, but there was a plume of anger billowing within me toward Ve'tani.

"Why don't you let me go?" My eyes flickered with rage. "Why don't you find another more suitable to your cause?"

Ve'tani bent over, shook the edge of her cloak just above her ankles, and smoothed a hand down across the fabric. "I like you," she said, simply and matter-of-factly as she stood up and brushed a stretch of her sash. "I value your strength... your youth and your beauty. You know this."

"I am merely a jewel in your crown." It was obvious she kept ties with me because I was a trophy in her eyes—a symbol of her capabilities as a maker.

As much as I tried to push the thoughts of Kathera from my mind, they lingered strongly enough for Ve'tani to sense.

"Your judgment is impaired by guilt," she croaked. "You *need* me. And now, you need to get rid of *her*. I demand you kill her or I will see to it that it happens."

I clenched my teeth and growled. "I will not steal her life from her."

"Perhaps you should have considered that before you got *involved*," Ve'tani spoke; her cold stare held me captive. "You have been given a chance to redeem yourself of your mistake. Don't make me do it for you."

Arguing with her was pointless, so I kept quiet as she absorbed her false sense of victory.

"Good boy." She beamed and then tucked her thick hair back behind her neck and tossed her hood over her head.

"You still know your place."

She turned away from me and disappeared into the night.

I was glad to see her go.

What was I to do about Kathera?

I thought long and hard and came across a solution that *could* keep her alive. If I could find a way to put her out of my mind, it would put her out of Ve'tani's, as well. She would forget about her if I could keep my feelings contained. But that would mean letting go and forgetting about Kathera myself.

Forget her smell.

Forget her taste.

Forget her friendship.

Her friendship... and the words that had struck me as tragic and yet heart-stoppingly familiar. Age was playing tricks on me for sure. The memory of Kathera kneeling mournfully on the ground, her hands in her lap and her eyes swollen with tears, began to remind me of Kathryn.

In the end, I had not walked away from Kathryn. I should have. My star-crossed arrogance had brought me to my sorry fate without her.

I lifted my face toward the brightly lit moon. Kathera was lucky she had someone to hold her close in my absence. I had tasted their attraction vividly in the scent of her skin and there was no doubt in my mind that Derek would quickly earn her devotion with me gone from her life.

Yes. That was the answer to the riddle that plagued me.

Stay out of her life...

13

KATHERA

I HAD always been afraid to die. I feared that unstoppable moment when my heart would beat its last.

But what was I going to do without him? Would I waste away after my last chance for a new life had turned his back on me? I was fragile, and Matthaya's refusal to take me with him had been more than enough to push me over the edge. He could have saved me from this end. He could have taken me with him.

Twinkling lights flashed below as the streetlamps shuddered from the storm. Wind gusts taunted me with snickers of ridicule, nipping at my cheeks with icy jaws while the unforgiving rain splashed against my face. Frustration choked *every last tear from my eyes and, for once, the darkness had become uninviting.*

With my last inhibitions tossed aside, I considered the worst.

No one would notice me gone.

No one would mourn my end—my scattered remains beneath the dying city lights. Some people do crazy things when they reach their breaking point. I had begun to understand why. My body lacked the strength to go on without Matthaya, but in truth, I was too afraid to die alone.

I stood and looked around the city rooftop, staring into the darkness of the clouds. There was so much solitude in the inky blackness above. So alone.

"So this is insanity?" I said to the sky. "This is the feeling of the end before death?" My tiny world crumbled in my hands and the storm was washing away any hopes of starting over.

I watched hundreds of busy lives darting along the streets to and fro, oblivious to the chaos all around. Thousands of people were building their lives, starting fresh, living, dying, growing, and fading. There I was, throwing it all away because I was afraid of life. In the short time Matthaya and I had been together, I had felt an extraordinary connection forming. He wouldn't admit it himself, but I saw it in the way our eyes met, his gaze no longer quick to break away from mine.

Perhaps I had taken it for granted that he would always be there.

Now he wasn't.

Loneliness taunted me, daring me to make my nightmares of suicide a reality.

I wished there was another way. I tried not to visualize what I would look like after the fall.

Once you enter a roller coaster car, strap yourself in, pull down the lap bar, and start moving, you have no choice but to hold your breath and wait for the fall you know is coming.

Once you reach it, however, you're never prepared. No matter how hard you try or how much you anticipate it, you never know the feeling until it hits you. It comes at you fast at first, and then you catch a glance of the hill leading toward the decline. Once you reach it, go over, and start to fall, your life seems to break into frames. You spiral down against your will. You hold your breath for what seems like forever and your heart skips a beat.

You're still shaking when it's over and you start to regret, but it's too late. Days pass and you forget how frightened you were. Later, you're willing to do it again, ignorant of the bullet your body took once already.

It didn't work like that.

In life, there's no lap bar.

All we can do is fall...

My infatuation with Matthaya planted new and different nightmares in my sleep. For weeks after our separation, I suffered through them and hesitated to discuss them with another living soul.

They pushed me into darkness. Depression. Thoughts of death and worthlessness plagued me, but I fought back the only way I knew how. I remembered him. I remembered Matthaya and knew my blood needed to serve a higher purpose than staining a sidewalk. I knew he wouldn't want me to die.

It had been weeks since I had paid my mother's grave a visit, and I despised myself for allowing such selfishness to keep us apart. She deserved better, but then, so did Derek.

Derek's embrace helped to soothe the pain... in time. Eventually, my heart had finally stopped aching. He cared for me much more than he should have, offering me a room to myself in his house while I recovered so I could get away from the bad influences of my stepmother. I was hurt and confused, and in that state of impaired judgment, I had accepted his help. With Aldréa out of the picture, my life had become less hectic and I was finally able to put my future in better perspective.

I don't know how Derek put up with me, or what possessed him to give himself so fully, but he used his patience to earn my trust. In return, I eventually found my heart growing fonder of him. Being beside him began to feel natural.

Still, when he wasn't around, I often lost myself in tears of remorse and anger. Tears that I hid from the world.

What had I done to make Matthaya push me away?

≋   ≋

I awoke unexpectedly in the night, painful memories stealing the breath from my lungs. I wiped a damp trail from my cheek and then slipped my feet off the bed and onto the floor.

My room was down the hall from Derek's. He had been honest about his honorable intentions and I trusted him more than I had imagined I could ever trust any man. It was nice being alone in the cozy guest room of his house. I had it all to myself, and sometimes even the entire house when he was out.

Aldréa's concern for me had withered after I had gone away and my father was resting assured by my faith in Derek.

After waking from yet another horrible nightmare, I decided to tell Derek the truth. I stood up from the bed, tugged my robe off the bedpost, and then slung it across my shoulders, tying the sash loosely around my waist. It was usually comfortable in the house, but my tank top did little to keep my arms warm on this frigid winter night.

The hardwood floor was cold against my feet as I crept quietly down the hallway toward Derek's room. I listened at his door, which was open a few inches, and heard nothing, so I knocked lightly.

"I'm not asleep either, Kathera. You can come in."

We were both so accustomed to working late and odd shifts that sleep never really came easily for either of us.

"Why don't you sit down?" he said, patting a hand on the edge of his bed and then reaching to his side to switch on a small lamp. A yellow glow filled the room. He sat up, put his hands behind his head, and lay back against his pillow. "What's up?"

I took a seat beside him and pulled my knees up onto the velvety comforter. I knew there was tension in him as he struggled to keep his feelings locked down while my broken heart recovered. I also knew how much he wanted to be a part of my life and how he had given everything in hopes of eventually convincing me to return the affection.

It had all been overlooked so easily in the past—before tonight. In the warm light and shadow, he looked… different. I moved closer to him and rested my hand against his bare chest. The feel of his smooth, warm skin calmed my restless fingers.

Even in the dim light, I could make out the brief smile that came across his lips.

He was always so patient with me. Too patient, maybe.

"Derek, I don't understand what's happening to me. I keep having terrible dreams over and over again." I closed my eyes and sighed. "I'm scared. I-I don't want to be alone…"

I felt his chest rise and fall beneath my hand.

"You don't have to be." He sat up and bent a knee for balance as he lifted a hand to cup my cheek. Then he leaned in and kissed my neck without asking.

A gasp caught in my throat.

No. I didn't want to—

His other hand slid across the collar of my robe, teasing the strap of my camisole.

"You'll never be alone, Kathera," he whispered. The heat of his breath on my skin made me lightheaded.

Derek, I... The words didn't come out.

My skin tingled and I flinched at first, wanting to revolt against his actions, but... his touch was gentle. He pulled back from my throat and looked me in the eye. Butterflies made my body shake.

"Kathera?" He held my face lovingly. "If you don't want me to leave you, I never will."

He pulled me into his arms and, in an outpour of organic passion, kissed my lips.

Again, I let him.

I let him take my breath away with his heated whispers, and I stopped worrying about the things I couldn't control.

I relaxed my shoulders into his embrace and my robe slid down my forearms. I climbed completely up onto the bed and he lay back, cautiously bringing me with him. My hands slipped out of my sleeves and the fleece robe fell to a pile on the floor beside the bed.

Persuaded by a primitive, instinctual force, I climbed on top of him, straddling his hips with my legs. I was tense at first, shaking with anxiety and uncertainty because I'd never done such a thing before. Then my muscles eased into Derek's arms as he pulled me down into another kiss. I was so close, the beat of his heart resounded through my fingertips.

His hands trailed down my sides and came around to my

lower waist where they remained, although it seemed painfully difficult for him to keep them there.

His chest was sensationally hot and taut beneath my palms. I didn't even know what I wanted from him anymore. Or did I?

My mind could barely fathom the rawness of the emotions crashing through me. I felt the muscles in his arms flex as he held me on top of him, gently but with absolutely no intention of letting go.

Then his fingers sunk an inch lower, his thumbs caressing the jut of my hipbones, pressing my hips deeper into his until desire raged inside me.

The heat of our bodies so close together made the room uncomfortably hot. I gasped faintly as a bead of sweat dripped down my forehead. His lips pressed into my throat. Our curves complimented each other and it became clear—we were *meant* to fit together. The room blurred and all I could see was him. All I could feel was Derek's insatiable hunger infecting me like a virus—blinding me with the sudden wants of my body.

He knew exactly what he was doing, and his skillful touch and the way he boldly wrinkled up my shirt to get to my bare skin made me pine for him. The trail his fingers made across my ribs had been firm but gentle—passionate and careful—a perfect combination. And now his fingertips remained just below my waist, lighting a fuse of sexual desire, which made me writhe. The sensation charmed my senses, clouding my mind. Making me vulnerable to his needs.

Or were they *our* needs?

Right then and there, Derek wanted me and *only* me. I felt it in my blood.

I wanted to let go completely.

I wanted to forget everything and be his.

His lips lingered on the hypersensitive flesh of my throat and an involuntary groan slipped out of me as I trembled. Derek's grasp tightened in response, his abdomen tensing and unconsciously pressing closer against me.

The rhythm of our breaths grew heavier. A hand cupped the back of my neck and pulled me into another kiss, even more impassioned than the last. He tasted powerful. *Real.*

His lips slowly explored my jawbone, until I felt a heated breath and a fiery stroke of his tongue behind my ear.

His hardened body pressed against me had me yearning. I found myself imagining things I hadn't before...

Our bare skin sliding together.

"Kathera," he whispered in a labored breath. "Say you want me." His fingers traced my hips. "Because I need you right now, more than anything." My mind went blank and my body flinched at the sound of his words. The sexual impulses were driving out all reason and conscience.

"Kathera?" He kissed the hollow of my throat.

Yes. I wanted him.

Didn't I?

His chest felt so good against mine and my fingers wanted to stay nestled in his soft hair. Maybe I did want to be his.

Yes. I did.

I wanted to taste him. Breathe him in. Be his. Be *all* of his.

All I had to do was give in... and let him take me.

Take me?

Wait...

What was I thinking?

I froze.

A breath caught in my lungs.

My mind cleared.

No.

I struggled to regain my wits as my body throbbed with an urge to become part of him—to *literally* let him in.

But I wasn't ready for this.

"I can't." My voice was shaky from the adrenaline. "I-I can't do this, Derek." His grip loosened almost instantly and I slid off to his side, recoiling a few inches away from him on the bed. I was shocked at how quickly he had let me go, but I think he was deathly afraid of doing anything that could make me fear him.

"Kathera." He used his free hand to wipe sweat from his forehead. "I'm sorry. I didn't mean to scare you." Derek rolled over toward me and touched my quivering face. His eyes widened with concern and he shook his head. "I wasn't go-ing to make you do anything you weren't comfortable with. Please, believe me. I'm sorry. I just—"

"It's okay." Thoughts were hard to gather with my head still spinning. My insides were quaking and unsatisfied that we had stopped. God, I wanted him so much it made me feel unfulfilled and angry at myself. No. My body wanted him, but I wasn't ready to give him the one thing I'd tried so hard to keep.

"I... want to wait. Please." I stumbled over my words though I knew what I needed to say. "I... want to wait until I'm married." My face felt hot. The request shouldn't have been such an embarrassing thing to tell him, but it was. "I'm sorry I gave you the wrong impression."

"No. No." He shook his head and thoughtfully stretched his fingers out to slide the stray strap of my tank back onto my shoulder. "It's my fault. I'm sorry that I would even assume anything from you. I couldn't help it, Kathera. I—"

"I led you on and I apologize for it," I said, looking away.

He hadn't assumed anything. For a moment, I did want to have sex with him, and if my nagging conscience hadn't been so strong, God knows I would have.

"I don't want to do anything to push you away." He rested a hand over mine.

"I'm not upset. Really," I assured him softly.

I'd be lying if I tried to downplay Derek's talents. He had me under a spell and I'd have been a fool to not covet such a capable lover. I just wasn't ready for it all so quickly.

Maybe I should have spent the rest of the night alone.

That would have been the *rational* thing to do.

But, I thought that if I had left him just then, it only would have made things worse; it only would have hurt him more—trying to sleep while being tortured by the idea that he had done something wrong to me.

Derek had tried very hard to treat me the way he thought I had wanted to be treated. It wasn't his fault that I had let my own inexperience get the best of me.

"Would you be upset if I wanted to stay with you tonight?" I scooted a little closer. "Please? Just... hold me close. If it's a stupid thing of me to ask, I'll—"

His arms wrapped around me again and he didn't hesitate to pull me to him.

"Thank you," I whispered, nuzzling his chest as my anxious heartbeat calmed.

He was quick to forgive.

He lay back and I cuddled up against his side. Pressed so close, my fingers unintentionally grazed over some of the scars on his chest. They were mostly small lines from cuts and scrapes he had likely gotten in his old fights. The swirling tribal dragon tattoos down each of his shoulders disguised most of them during the day, but right against his body I could feel them as sure as they graced his skin.

He had told me about the girl who had nearly gotten him killed—the one he had fought so hard to keep, only to discover that she had been cheating on him. The scar running down his side would be a constant reminder of his misjudgment. He had put his trust in the wrong girl back then; it had taken him years to get over, and I truly respected his decision to trust *me* now.

It had changed him greatly, though—his experiences. He had hurt many people including his parents, and he had been paying the price for most of his life, even after he had made the difficult decision to change.

I couldn't imagine him with a dark streak. His touch was careful and reserved with me and, despite what had almost happened, I still felt secure in his arms. I knew he would keep me safe at any cost.

I rested my fingers on his skin. Scars had always fascinated me. Perhaps because each one holds a story only the bearer can really tell. They weren't imperfections, they were embellishments.

One of Derek's hands brushed a trail down my cheekbone. I smiled and knew he did the same. We had our differences and we had things we needed to sort out still, but there was no denying how good we felt in each other's arms.

Morning came. Sunlight shone through the partially opened blinds and I blinked several times to adjust my eyes. My fingers uncurled from the edge of a soft blanket that had apparently been pulled over me as I had slept. I sat up and looked around the empty room.

Derek was gone, but my robe had been neatly laid out flat across the other side of the bed. There was a small note folded up next to it that read:

"Take it easy today. I went in early to get some things done. Forgive me for last night. You're worth more to me than that."

It was signed simply in a cursive "D." There was a small,

artistic heart scribbled beside his initial that made me chuckle. He was an artist, too, after all.

Our days and nights continued much like the first night we had ended up sleeping in the same bed together, only with him knowing exactly how far to take things and graciously accepting the consequences of his sacrifices. Derek listened to me and he respected my decision to save myself until marriage, but I sensed how excruciatingly difficult it was... sometimes for *both* of us. Maybe it was selfish of me to deny him the inevitable, but I couldn't ignore the voice in my head that kept telling me to wait.

Still, he never hesitated to spend a portion of each night holding me close and pledging faithfulness to me with every kiss and earnest whisper. He was in love with me and not afraid to say it.

He had professed his feelings many times already and, to refrain from being insincere, I had explained my discomfort in returning the sentiment. It wasn't that I didn't feel the same way; I just couldn't bring myself to tell him that I loved him in return until I was sure with all my heart and soul. My heart swore his embrace was meant to hold me, but my soul harbored unjustifiable doubts.

The knob squeaked as I twisted it and the water stopped

running. I stepped out of the shower and grabbed a towel to wrap around my body. My wet feet formed shallow imprints in the bathroom rug as I wiped them back and forth a few times to dry them. I bent over, wrapped a second towel around my scraggly, damp hair, and then flipped the whole bundle back behind my shoulders.

It was quiet outside the bathroom door. Derek had left for the shop probably no more than twenty minutes ago and he would be back later in the night. I hadn't been scheduled to work tonight, so the entire house was mine for the remainder of the evening. It felt nice to pry open a few windows and let in the fresh winter air. The days became dark earlier, and I tried to enjoy the sunlight while it was there, because it vanished all too quickly.

I slipped my arms through my soft t-shirt and pulled my jeans on. There was a chill in the air from the breeze, but I liked it. Nothing my dark-gray hoodie couldn't stave off. I pulled open the top drawer of the large dresser in the guest room I usually stayed in and slid out the folded-up hoodie. I shook it out and looked it over. There were a few wrinkles from storage, but it felt and smelled as comforting as ever.

I had barely finished tugging the sleeves down my wrists when I noticed it.

There... on the dresser.

A note.

And a small black velvet box.

I gasped without even considering what the note contained because I knew what the box did.

I stepped back, unsettled and afraid to open either of them.

My knees shook as I stretched a hand out to take up the note.

An elegant, soft yellow parchment envelope contained a matching paper note with hand-written cursive in black ink—the deliberately refined form of Derek's handwriting.

My hands trembled as I lifted up the letter to read it.

14
MATTHAYA

FOREIGN FRUSTRATIONS tingled in my blood, imbuing me with the agony of another. My senses heightened and I felt a twinge deep down in the darkest regions of my soul.

She was torn and anxious. I could feel it in the marrow of my bones.

Why was I hearing her?

More importantly, why was I feeling her pain?

I had no choice but to follow my instincts back to the source—the very source that had caused a rift in the link between Ve'tani and me to begin with. I could not let it go unnoticed... but I struggled with the thought of endangering the life of the mortal I had grown so close to. Ve'tani had ordered me to kill her, and I had refused, but... I needed to see her again.

Kathera needed me.

The sun had barely begun to set, but I was aware of the risk and sacrifice it would take to leave just then. There were few clouds left in the sky and a brilliant violet hue stretched across the horizon with softening edges of sapphire and rose. It wouldn't kill me to go, though the discomfort measured one notch above a cloudy evening and my eyes stung from over-stimulation. The rich saturation of the fading light was at the brink of intolerability, but it vanished quickly and relief melted through me as my skin cooled.

A light breeze carried a hint of Derek's musky scent. It was distant; he had left many hours before I had arrived. More potent was the scent of intense sadness and doubt brought alive by a heavy rain of tears. I could smell them a dozen steps before she even knew I was there.

A distressed patter rose from the back yard of the house and I headed in the direction of the sound. It was silent all around us, aside from the heaving breaths she made; this part of town was quiet compared to the rest, and I could be at ease knowing that no one would see me.

I watched her from a distance.

Kathera sat on the third stair up on the back porch, hunched over, her face half-buried in her hands. Curly stray strands of wet, frizzy hair framed her face.

"I can't," she said, weakly, wheezing. She rocked back and forth and groaned. "I just can't."

"Can't what?" I revealed myself and took a step toward the stairs.

She yelped.

Once she recognized me, her irises grew dark and ecstatic. She pushed to her feet and wiped her palms on the sides of her jeans.

"Matthaya!"

I backed away, surprised she seemed excited to see me.

"I'm not here for pleasure," I warned stiffly. "What's wrong?" The tension in her veins put even me on edge. There was a soft rustle of paper as Kathera slipped a small card from her pocket and offered it out to me with a shaking hand.

I took it from her as cautiously as she gave it to me and unfolded the note.

It read:

"Kathera:

I wake each morning knowing you are never far, but each moment I breathe without you in my arms makes my heart ache. I know that you want more from life than I have been able to give you in this friendship, and I don't know how much better it will become—but I know that if we were to spend that life together, it would make me a better man. And as that man, I would sacrifice everything to make your hopes and dreams as real as possible."

"It was next to this." She uncurled her fingers to reveal a

small, black jewelry box.

I recognized where this was going and tipped my head in understanding. There wasn't a lot I could say.

"Why is this such a painful thing?" I asked. "You can't tell me you haven't taken pleasure in your share of nights with him."

Even fresh from a shower, she could not mask the stench of their passion. She had tasted him willingly. It was on her breath. In her skin.

"I *thought* I was falling in love with him," she started, staggering back toward the steps. "And then... this. Now I can't stop having second thoughts. I can't stop thinking I've made a mistake."

"This happens often, Kathera." I handed the note back to her and leaned down closer to where she sat. It was improper for me to stand over her while she sat on the porch stairs. "It doesn't mean you aren't in love with him. You're simply frightened of the unknown."

"It's not fear," she continued. "I thought it was going to work, but now... I don't see him being the man I'm meant to marry." Her fingers folded together in her lap and her head fell. "Yes, I've been happier since I began staying with him, but I've been having more dreams than ever."

"Good ones?" I moved closer to her and then pulled back as I caught myself.

"Some good. Some bad."

"The bad ones?"

"Suicide, again," her voice broke. "But when I wake, the thoughts just linger in the back of my mind, haunting me throughout the day. I've even found myself dwelling on them.

Wondering if they could become reality."

Suicidal visions? Still? Why?

She shifted her weight on the step and looked back at me for a response.

"And the good ones?" I asked, changing the subject. "What about those?"

"I'm with you." She smiled a thoughtful, serene grin I hadn't seen cross her lips before. She looked off into the distance and sighed. "We're sitting together in a meadow of flowers. Spring leaves rustle, the breeze whips through our hair, and things are different than they are now." She chuckled. "There's even a horse grazing nearby. I grew up in the city, Matthaya, I've never even seen a horse up close before. Can you believe that? And it's so real. I can almost reach out and pet his bristly snout." Her eyes met mine and she shook her head. "It's such a beautiful place, too. I never want to leave. The sun is shining, the air is peaceful, and..."

"And?"

"You're holding me in your arms and..."

I was charmed by how she described a fading memory of my past with uncanny detail.

"And?" I prompted a second time.

"And you're happy." Her eyes scanned my face for a reaction and then fixated affectionately on my gaze. "Matthaya... you're *genuinely* happy in those dreams."

I *had* been genuinely happy when I had been with Kathryn. Frightened of the future, but truly content despite the risks involved in spending time with her.

My stare broke away from Kathera's and met the door behind her.

"I had a long, hard conversation with myself this afternoon," she continued, "and I realized... that no matter what happens, I will never love Derek with the honesty and depth that he loves me. I just can't, because I'm still in love with *you*." She stood and I did the same. "Whether or not you do or even can feel the same, I am in love with *you*, Matthaya, and I can't even explain why."

"And what if I had never come into your life?"

"Then I would love no one and Derek would never have made it into my heart the way he has. Still..." She twiddled her fingers nervously.

My ears twitched.

"I can't hurt him," she added, pressing the folded note close to her chest and closing her eyes.

"You already have." Derek stepped out of the back door and glared threateningly toward the both of us.

Kathera was startled from behind and nearly toppled off the staircase in surprise. She grabbed the banister to steady herself.

I had known for several minutes that he was coming, but there was no point delaying the inevitable. Derek had heard most of her last few sentences and was fuming. There was nothing I could do to change her state of mind and there was no use hiding what needed to eventually be said to him.

"What the hell is he doing here?" Derek's nostrils flared

and his lips wrinkled angrily as he came closer. "No, wait." He turned to Kathera and stared at her judgmentally. "What the hell are you doing here *with* him?"

"Derek, I-I can explain." Kathera took a step down from the porch as he approached her.

"I bet you can."

An aura of dark energy radiated from him and he formed trembling fists with both hands.

"After all the screw-ups in my life, I was sure I wasn't making a mistake with you, Kathera. Apparently, I was wrong about that, too. Everything I've done for you, and this is how you repay me? You're still seeing *him*?" He turned toward me. "And you, you told me yourself that she was never yours. *You* walked away from her. *You* broke her heart and left *me* to put the pieces back together."

The heavy pounding of his vengeful heart affected my equilibrium. My ears amplified the sound a thousand fold.

"Derek, please." Kathera came between us. "Please, let me—"

"Stay out of this!" He grabbed her by the arm and jerked her back behind him.

She grimaced and withdrew. "Derek! What's wrong with you? Why won't you listen to me?"

He veered back at her. "Because one bitch in my life was enough."

She gasped sharply.

"I sacrificed everything for you, Kathera! And you're still in love with this guy?" Derek turned to face me. "Do you have any idea what I've had to deal with? Where the hell were you when she was crying in the middle of the night? Where were you when she was scared and afraid and needed someone?" He began breathing harder, fighting back the bitterness and pain shaping his face. "But here you are. I bandaged her up and now you're here to take her back as if you never damaged her at all."

He paced in front of me, boiling over with anger. He shouldn't have judged her so quickly.

"Say something!" His face was barely an inch from mine and the heated breath grazed my cheek. "What have you two been doing behind my back?"

"Nothing." I crossed my arms.

He switched his focus back to Kathera. "That's the real reason you held back from *me*, wasn't it?" He stepped closer to her. "Because of him?"

"No." Kathera backed away.

"How could you do this to me? I would have risked my life for you, Kathera." He pointed at me. "Would he?"

"Derek, stop!" I raised my voice.

He froze in his tracks, each stressed huff of breath audible. His jaw tightened and he squeezed his fists. "Don't tell me what to do," he muttered.

I took a single step closer. "Derek? Please." My fingers stretched toward his quaking shoulder and his heart thumped against his ribs.

He twitched, spun around, and hurled a fist at my face. It made contact and sent me reeling.

In a split-second, I swerved toward him again, a thunderous growl seething from my gritted teeth. My eyes sparked with luminescence and the shapes and sounds around me came into vivid focus.

"Matthaya!?" Kathera shrieked at the sight of my full-blown rage.

"Stay back!" I hissed, baring my fangs at her.

"Wh-what the hell are you?" Derek stammered, stumbling backward. "Kathera, what is he?" He glanced at her and she whimpered.

Jagged lines of red and yellow light fringed the edges of their silhouettes, highlighting their actions so I could predict their next moves. The heightened senses also distorted my reasoning, blurring the line between friend and foe. I had to remain vigilant to keep it under control.

"I don't want to fight you, Derek," I snarled, trying to shake off the itch to lunge at him.

The clinking of metal drew my attention.

"No!" Her essence rushed through my veins with the force of a tidal wave.

She was there. Why hadn't I sensed her sooner?

"Matthaya?" Kathera had quickly dodged past Derek to get close to me. "Are you okay? What's happening?" Her fingers brushed against the back of my hand as I searched the air.

Damn. It was *her*.

"Couldn't keep this to yourself now, could you?" The thickly accented voice was undeniably Ve'tani's.

The jingling of her bangles sounded several paces behind Derek as she leapt down from the roof of his house. He turned to confront her, hearing the sound of her bodyweight landing on the ground nearby.

"You're causing quite a scene, Matthaya," she crooned. "Really? Is all this drama necessary?"

"Who is she?" Derek asked, the faint scent of his growing fear teased my nostrils. No doubt Ve'tani smelled it, too.

Kathera latched tightly onto my arm, her eyes glittered with the same question. I caught a glimpse of Derek creeping a hand down into his side jacket pocket in search of something. He was a fool to think he stood a chance against *her*.

"It could have been simple, Matthaya. All you had to do was kill her." Ve'tani gained ground, coming closer to Derek, and flashed a wicked, tawny gaze his way. "Now you're doing exactly what I thought you would. You're involving *me* in your little mess and now I am going to have to clean it up."

"Did you have to involve your mom in this, too?" Derek flicked open a long, black butterfly knife and planted his feet, steadying himself. "Don't screw around with me, you two. I won't stand for it."

Ve'tani grinned callously. The amber fire in her eyes brightened excitedly. "Oh, he wants to play," she said, rubbing her hands together. "Foolish boy, human toys pose no threat to our kind."

I had to stop her before she said anything more. If she told him what we were, he was as good as dead.

I offered a comforting glance at Kathera and touched her

hand in a fleeting act of reassurance, nudging her to let go of my arm. She did as I had hoped and stepped away from the three of us. She backed herself against the fence and watched.

"Surely they should know the truth… *before* they die." Ve'tani tilted her head at Derek as if she were a bird sizing up its prey. Then she smiled an exaggerated, toothy grin that showcased her sharp, elongated incisors. She always enjoyed playing cat and mouse. It was disgusting to watch her savor others' fears, as I had outgrown her twisted ways.

The knife cut the air back and forth as Derek waved his hand from side to side. He was brave, but I sensed the panic overwhelming his body. His temperature had dropped and the color of his face was pale with his uncertainty.

"We are vampires!" Ve'tani bit the air, snapping her teeth down with a click. "It's been a while since I've had prey fight back, but, now that we're here… do humor me."

In a rustle of leather, Derek lunged toward her with his knife. She dodged, but his timing was good. He managed to split a trail down her velvet cloak at her shoulder.

"Ah!" she yelped like a little girl and parted the slice in her robe to reveal a splash of blood hidden beneath it. "This is my favorite robe. You little bastard!" She took fast steps toward him.

"I told you not to mess with me." Derek narrowed his eyes.

"Leave him alone!" I yelled. He was no match for her.

"Oh?" She turned mechanically and jerked her head, locking onto a new target. "Would you rather I kill *her* first then?" Ve'tani's eyes flashed with golden light and she rushed the porch staircase, covering the short distance in an instant.

She leapt and took hold of the wooden archway of the porch, scurrying up and over it like a wild animal. Her nails dug into the wood rafters and she slid down a foot or two, shredding a set of claw marks down the sides before thrusting herself off in Kathera's direction.

I threw myself between them, blocking the attack with a thrust of my arms. Ve'tani hit the ground and rolled back onto her feet. Her neck bent back and a piercing screech had the two mortals covering their ears in pain.

With Kathera now trapped against the fence line, I had to move fast. I had to gain the advantage.

I peeled off my coat and shrugged my shoulders back. There was a powerful snap at the joints as a pair of gray wings burst free from the back of my shirt. They unfolded from the deep indentions beneath my shoulder blades and cracked as they spread out to the sides. Blood flushed through the membranes, smoothing and stretching the dry, leathery skin, allowing them to return to their full size.

The hook-like claws crowning the top of each wing were as sharp as knives, and despite their compact structure against my spine, my wings were massive and strong when fully opened. Their double-jointed nature made them as dexterous as human hands.

"What kind of demon are you?" Derek shouted, drawing the attention of Ve'tani once more.

"We're *not demonsss*," Ve'tani hissed. "But, if that is what you want me to be..." Her voice trailed into silence and her fingers curled and stretched restlessly. She flared her lips and roared.

I couldn't protect them both, so I stayed in front of Kathera.

Ve'tani came behind Derek and snatched him up by the thin scruff of his neck. He let out a painful yowl and I extended a wing to keep Kathera behind me as she struggled to go to his aid.

"You can't fight her," I warned, pushing her back.

"Then help him!" She shoved me hard in the back.

"You insolent boy!" Ve'tani scolded and shook Derek like a rag doll. Agony creased his face.

With Kathera pushed back, I lunged into the fight. My wings propelled me forward. I leapt up to gain the advantage and then came down on top of Ve'tani with a brutal thrust, slamming her to the ground. Derek fell from her grasp and hit the dirt hard. The smell of blood saturated the air and my senses spun into overdrive.

He managed to scramble to his feet, though not without a struggle. There was blood running from the back of his neck where she had held him, but he appeared otherwise unharmed.

"He will die, Matthaya!" Ve'tani's eyes swore her determination. "And so will she," she added, knowing very well that I could not protect them both at the same time.

Her hatred toward Kathera saturated every crevice of

her brain, but I couldn't detect which target she would choose first. She masked her thoughts well.

Again, Ve'tani rushed toward Derek, and this time pounced on him full force, sending him tumbling to the ground beneath her weight.

I flinched. There was a brief break in the mind link between Ve'tani and me when Derek's knife pierced her flesh. She screamed in pain and brought a rain of sharp claws down across Derek's chest. In a rage, she tore through the flesh of his ribs and I watched in horror.

"No!" Kathera cried out from behind me. She lunged toward him again and I flapped a wing back to keep her where she was.

Shreds of Derek's shirt curled at his sides and his cries for help were swiftly dampened by blood loss. Ve'tani rose from the ground and wrapped her fingers around the hilt of his knife—still sticking out of her chest. She jerked it stiffly from her ribcage and twitched, clenching her teeth and firing her gaze at me.

Kathera ran in the other direction and then came shooting past me. I snatched at her shoulders and pulled her back against my chest, bringing in a wing to secure her there. I was stronger than her, but she flailed and twisted her body in an attempt to break free.

"Kathera, no." I used everything I could to hold her back without harming her, but she risked dislocating her shoulders with her blind adrenaline-driven struggle.

"Derek's dying!" she screamed, oblivious to the severity

of his wounds.

Yes. He was. And it was too late for him. The growing pool of blood surrounding him affirmed it.

"Let her take her revenge," Ve'tani taunted, bending a finger inwards. "I'm enjoying this game."

Kathera kicked free, ducked under my wing, and darted after her. Ve'tani grabbed one of Kathera's thrashing wrists and then the other and flung her onto the ground, forcing the breath right out of her. She jerked Kathera's hands up over her head and knelt down, pinning them beneath her knee.

"Ve'tani!" I charged forward but stopped at the sight of Derek's knife glimmering in Ve'tani's grasp.

"No! Please, Ve'tani!"

The thrill of the battle gleamed in her wild-eyed grin. She drew the blade across Kathera's wrists and split flesh open. Kathera released a bloodcurdling cry, writhing frantically in pain. Even *I* felt a sting of the horrible ache that was her blood spitting from the wounds.

"I'm finished playing with your little toys!" Ve'tani stood and tossed the knife into the grass.

I dropped down at Kathera's side.

Ve'tani straightened her cloak down along her arms and flattened her hair against her neck. "Someday you'll learn to obey," she snarled. Then she shook her head with disappointment, pulled up her hood, and fled from the scene without another word, leaving me to watch Kathera die.

I lifted her up into my arms and felt the heat of her body

rushing violently from her. She trembled, growing colder by the second. The short, choking gasps from her lips made me cringe.

"Help me." She coughed weakly, turning to look at one of her wrists as it poured blood onto the grass. "Please."

I couldn't.

Her eyelids fluttered as she drifted in and out of consciousness and she tried to reach for my face, but she was too weak and the tendons in her wrists had been severed.

I'd witnessed true mortality many times over in my lifetime, but Kathera's young death was all my fault. Blood collected on both sides of me as I held her up in my lap and pressed my fingers firmly against the deep lesions.

Her skin grew paler and the soft locks of hair tumbled over her shoulders, its red color enhanced by the fresh blood. My thumb brushed across her quivering cheek, leaving a streak of crimson. She *would* die soon.

Beautiful Kathera would die in my arms.

I traced the scar-like smudge on her cheek and closed my eyes, raising my face to the sky in hopes of an answer.

The sweet scent of her innocent blood teased me; I had smelled it once before. Though it had been old and dried at the time. It was back when Aldréa had struck her and... I had been able to heal it.

No. This was far more complicated than that. I couldn't simply lick the wounds closed. Still, I couldn't let her drift away in my arms. I had to try something.

Saliva can heal an external wound. Could blood heal an

internal one?

I carefully laid her body down. She was quaking violently, even in her weakened state. Her head fell back against the wet grass and her arms twitched as a fever of chills swept over her, shaking her like a seizure.

I straddled her waist with my legs and took her hands into mine, lifting them and laying them back down against the ground parallel to her shoulders, palms facing up. My wing stretched out to the side and dragged Derek's knife from the dirt beside us, bringing it to my hand. Tightening my grasp around the hilt, I raised my other palm, spread open the fingers of my empty hand, and pressed the blade into my skin, swiping it swiftly and deeply across the indention of soft flesh. I switched hands and quickly did the same to my other before too much blood squeezed out. It stung, but the sensation couldn't be described as pain.

Blood oozed out of the wound and hit the grass in splashes of deep burgundy, a color much darker than her mortal red. I leaned over Kathera, whose breath was hardly audible anymore, and could barely hear her soft heartbeat.

I extended all of my fingers and flattened the palms of my hands down against her wrists.

Her eyes widened and she howled in pain, her back arching and her body coming up from the grass a few inches. My blood surged from my body into hers. I pressed harder and harder until the blood from her wrists stopped seeping from between us and her squirming ceased.

The exchange of blood made my own body ache and churn

with an unnerving sensation. The colored fringe faded from around her body, as I grew hazy and disoriented.

Some of her color was returning to her skin and the wounds were shrinking beneath my palms. Kathera gasped and pushed against me, then her eyes rolled back into the whiteness and she blacked out, her body going limp and falling back into the grass. I shifted my weight and took a seat beside her, sitting back against my heels. A sweep of my tongue across my bloody palms accelerated the healing of my wounds and I watched as the flesh regenerated itself from the outside in, sizzling before fading into fresh skin.

She would live. I could feel it.

Saving her life, however, would come with a cost. Ve'tani wouldn't tolerate Kathera *not* being dead.

I'd seen horrible things in my many years, but I had forgotten what it was like to watch people you know suffer. My clothes were soaked with red, the ground was covered in blood, and Kathera had nearly died.

And Derek...

I felt weak. I felt sick. My veins pulsed with hunger and my head spun with a million impossible-to-answer questions. What would become of Kathera now? How could she *ever* forget this? How could she forget what she saw? How could I tear myself from her world, now that she and I shared the same blood?

There was so much more to it than that. I stretched my fingers down into my shirt collar and slipped the golden cross pendant out, holding it between my bloody fingers. I'd never believed in fate before, but Kathera and I had far too many things in common for them all to be coincidences. When I had kissed her, I saw Kathryn. When I left her with Derek, she cursed me with the very same words I had heard as a mortal trying to dismiss Kathryn's love. And then... the dream of us in the meadow together. It wasn't a dream at all.

She was remembering things.

Her life.

Her death.

Me.

Perhaps she wasn't just a girl in love with a curious stranger. Perhaps she *was* Kathryn.

15

KATHERA

CLACK...

CLACK...

CLACK...

The window shutters flapped back and forth in the wind and the banging sounds woke me abruptly from my sleep.

Who left the window open?

I wiped the back of my hand across my warm, sweaty forehead. My stomach grumbled, but I felt very sick and even lightheaded.

I couldn't remember what had happened before I had gone to sleep—how I had gotten to bed, why I was back in my old room in my dad's house, or where Derek had gone. I felt stupid that I couldn't recall anything, but I couldn't concentrate long enough to remember. Every inch of my skin ached as I moved and my face radiated feverish warmth. I tossed the covers off to the side and put my feet onto the floor.

"Ugh." I cupped my face in my palms. "My head." It was pounding. My eyes burned. My inner ears hurt.

I pushed the feeling aside, made the short walk into my bathroom, picked up my brush from the sink, and started to comb my hair. It was thick and matted, but I assumed it was from the sweat.

Why was I feeling so sick?

The hair on my arms and neck perked up and I sucked in a sharp breath. I could have sworn that I wasn't alone in the room. It felt like Matthaya was there with me. I veered around to check, but there was no one there.

I turned back toward the sink and took a deep breath. It had been months since I had seen him last. I missed him so much.

I set my brush down on the bathroom sink, opened my eyes, and screamed.

My hair was caked with a dark, rusty-colored substance—blood!

I shrieked and jolted backward from the sink, slamming my body into the bathroom wall. My head throbbed twice as violently.

I looked down. My clothes were soaked with red.

What the hell had happened to me?

A violent stabbing pain struck deep inside my stomach

and I doubled over, crying out to deaf ears. It felt like my intestines were being coiled into a tight knot. My spine ached and I wrenched back and forth, moaning uncontrollably as invisible nails were driven into me from every angle.

Someone knocked on my bedroom door. Each thump made my head pulse.

"Kathera? Is that you? What the hell's going on in there?" Aldréa asked, her voice muffled and distorted by the closed door.

I gasped again and stumbled out of the bathroom. My hands shaky, the knob was difficult to turn, but I managed it after a moment of trying.

"So you're back already?" Aldréa crossed her arms and sneered. "What's wrong with you and why are you covered in... blood?"

I bent over and held my stomach while another wave of needles pierced my insides. My ankles weakened and I toppled over onto Aldréa's feet.

"Get off me!" She yanked her shoes out from under me and backed away.

Was I dying?

"I need help," I uttered, the words barely coming out. My eyes began to water and violent chills rippled through my body.

"Deal with it," Aldréa huffed, turning away from me.

"Come back!" I reached out toward her. The sight of her back made me anxious and a rush of adrenaline pushed my pain aside.

"Damn you," I seethed, coming to my feet.

"What?" She turned to face me again. "Don't you talk to me like that, you little bitch."

I held myself and stumbled closer to her, dragging my feet as the stinging slowly subsided. The pain went away for a moment and then returned. It came and went in sharp bursts. The anger brewing inside made my heartbeat spike and I was intimately in tune with each new wave of pain.

I approached her and the bright hallway lights made me squint. I blinked several times. Every cell in my body pulsed with strength and pain simultaneously, but with each flutter of ache came a new sensation—*fearlessness*. I hurt everywhere, but I feared nothing. "Don't call me that," I hissed.

"I warned you about talking back to me, Kathera," Aldréa snapped. Her hands curled angrily into fists.

I bolted at her.

She choked as I caught the base of her throat within my grasp, squeezing until her eyes grew black with fear. She squirmed and wriggled in vain, her hands feebly pawing at my own in a sorry attempt to pry my fingers away.

I coiled all of my weight together and tossed Aldréa down on the floor of the hallway. She slid several feet across the hardwood and then bashed against the banister at the top of the staircase.

Her high-pitched yelp made me smile. I took slow, deliberate steps, one foot in front of the other, staring, glaring—mocking her in return for all the times she had crossed me. The scent of her fear tickled my nostrils and made my grin grow wider.

I could taste it. Absolute terror rushed through her veins and I relished it.

Aldréa scrambled to get back onto her feet, but I rushed toward her again and hurled myself at her like a bullet. The pounding of her heart thumped through me as I held her down beneath my weight.

I wanted revenge.

The world would not stop me from taking it.

I hungered for it.

I hungered for *more* than just that.

She cried out. My nails sunk deeper and deeper into her flesh and the blood was warm against my skin.

"Kathera, no!"

"Beg all you want." Her words annoyed me. I leaned down and breathed a whisper into her ear. "How does it feel to be afraid?"

She gasped, and then my teeth clamped down onto the side of her throat; the taste of hot iron rushed over my tongue.

Then the house became wonderfully silent again.

I awoke on the floor of my room, my face damp with sweat and my heart beating a million miles an hour.

What the hell kind of dream was that?

There was a pounding in my head and a strong metallic taste in my mouth. I swallowed the acid creeping up my throat and felt like I was about to throw up. I rushed into the bathroom, turned on the faucet, and tossed cold water onto my face. Then I retched. Dry heaved, but so close to the real thing.

I lowered my head and my eyes grazed over a thick brownish-red trail by my feet. I stepped back in fear and slammed into the bathroom sink. "No!" I brought a hand back to rub the sharp ache at my hip. I poked my head out of the bathroom to see that the stain extended all the way into the hall.

I heaved again, this time coughing up red. My gaze shot up to the mirror.

Blood! Everywhere!

My mouth tingled and I dragged my forearm across my crimson lips. My stomach tightened at the sight of the damp red smudges that appeared and I gagged and choked again, only spitting up even more red into the sink.

I rushed to the window and looked out. Aldréa's car was still in the driveway.

"Aldréa!" I called for her, but I didn't know why.

It was just a dream. Right?

But the bloodstains were unmistakably real.

What had I done?

"Aldréa!" I called out again, for once praying for a reply.

I wanted to know that she was there.

She wasn't.

My clothes were soaked—stiff with dried blood. I returned to the bathroom sink and twisted on the hot water faucet. I scrubbed my arms and neck with a damp washcloth until the sink was full of brown water. I couldn't stop shaking as I squeezed each handful of color from the rag into the sink.

What was I going to do? What was I going to tell Dad? Where the hell was Aldréa? Or... her body?

Should I call the police?

I crept out of my room again and looked around. The blood trail stopped at the top of the staircase, so I went down to the first floor and flipped on the hallway light.

Matthaya?

"Come," *he* said, firmly.

I had sensed him a split-second before I had even heard his voice. Immediately, I turned and saw him standing in front of the open sliding patio doors. His hand was outstretched toward me and his eyes were darker and more demanding than I'd ever seen them. A sparkle of green light flashed through his irises.

"Matthaya! You have to help me," I cried, running to him.

"I know," he replied, taking my hand. "You must come with me. Now."

"Where is Aldréa?"

"Her body is not far from here," he answered with a scowl. "I caught the scent of it as I approached, but I am certain you will not want to see it in the condition it is likely in."

The condition...?

His grip on my hand tightened and he pulled me out the door with him.

It's over for me, isn't it?

Derek was dead.

I had apparently murdered my stepmother.

Police sirens echoed in the night from all angles. I'd heard them countless times before, but tonight, it was terribly different.

Tonight, some of them were probably searching for me...

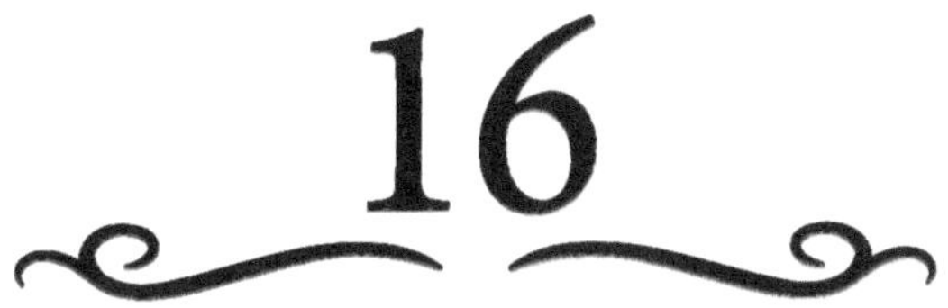

16

A CHILL ruffled me and I wrapped my arms around myself as I stepped inside the house.

"It's very cold in here," I said, rubbing my hands together briskly. My fingers were always the first part of my body to get cold.

"I'll put on a fire." Matthaya motioned for me to walk into the room up ahead and then he shut and locked the door behind us.

As thrilled as I should have been to actually be in his home, there weren't many interesting things inside the place. The walls were old and the wallpaper was fraying in many areas. Cobwebs blurred some of the archways beyond the staircase beside the entrance and it felt empty and unwelcoming. The new sights were distracting, though, and helped ease my stomach a little. The nausea had settled a bit and I didn't feel quite as threatened by the urge to vomit anymore.

As I scuttled my way into the living room, I continued to investigate my surroundings. All of the furniture was covered with plain white sheets and looked untouched.

"For some reason, I never imagined your home would be this large," I commented.

His eyebrows furrowed. "It's not my *home*." The pitch of his voice rose slightly with his reply. "It's only the place where I reside for the time being." He tossed a few chunks of wood into the large stone fireplace and pulled a box of matches off the mantle.

I felt stupid. A house. A home. I guess they are very different things to some people.

Matthaya crouched over and lit a bundle of paper in the fireplace. A large flame grew quickly from them, dancing over the logs as they blackened the crumpled sheets.

There, above the mantle, sat a painting of a young, red-haired girl with the fairest porcelain skin. "Did that painting come with the house?" I asked, studying the girl's faint, secretive expression. I shifted my gaze to meet hers and was unsettled by a striking familiarity in the color and shape of her blue eyes. It sent a wave of goose bumps up my arms. I'd looked in the mirror enough times to recognize my own eyes anywhere.

Matthaya paused for a second and then stood up from

the fireplace. He turned to the side and acknowledged neither me nor the painting.

"There's something I need to tell you," he said lightly, his gaze focused on nothing. "It may take a while. We should sit."

He pulled a large white sheet from the couch behind us and tossed it into the corner. Dust flew into the air. I coughed and covered my mouth and nose with my forearm.

"I'm sorry." He tipped his head in apology and then walked out of the room. Moments later, he returned with a thick bundle in his arms. "Sit down, Kathera." He waited for me to get comfortable on the rather old and springy couch and then unfolded the blanket he had brought over me, pulling it up to my shoulders. I shivered again and rubbed my arms.

My fingers stroked the soft curls of the fleece. I felt warmer already and the fire was growing quickly, the comforting red-orange light adding a welcoming glow to my surroundings.

He sat down beside me and finally allowed himself a glimpse of the mysterious girl on his mantle. I could see a deep pain resonating from within him as his jaw tightened.

"Before I can go through with any of this," he started, his voice cracking, "there's something you must understand. That painting is invaluable to me." He cleared his throat. "It is one of my few possessions and it took me many years to find."

The painting wasn't very large, maybe 16" by 20" or something to that effect. Surprisingly, for such a valuable piece, it was unframed and displayed simply in its original condition as a stretched canvas. The style reminded me of the Renaissance. There was no doubt it was from many centuries ago; still, overall it appeared to have been well-kept, although some paint was faded and scuffed around the edges. The expression on the girl's face made me wonder what secrets she was hiding.

"Why is it so important to you?" I asked thoughtfully, still intrigued by the familiarity of the girl.

"You see it, too, don't you?" he replied. "The look on her face? How she hides something from us?"

I nodded and looked back at him, only to witness his eyes grow heavy and pained.

"No matter how hard she tried, she could not hide it from the world."

"Hide what?" I moved closer to him.

"Her lover."

Maybe it was a crazy thing to ask, but after everything else I had seen recently, the question wasn't too far fetched.

"Did you know her?" I shifted my weight and pulled my legs up onto the couch cushions.

He nodded.

"I... loved her."

Matthaya had clearly seen many things in his life, but I had not pegged him for the Romeo of a romantic tragedy. It saddened me and made me realize why he was so cold and distant.

"I'd like to know more about her. Please." I poked a hand out from beneath my blanket to press it over his cold fingers.

He looked me in the eye as if it had surprised him. "Please, Matthaya?" I smiled. Another wave of nausea washed over me and I grimaced. He covered my hand with his.

"Of course," he said, smiling though it was bittersweet.

He proceeded to tell me the story of his lost love. Of the struggle they had endured and the sad irony of their separation; how he had had to watch her perish because the curse of vampirism had left him without the sense to do anything more. He explained to me how Ve'tani had bitten him in his wounded state and forced him to become her companion for the years that followed. How she had filled his head with the lies and brutalities he'd require to keep himself alive in the world of mortals.

His face twisted and changed many times as he struggled to hide his feelings. It hurt him so much to remember, yet he felt some deep desire to share his story with me regardless of how many wounds it reopened. I watched as his face came to the brink of tears, but none fell. Nothing glistened in his eyes or ran down his pale gray cheeks. Still, I imagined how his face might have shimmered with them if his body had allowed.

He regretted his past, even hated it, with a passion far greater than his devotion to her. Centuries of knowledge had filled no voids within his broken heart.

My chest ached as tears filled my own eyes and I cried into my hands. Midway through his story, my stomach became sickened and weak again. Images flashed through my mind like faded memories of a nightmare I had barely woken from. It was as though I could see every face and re-live every scene of the life I had never lived.

Matthaya noticed the fire getting smaller and quickly tossed more logs into the flames. Meanwhile, I continued to cry uncontrollably to myself on the couch. My tears satu-rated the curled end of the blanket I was using to wipe my face and I felt absolutely helpless to restrain my emotions.

He returned, and this time sat close by my side. He drew a small scarf from his pocket and dabbed the corners of my eyes with it. The gentleness felt nice against my skin.

He never even questioned my outburst.

"Why didn't you return for her sooner?" I asked, still caught up in the thought of him leaving Kathryn to her tragic death.

"I tried... but by the time I returned—"

"She was too far gone," I interrupted, murmuring be-neath my tears. I sniffed hard and wiped my cheek again.

"*I* was too far gone," he added solemnly.

My chest tightened and my heart burned with insatiable pain as the visions in my nightmares mirrored what he was telling me. The green eyes looking back at me. The water swallowing me up. My lungs hurt and I kept taking in breaths, but it felt like I was getting in no air at all.

"Why do I feel as if I know *exactly* what happened to Kathryn?" I whispered. My breath quivered. "Why do I feel as if I *remember*... what happened?" I choked.

He pulled my trembling hands out from beneath my blanket and wrapped his own around them.

"Kathera, the reason why you could never bring yourself to love Derek, was because you have always been in love with me."

His grip tightened.

"I didn't understand at first," he continued, "but then things changed and the coincidences weren't simply coincidences anymore. I believe you somehow possess a spirit that has transcended many centuries. Somehow, you've come back to me."

He released my hands and undid the top button of his shirt.

"This necklace," he gestured to his golden cross, "was Kathryn's—*yours*, and I once swore to return it to you."

He unclasped the chain from around his neck.

"We were bound to each other in that world. Despite how violently life tried to tear us apart, I believe our souls have found a way to reconnect."

He offered the necklace to me with an open hand.

So the dreams weren't nightmares, they were glimpses of my past. And that explained why I never really felt threatened by him. It wasn't curiosity I had felt before; it was fate.

"Would you, please?" I asked.

He placed the necklace around my neck and the tiny gold cross fell just past my collarbone.

"So, if I'm Kathryn, can you help me, Matthaya?" I said, my eyes piercing his.

"I didn't think I could," he replied quietly. "We can't simply make others like us."

"Then why did you bring me here?" I swallowed, tasting blood again. "I'm dying, Matthaya. I can feel it. Derek is dead and I've done something unspeakable to Aldréa. You have to help me."

"I will not let you suffer my fate. I won't allow this curse to take you, too."

My body felt empowered as the intensity of Kathryn's love filled me. I wrapped my fingers around the cross at my neck and stared intently into Matthaya's eyes. "The world may be a different place, and time may have changed you, but if you have a choice this time, Matthaya, don't let me die alone."

"I never meant to let Kathryn die alone!" His eyes grew bright and fierce with guilt. "I never meant to leave you. Do you think I wanted to change? That I wanted Ve'tani to take me and turn me into this-this *thing*?"

Matthaya's voice rumbled with regret and his fangs flashed angrily as he spoke. "I watched you kill yourself because I didn't have the sense to try to stop you. It wasn't as if I wouldn't have given my life trying to save yours. I would have, but this... hell Ve'tani put me in had left me indifferent to the world and helpless to see anything beyond the blood I craved."

The green of his eyes radiated with the eerie luminescence that I had only seen a few times before.

I looked away and sighed. "I didn't mean to upset you."

"Kathryn..."

I grinned faintly, but he corrected himself quickly.

"Kathera, God knows," he paused and rolled his eyes skeptically, *"if there were a God,* that I would have done anything to save you that night. I've hated myself for centuries for letting you slip away from me, but then I realized something. If I had attempted to pull you from that watery grave, it would have been only to feed on what remained of your life. I wouldn't have had the will or the conscience to have done otherwise."

"But now you do," I said, placing my fingers onto his troubled face.

The light of his eyes dimmed. "I know," he replied solemnly, averting his gaze.

"You're afraid. Aren't you, Matthaya?"

He rested his cheek against my palm and pressed his fingers over my hand.

17

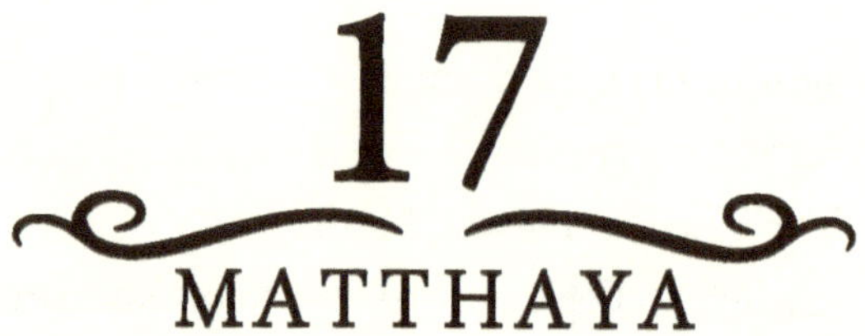

MATTHAYA

YES. I *was* afraid.

The horrible taste of Aldréa's blood still lingered in my mouth, even though I hadn't been the one to draw it. It was everywhere—inside me and all around me. I couldn't escape its bitterness.

My awareness of our growing bond was stronger than ever, and I was dizzied by the rush of Kathera's thoughts. It was even greater than it had been earlier in the night, and my connection with Kathera was becoming supernatural and binding.

But, I hadn't thought it was possible.

It is said that the Taken cannot sire and that the

sterilization allows only the oldest to choose the best and most appropriate bloodlines for the species. I have grown and changed in many more ways than are common for my kind. My mutations granted me wings and with them greater strength and advantage. That power was what had made Ve'tani such a difficult comrade through the years. The genes in my body formed a more than suitable host for the disease and it has changed me to its will. Perhaps, even beyond that.

The Sire and Taken can sense each other and are unconsciously and inherently drawn to the same locations by a bond much stronger than blood. The feelings I was getting from Kathera echoed the psychic flashes of thought often exchanged between Ve'tani and me. Those feelings proved true what I had thought was impossible—that I, too, had the ability to sire.

I had been certain it could only spread through venom, but perhaps I had been mistaken. Though never bitten, she had somehow been infected and the virus had begun a slow and deadly path through her system. Healing her wounds with my blood must have sparked a catalyst of change and a process with no sure end without *thorough* infection. The vampire blood could not function properly in a living host, and in order to bind myself to her, I would have to take her blood into my body, as well.

I would have to *kill* her.

No matter how it started, I would have to finish it. I would have to take her blood in order to change her completely.

Else she would die a slow and violent death as an infected mortal with the urges of a vampire. She would not be able to resist the bloodlust and her body would not be able to endure it.

Still, there was the harsh reality of eternity upon us, for once I chose her, she would be unable to break our bond until I took another. Given the opportunity, I was prepared to share immortality with her, but was she prepared to accept it?

Could Kathera truly fathom the depth and darkness of *forever*?

But it was only I who had the power to save her—to shape her fate. With Derek lost forever—in a more blissful sleep than I—there were few choices left.

I recalled my own experience and the trauma of it all. Being taken was a vicious process and it wouldn't be as easy as she probably thought. Certainly I would do it with more grace and consideration than Ve'tani had given me, but regardless, it wouldn't be easy or pleasant.

She would be the first I had ever taken and it would be a serious risk to her life if I did it incorrectly. There was no way of knowing exactly what the consequences would be or—if she survived—whether or not I would even be able to control her afterward.

Or, if she would even be able to control herself.

"I want to be with you," she whispered. Her warm fingers on my cheek were so tender and her blue eyes looked upon me with such longing.

My heart had grown so numb and desiccated by the years of guilt that it was difficult to reciprocate those feelings. With her blood still warm with the delicate aesthetics of affection and passion, she wanted something I couldn't give her.

I could almost recall what it had felt like—that desire—that lust I had once had for Kathryn. Now, those feelings were cloudy and blurred by distractions beyond mortality.

How badly I had once longed to hold her in my arms—to feel her naked body pressed against mine and the warmth of her sweat in the night. It was easy to envision but impossible to reenact. Now, I had a new sensation of lust within me and the thought of her warm blood against my lips taunted the animal inside.

It would be so easy to take what I wanted from her—to kill her and drink the innocent blood I could already imagine tasting so eagerly. Just the sweet smell of her body made me quake with anticipation. It was, in a sense, the very same feeling I had felt for her before. Only now, it was twisted and mangled into something so sick, so violent, that I hated myself for every moment that I spent feeling this way. I still wanted her. Now, more than ever.

"Matthaya?" Kathera stared thoughtfully at me. "You can tell me if you're scared."

It wasn't fear; it was apprehension. I knew she didn't have many choices—or *any* choices for that matter—but I still needed to hear her say that she *wanted* this from me.

"I only want you to understand what it is I must do," I said. "In order for me to bring you into my world... you will have to die and I must be the one to take your life. Although I will try to make it brief, it will be painful beyond your imagination and the process cannot be stopped or reversed once it takes you. Are you certain you want this?"

"Yes," she replied quickly. "And I am willing to give up everything for that. Even if it means giving up what's left of my life now." She shook her head and shrugged. "I didn't want to tell you this, but I'm frightened, too. I murdered my stepmother." She swallowed hard at the thought and her eyes began to redden around the edges. "Aldréa was a very evil woman, but what I did to her was unforgivable. My hands are stained with blood and I will never forget the taste of it." Her fingers wrapped tightly around the blanket's edge and she trembled. "Oh, I don't feel so well, Matthaya."

Color was draining from her face and I could hear her heartbeat softening. Time was running out. I knew what had to be done but couldn't bring myself to do it until I was sure I had complete control over the primal hunger. I wouldn't risk letting Kathryn die a second time.

I got up to put several logs onto the fire and then sat back down next to Kathera again. I moved down the couch and motioned for her to lay her head in my lap.

"Get some rest, Kathera. You'll feel better when you wake up." I smiled earnestly and caressed her forearm with my fingertips.

She made herself a little more comfortable and pulled the blanket up as she rested her head against my leg. Her narrowed eyes indicated she was thinking quite intently.

"Matthaya?" She lifted her face and looked up at me; I couldn't see them beneath the blanket, but I heard her fingers rubbing the cross pendant between them.

"Yes?"

"You once told me that you would never love me," she whispered. "Did you mean it?"

I hadn't. But, at the time, I had had no other choice but to lie to her.

"I once thought I would never stop loving you," I replied, remembering my vows to Kathryn. "And that is still the truth."

Without further response, she lowered her head and closed her eyes again.

I brushed my fingers through her soft, flowing hair and listened closely to her every breath. I marveled at the fairness of her skin—the beauty of her resting eyes.

The two girls clearly had their differences, but Kathera was beginning to look more and more like Kathryn to me now.

Minutes passed and her breathing became shallow and slow as she fell deeper into sleep. The fire was beginning to dim, but I couldn't wake her just yet. I slipped the sleeves of my jacket off and pulled my coat from my back.

I bunched it up into a ball, carefully lifted Kathera's head from my lap, and then laid her back down onto the makeshift pillow. She quickly accustomed herself to it and curled her fingers around the edges of it. I put more firewood into the fireplace and went off into one of the rooms to make preparations.

It was an old house and there was another fireplace in the master bedroom that would serve well for the occasion. I made haste to set another fire ablaze while she slept peacefully on the couch.

The scenario I had planned would not be perfect and my heart still ached at the thought of harming her, though it had to be done. She was dying, and I wasn't going to let her go this time.

All I could do was hope I had enough power to satisfy her mortal heart.

I could trick her mind... if she let me.

We were already bound by blood and fate to do it, but it could only take place if she gave in completely to my will. Kathera *and* Kathryn had to give in to make it work the way I had planned.

Hypnosis was one thing, but to truly bring to life her deepest imaginings would take much more than the power of suggestion—and seduction. She had to see exactly what I wanted her to see and feel exactly what *she* wanted to feel. For the short time I would be in control of her mind, Kathera would believe she *was* Kathryn, and Kathryn would believe I was human.

It was going to trigger an unpredictable outcome, but it was the least I could do to dampen the true horror of what was about to happen.

I began by visualizing all the wonderful things the world had graced me with as a human—the things I had taken for granted. My body would feel warm to her touch as she sank closer into me. My heart would beat as though it longed to leap from my chest and consume her with its hunger and passion. And my skin... my skin would glisten with a youthful glow and vigor as if kissed by the sun's golden rays. It would not be cold or gray, and in the end, she would get what she wanted.

Surely the pain would take her out of the trance regardless, but until that point, I had to keep her in *my* mind; I had to retain control over her thoughts.

"Kathryn." I knelt down on the floor beside where Kathera slept on the couch and caressed her cheek. She twitched slightly.

Holding my face next to hers, I whispered into her ear.

"Close your mind to all that you know. Forget this place. Forget this time. Remember only me... and give in."

As I spoke softly, I felt her letting go. Her breathing deepened and she was releasing herself to my will.

"Kathryn, wake up." I gently nudged her shoulder with my fingertips.

She opened her eyes and looked around. The room was not as she had left it. It was no longer dark and gray with undecorated walls and dusty floors. It had become warm and accented with elegant reds and golds, satin draperies softening the window frames and an elegant tapestry hanging where Kathryn's painting once had been.

An illusion that trumped all illusions.

She sat up on the couch and remained silent and awestruck.

At her ankles rested the edge of a long white dress, which she kicked at with her bare feet, ruffling the hem with her toes.

There was confusion crinkling her brow.

"Come with me." I offered her my hands.

Her fingers slid instinctively into mine and I pulled her up and into my embrace.

She would not see my fangs or the folded wings that lay dormant within my back, and my flesh was as warm and real to her as it had once been. Kathera—sincerely wanting the past to live again—drifted deeper and deeper into the trance.

The room began to glow with the light of the distant illusory sunset as I led her to an open balcony, much like the one we had stood upon years ago. I wrapped my arms around her and embraced her just as I had done then.

"How can this be?" she asked, breaking away and turning to face me.

She slipped naturally back into her Irish accent—a surprise to even me. Centuries had passed, but I had to quickly try to remember my own.

"Father will come after us!" The undying fear overwhelmed her and her eyes widened. She took hold of my hand in desperation. "We cannot be seen like this."

The fantasy was under *my* control.

"Yes, we can." I brought her left hand up to eye level and grasped her palm firmly. There on her finger was a fine golden band gleaming in the sun's fading rays.

Kathera gasped in disbelief and pulled back from me.

"I feel so ignorant." She cupped her hands around her

face and sighed heavily. "I do not remember any of it," she muttered, rubbing her eyes. "How can I not remember such a thing as our wedding?"

Her doubts had a devastating impact on our surroundings. The images around us began to flicker in and out of shadow and light; red became gray and the sun became pale and white. The colors faded back into reality as she slipped from my control.

"Do not think about the past right now, Kathryn," I said. Quickly, I took her arm and pulled her back to me, putting a hand softly on her face, locking eyes with her and keeping her focused on me. "The day has been long. You will remember it. Give yourself time."

She trusted me with her life and it showed in her expression as the fear in her eyes dissipated with my words. The illusion took shape again and the disturbance in her vision had gone unnoticed.

"I will protect you with my life, Kathryn," I promised. "I will protect you *forever.*"

The sunset faded into the horizon and the house became dim as the reddish glow of the fireplace beckoned to us.

The tips of my fingers playfully coiled around the blue lace that graced the short sleeves of her gown. She grinned coyly and fiddled with a flower that was nestled in a ribbon that had been braided into her hair.

I rested my weight against the nearby wall.

"Now that the sun has set and the darkness implores us to spend the night together, tell me, Kathryn, what is it you want?"

Kathryn's eyes met mine for a split second and then darted away in a pointless attempt to shield her thoughts. A brief and vivid image escaped her mind and penetrated mine—*her body pressed helplessly up against the wall—me holding her there and kissing her breathless as our naked skin met and our fingers entwined.*

She spun the wedding band around the base of her finger and shrugged.

"I already have exactly what I want, Matthaya," she said. "Don't you?"

"You and I both know that is a lie." The vision I had just had and the wild flutter of her heartbeat spoke the truth even when she refused to share it. She was stubborn but powerful, and for once in her life, she was at a loss for words. I knew what she wanted. *Kathryn* knew what she wanted.

In our past lives, we had tried to be together. The complications of our situation and the impossibility of marriage at the time had clouded our young minds and sent us spiraling into catastrophe.

Given the chance, I would have never let her go, but the last night we had spent together had left us broken—devastated. Now, the physical distance induced by the hormonal dampening effect of vampirism made me uninterested in sexual needs. It was difficult to express how very desperately my body had once longed for hers—and how often I had dreamt of making love to her and knowing she was completely mine.

Kathera coughed hard and a strained wheeze resonated

within her lungs.

The clock was ticking.

She came closer to the wall I was leaning on and backed up against it, obviously allowing ample opportunity for me to take advantage of her. I moved, cornering her against the wall as she had fantasized. Her breath trembled as I took her hands into my own, tightening my grasp and pressing my weight into her. My lips lowered to the side of her neck and she tilted her face to the other side, welcoming the gentle kiss against her throat. It was enough to provoke a quiet, breathy groan from her mouth and a smile from mine.

My mind had indeed witnessed what she had thought she wanted.

But I could do better.

18

KATHERA

THE SENSUALLY darkened bedchamber enchanted the breath right out of me. Flushed with red velvet, romantic shadows, and dancing candlelight upon the walls, the room called to us.

Matthaya brought his hands up to cup my face and I again noticed the gleam of the ring on his finger. He brushed his thumbs across my cheeks and smiled.

It was a lovely smile—honest and pure. His face looked so young and beautiful as his eyes sparkled with amber light from the fireplace. He drew closer and I tilted my head and lowered my lashes as our lips met in a long-awaited kiss. It was soft and sweet and I melted into his grasp as his hands slipped down to my waist, where they held me tightly, pulling me gently nearer.

I wanted to taste him—only him—forever. And in that moment, he couldn't kiss me long enough—or deeply enough—to satisfy the overwhelming hunger I had for him. I wanted the world to disappear.

His fingers loosened; he cupped one of my wrists within his hand and raised it up to my eye level, caressing the sensitive flesh with his thumb. His face tipped and he pressed into my palm a slow and deliberate kiss. The heat spread and his eyes closed with a second kiss sliding down to the delicate inside of my wrist. I choked on my breath as the sensation made my chest tremble. Hot breaths teased my skin.

His lashes came up with his face, our eyes met, and he rested my hand on his shoulder.

The rapid beating of my heart made my breaths fluttery and anxious as he bent down and swept me into his arms. He carried me toward the bed and I was hesitant to take my hands off his neck as he laid me down onto the soft linens. In a moment, he was there beside me again, leaning over my body with an intense, hungry gaze fixated on me.

I reached for the buttons of his shirt and undid them one by one. When the last button came free, he sat back on his ankles, slipped the shirt down off both arms, and set it aside. The fair, golden color of his skin was exquisite and my fingers gravitated toward him again.

Then I felt *them*.

The scars...

They had long since healed, but the marks of my father's rage would forever adorn Matthaya's back and the ridge of both shoulders. I couldn't help but trace them with sympathy. They weren't ugly to me. They were beautiful. But tragic.

"I'm sorry," I apologized again for what had happened. They would never fade.

"They are part of me now," he replied calmly. "They have made us who we are."

He pressed one of my hands more firmly against his skin.

"And you are as beautiful as you have ever been to me, Matthaya," I added, massaging my fingertips in a thoughtful line along his shoulder. "They are part of you, as am I."

He inched closer to me and his fingers crept up along my arms where he slid the sleeves of my dress off one shoulder and then the other. The tiny hairs on my neck stood on end, but the sensation made me squirm happily. I reveled in the soft, velvety sheets against my skin. Matthaya was *finally* mine and I could think of nothing but giving him all of me.

His hands trailed down the sides of my waist and then down to my legs where he pushed up the lacy hem of my skirt and bunched it across my hips. My chest shook with tiny gasps and my fingers drove through his silky hair as his palms wandered up my legs, followed by soft kisses against the inside flesh of my thighs.

The taste of his kiss came once again to my lips and Matthaya's body pressed against me; my knees trembled as they pressed back. I imagined my legs squeezing him in closer and felt my grasp tighten around his belt as my fingers quickly worked to unclasp the buckle. All the while, his kisses trailed down my neck and across my collarbone; the anticipation of his touch cloaked every inch of me in heightened sensitivity. I was powerless to contain a heaving groan of need.

The belt slipped out of my hands and to the floor just as he came down on me again. His mouth encased my lips beneath his and his tongue grazed mine.

Sweat beaded on my brow. Lust and instinct took over, driving my body to pulse and writhe as if under a spell.

My mind was in a thousand places at once—all of them, with him. I was hot, woozy, and disoriented, but desperate to be made his. I *wanted* the pain and I was ready to endure it to be bound to him always.

"Matthaya, please." I exhaled a heavy breath close to his ear. My fingers danced across his naked back and then tightened at his waist. I felt the firm flesh of his abdomen and embraced the subtle curve of his hips with my palms.

The soft skin of his neck was inviting and I licked a trail of kisses across his throat.

He gasped.

It made me smile.

And just when I had thought that he was helpless in my grasp, his eyes met mine. A warm hand rested against my thigh and I froze, sucking in a quick breath.

"Don't be afraid," he said. The tone of his voice was melodic and soothing.

Perhaps, deep down, I *was* frightened, but the fear of it could not compare with the *need for it.*

"I will never fear you, Matthaya." My words were bold and true.

The corner of his lip curled into a grin and he lowered his head to bring a powerful kiss down against the sensitive indentation behind my ear. Delicate bites to the base of my neck aroused and consumed me, the gentle pain making it difficult to breathe.

The heat of his skin sliding over mine sent a jolt through me, making my body arch to meet his. My arms tightened around him and a short cry escaped me as my flesh gave in to his. I lost my breath and a ripple of emotion rushed through my veins as he sunk deeper into me. My fingers tensed against his shoulders, nails almost scratching him too hard. Restless and unable to let go.

Every action became involuntary and instinctual. His movements complemented mine and the flow of our passion became completely unrestrained and sacred.

It was unbelievably right... having him inside me.

I quivered and filled my lungs with short, swift breaths as his body possessed mine...

19
MATTHAYA

WITH THE deepening of my kiss to her neck, hints of her unadulterated blood tantalized me and reminded me evermore of my hunger. Still, the sound of her passionate breaths and the soft, pleasured sighs were as charming to my ears as they had ever been.

I savored the lush curves of her lips with my tongue and then kissed her again. In what appeared to me as flashes in and out of reality, I lost myself in the darkness of our lovemaking. The impassioned, airy groans that escaped her sensually parted mouth filled me with resurrected desires. I imagined my body, warm against hers, a soft friction between us. I wanted to take her as my own. I wanted to lose myself inside her.

If only ...

What I would have given to be human enough to taste the sweetness of the warm sweat beading up across her breasts and to inhale the captivating scent of her tousled red locks. It truly was Kathryn's blood pumping through her veins, and the depth of her passion drove me mad as she surrendered completely to me.

I regretted being so naive in my youth. Our encounter now would never be what it would have been when were young and I was still *alive*. My honor and guilt had led me to preserve Kathryn's innocence for so long—until it was too late. Now I struggled with that decision, as my body participated little and gained no pleasure from her ecstasy. It was all in our minds alone.

If only we hadn't been stopped.

If only we had been able to share that night together.

I had imagined her body having been made to fit mine as if we had been two rare pieces of a puzzle. Hers needing mine to be complete—and taking me in and swallowing me up inside her warm flesh.

How I had once fantasized...

Now, I would take her blood and make her part of me forever.

Kathera's heartbeat hastened and her breathing became labored.

I wanted her.

More than ever.

Her body writhed blissfully with the vision of our entwined flesh, but I selfishly yearned only for the satisfaction of my fangs burrowing into her throat—of her blood mingling with mine.

Her... blood... inside me.

I licked a path up to her throat and then gritted my teeth as Kathera called out to me again. The vampire instincts amplified the sounds of her heart with vivid exaggeration. Each beat throbbed and pulsed through me, leaving my bones rattling with tension. They reverberated through my brain incessantly until—

It was a swift bite.

My fangs sank into her neck and her fingernails into the flesh of my back. She let out a desperate cry as my teeth pierced her throat and blood spilled onto us both. The colors of the room became muted momentarily and then burst back and forth from gray to red, flickering in and out of reality and fantasy.

Her pained screams were drowned out by the seductive thrill of her body falling victim to mine. Deafening the sounds of dying prey to our perceptive ears was a feature of the curse that softened the blow of killing, but only by a thread.

Within moments, I lost power over Kathera and the illusion flashed violently in and out, faster and faster. The poisonous glow of my eyes reflected in her dark, terrified pupils.

I couldn't let go.

Venom spread through her veins, infecting and attacking every cell of her blood with its paralyzing effect. The illusion vanished and the room became dull and gray again. Her nails dug helplessly into me, as she grew ever weaker from the poison. The arousal of the kill left me eager. Insatiable. My wings unlatched and stretched out to arch high above her body as the heat of her blood blinded me to her agony. The scratches she left would heal before she even remembered them.

But how her blood charmed me. She was wonderful. Rich. Unique.

How long it had been since I had tasted such perfection—since I had fed so guiltlessly. It was a necessary sin to make her mine, but how difficult it was to stop myself from bleeding her dry—from killing her with the pain instead of allowing the disease to take her first.

There was a delicate balance between the two and my inexperience left me guessing... and praying my instincts would perceive those nuances.

Her cries were quickly reduced to weakened moans and it was then that I gained the sanity to pull myself away from her, withdrawing my fangs from her bloody throat.

Kathera's heartbeat slowed significantly and her grip loosened. The blood from her wound seeped down her bare neck and off her pale shoulders, staining the sheets below us.

I lifted her dying body up into my arms and carried her closer to the fireplace, laying her carefully down on the large, plush rug nearby.

It wouldn't be long before her heart would cease to beat.

"Forgive me, Kathryn."

I kissed her forehead as she trembled. She was everything to me—in this life and the last.

"I love you," I whispered and then kissed her just as the last of her warmth dissipated from her skin.

Kathera's final mortal tears trickled down her cheeks and, after a final gasp of air, she stared into nothingness. I was filled once more with hate and regret. There was no way of knowing when... or even *if* she would reawaken.

I ran my hand over her face, closing her eyes. Dragging my fingers down her neck, I then brushed them over her pendant, wiping the translucent red glaze away from the gold.

God had not answered my prayers before, but never in my life had I longed so much for an attentive ear to hear me. In the quiet darkness, I was lost yet again to the solitude of my curse.

20

***HOW LONG** would it take for her to come back?*

Had it worked?

It must have...

There was a strange quietness to my thoughts. Ve'tani's essence and consciousness had vanished within moments of Kathera's death and I felt surprisingly lonesome without that connection. I had grown accustomed to it over the centuries.

Now, I felt empty.

Kathera remained cold and there was no way of knowing when she would awaken. Every passing moment of her silence made it harder for me to function. I wanted to sleep it off and wait for her return, but I was too restless. And I couldn't leave her to face the poison alone. I wouldn't let her face the darkness without me. I had to be patient. I had to wait.

I sat back in the nearby chair and rubbed my un-aging eyes with my palms. I used to feel things... emotions now so dead to me that I have forgotten many of them. Time erodes even the strongest of stones into dust, and the greatest memories into dreams long lost in the night.

Years—many, many years ago, back when I had still been killing for the fun of it—I had learned a horrible secret about the delicacy of life. There is an unfortunate moment, just before death, when your body becomes a mere shell hosting a fading life force.

Too many times have I gazed into the ambiguous eyes of death because Ve'tani had taught me to look upon humans with indifference. Anything else would cloud my judgment and make the kill difficult. She taught me many things in my young life which I now wish I had never learned.

It takes many years for a vampire to mature mentally once they have been infected—to reestablish a grasp on their humanity. Though many decades pass, many of us never do and I nearly didn't.

The first time I had recognized death in the eyes of another had not been when I watched my beloved Kathryn take her life, but when *I* had taken the life of a girl who had resembled her. Only then had the nightmare of what I was finally sunken in.

It all began following my resurrection. Ve'tani had

nurtured me like a lioness, praising my kills with more and more blood for us to share. She was a lost mother, tattered and torn from a past I would never come to know. Trying her best to train me as her own, she led me to an addiction to what I now know as "blood tapping"—feeding upon the most vulnerable and innocent of humankind: children. The ritual ingestion of immature blood of a youth leaves us feeling invincible.

Smooth. Young. Delicate.

Like an exquisite wine, the untainted blood of the young is something we lust for. It is fresh and potent, unlike its elder counterparts. The more mature the blood, the more toxins it contains and the less it curbs our hunger. Adolescent blood makes us strong but in the end, neither type of blood ever fully satisfies our thirst.

A vampire who kills to please him- or herself and never notices the eyes of the victim whose life they have stolen is a lucky one. I was not one of the "lucky" ones for long.

It's a wonderfully invigorating feeling to taste the flesh of a kill so close to your lips, and there is a power in that kill that makes one feel fulfilled. That is until you see the killer—yourself—reflected in their tears.

She couldn't have been any older than I had been just a few years before I had been taken. Her hair was an auburn shade from what I could tell, and her eyes were... empty. It was the moment before her death when I saw it as I pinned her down against the dirt road. With her last ounce of strength, the girl stretched a hand out past my shoulder and desperately toward the sky. It startled me, but I had already finished with her. I tore my teeth from the girl's throat and darted off.

Then, I heard someone approaching. Watching from a hiding place in the distance, I could see the horror and disbelief in the stranger's eyes as the girl's arm fell lifelessly back down to the side.

The approaching man dropped to the ground in aid, bellowing into the darkness for help, but no one was near enough to answer. I watched as the man vainly attempted to gain a reply from her corpse.

I could see it again and more vividly than ever—the eerie green light of my eyes reflecting in the whites of hers. It had pierced me like a blade; cutting a hole so deep that it had revealed an image I had long forgotten. It was the same reflection I had seen in the water so many years before, as I had watched Kathryn drown. *She* was reaching out to me.

The uninvited vision provoked me and I snarled, drawing the attention of the weeping man.

"Who's there?" he asked, frantically searching to find a face within the shadows.

Then a vision seized my mind: I was holding Kathryn down in the water, watching her drown and gasping for air as the blood from the tear in her throat filled the pool with crimson. My eyes... my green eyes... glowing with hunger and a lack of fear—*I* was pushing her to her death. Destroying her.

No...

It wasn't true.

But the girl I *had* killed—she brought about a horrible vision of something that had never happened—something more terrifying than ever.

I would never hurt Kathryn...

I coughed violently on nothing and spat blood onto the ground.

It felt like death was coming for me again. If my heart could have skipped a beat, it would have stopped right then. I drove my blood-soaked nails into my hair and let out a frightened howl into the night.

I ran.

Unable to escape, I fell prey to the arms of a frenzied Ve'tani.

"What has happened, Matthaya!?" she roared, blocking my path and digging her claws into my forearms.

I broke free, driving her away with a violent thrust of my arms.

"What have you done to me?" I continued to gasp desperately for the air I did not need. I coughed again and watched as more blood splattered the ground. "What's happening?" My hands trembled uncontrollably.

My coat glistened red beneath the moon and I could bear its guilty weight no longer. I tore the sleeves down off my arms and tossed it into the air, thrusting it far behind with the force of my wings stretching wide.

"You cannot escape this, Matthaya," Ve'tani warned, but her omen went ignored.

"You will not control me any longer." With that, I took off running into the distance. I had to get away, whether or not she pursued.

A forest blocked my path to freedom, but I knew that with the help of my agile wings, gliding between the trees was a swift alternative to navigating them on foot. I scrambled up the trunk of the closest tree and climbed quickly toward the sturdy midsection. From there, I leapt into the air, caught myself on the branches of the nearest tree, and then vaulted into those of the next. My nails dug into the bark of one tree, and then another, sliding, leaping, and gliding as swift as an eagle until I was as far away from Ve'tani as I could get in one night.

The air smelled familiar and my nostrils flinched at the scent of the salty seawater. I was at the shoreline that bordered what had once been Kathryn's family estate. It wasn't intentional that I had arrived there. Perhaps fate had sabotaged my fleeting attempt to hide from my past, forcing me to come face to face with the very place that echoed with Kathryn's death.

Many decades had passed since I had been confronted by the sea that had taken her away from me, and for the first time, I was not looking into an ocean, but a bottomless grave. As I crouched to take a closer look, my head jerked in the direction of a faint splash. A drop of blood sunk beneath the surface and disappeared below me.

My wounds had long healed and it was not my own. It

must have been blood from the girl I had recently killed. Her vengeful spirit mocked me and my loss. I lowered a wing into the water and quickly gathered the fading blood within it. I would not allow it to tarnish Kathryn's tomb.

I poured the pink liquid onto the sand at my side and plunged my cupped hands into the sea. I stared hard into the handful of water as it escaped my grasp, seeping though the cracks between my fingers.

Kathryn!

Again, I saw her! Screaming—flailing—reaching for me as she sunk beneath the surface.

"Kathryn!" I shouted, batting violently at the water with my hands and wings. "Kathryn!" I cried again. My feet slipped out from under me and I stumbled back against the shore. Ocean water crashed over me, leaving my wings mottled with traces of sea foam and my clothes drenched with saltwater.

I felt worthless and empty.

It was there that I stayed until the light of morning threatened my eyes with a fire beyond expression. I wanted to die then and there. I wanted the sun to burn me alive like the demon I had become.

Take me.

My insides churned and pulsed with a new kind of pain and I curled my fingers around a handful of sunlit sand as I pleaded for a swift end to my suffering.

A large, dark covering was tossed over me and a cloaked figure pulled me to my feet.

"I will not let you die here, young fool."

It was Ve'tani. She had traced me back to the water's edge.

"Let me go! Please," I begged, fighting her grasp, but the draining sunlight had made me too weak to do so.

"We all face this fear—we strong ones," she said as she dragged me to the safety of a nearby rocky alcove. "We all relive the pain of the lives we took and the life we left behind," she continued, pushing me to the ground.

"You have felt this way before? I don't believe it!" I knocked her hands from my shoulders and shuffled farther from her, kicking a plume of sand into the air with my feet. "You've never felt pain. You've never grieved for anything." My back pressed into the solid rock wall behind me.

"You know nothing of my past," she snapped, raising her claws and readying to lash them across my face. She hesitated. "You know nothing..." she lowered her voice, and then her hand to her side.

She wiped a drop of spit from her chin and looked away from me.

"I, too, have felt the fear that haunts you now—the fear of those you have lost in life and those whose lives you have taken."

"Then why do you not regard it?" I hissed, my body filled with sudden new strength.

"Because it will do you no good, Matthaya!"

"You lie!"

Ve'tani's pupils grew huge; black swallowed the amber of her irises.

"It will do you no good," she repeated. "You cannot deny your needs."

"But I can resist them."

"Hah! I'd dare you to try, but you would fail." She crossed her arms. "I have lived a thousand years longer than you. I have seen others fail and die. You, Matthaya, are more powerful than any of them." Her eyes traced the edge of my wing that poked out from the blanket draping across my hunched shoulders. "You are part of a new bloodline and one of the strongest, Matthaya. I will not let you die so easily. Fight it if you will, but our bloodlust is undeniable." She stared down at me. "You should be proud of yourself. In my thousand years on this earth, I have not allowed another the strength that you have." She scoffed lightly and smirked a half smile. "I only wish I had waited a few more years to take you."

"I would not have let you touch me, then."

Ve'tani laughed again. "Do you think you could have stopped me? You, a pitifully weak young boy, would not have been a match for my fury. And as for your little female—"

"I wouldn't have let you near her."

"She took her own life, Matthaya! Now, being what you are, you will never desire another to take her place."

"Damn you, Ve'tani!" I tossed the sheet from my wings and leapt at her. She dodged me, easily, and then shook her head in disbelief.

"Oh, I thought I had trained you better," she said, "but you have much to learn. Perhaps you need some space. I will find you again someday and we will continue this confrontation." She pulled the hood of her cloak over her head and chuckled. I followed her a few steps closer to the entrance of the cavern until she dashed out toward the sunlit beach.

"Ve'tani!" I lunged for her, but stopped as the sun's rays stung my hands. There was no use chasing her. In the past, she had left me for days at a time and I had never been able to find a trace of her. She was invisible when she chose to be.

But we were connected always, and if I stopped looking, she would find me... in time. My ability to sense her presence grew sharper over the years, however, and some days I wanted nothing more than to escape her ever-watchful mind.

As I sat back in my chair, I realized that it was for this very reason that I feared making Kathera my own. If she were an incarnation of Kathryn, then we were fatally connected to one another throughout the threads of time. Making her like me would stain her innocent hands with blood.

Already, a day had passed. The hunger grew inside me as I tired of the wait. The taste of Kathera's sweetness lingered on my lips and resurrected the desire for more. I had to sleep it off or it would only grow stronger.

It would take only another day, *perhaps*... I hoped.

Any longer of a wait would drive me to insanity.

The curse may have been alive inside her, but there was no denying the truth—*she* was dead. She was cold and still. The sound of her heartbeat no longer dizzied my senses, but the stillness of her body made my soul ache.

And then, there was all the blood. The scent was fading, but she was still covered in it. Though the bite mark had healed, her delicate white-lace top was sullied with rusty stains and her fair neck retained crimson traces of my sin.

All I wanted was for her to come back to me—to open her eyes and gaze into mine once more.

To speak.

To touch.

I wanted to know she was okay—that she would forgive me for it all.

I closed my eyes and willed myself to let go.

I had to sleep.

I had to make the cravings pass.

21

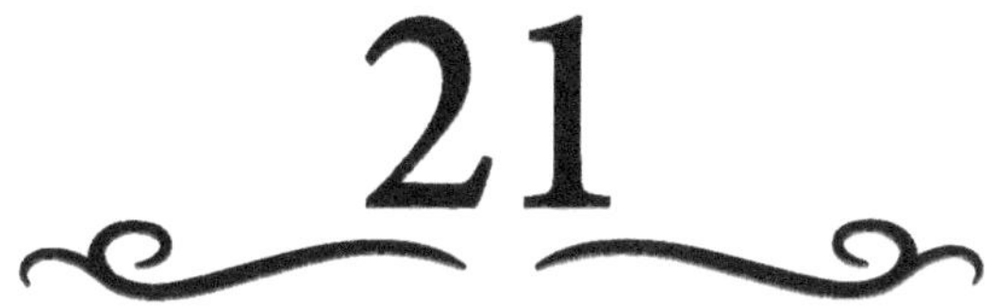

THE DARKNESS stirred and a bolt of color invaded my thoughts.

Kathera!?

I could sense her mind stumbling back into consciousness even as she remained sleeping. It was faint, but it was there—the light sparks of memory and instinct awakening in her brain.

Another look at her body made me grimace.

Crimson painted her skin.

I slipped my hands beneath her and scooped her up into my arms. With only the moon to join me, I carried Kathera out into the night.

I would not let her awaken to so much blood.

ℂ℁

I waded into the water until I was waist deep in the lake and then lowered her entire body barely an inch below the surface, letting a shallow ripple sweep over her face. Her mind was growing brighter and our link stronger with each passing minute. Like a pulse, her thoughts flashed in and out.

Reddish clouds drifted from her hair as darkened strands danced beneath the surface of the lake, and the stains in her shirt lightened, revealing a subtle hint of her skin tone beneath. I wiped a splash of blood from her throat and her lips parted.

Her eyes sprung open.

Fingernails pierced the flesh of my arms and her legs flailed and kicked violently against the water as I pulled her up. She thrust me away from her and the brilliant azure glow of her gaze left me stunned in a moment of regret.

Kathera's fangs flashed beneath the moonlight; watery reflections bouncing at her from all angles left her frenzied. She hissed and bared her teeth at me with a snarl.

"Kathera!" I called out to her as she waded frantically toward the shore and trudged out of the lake to get away from me.

The hinge claws at my shoulders unclipped and my wings flung open with a powerful flap. I used them to propel out of the pond and to the shore, but she was running on full adrena-line, and at break-neck speed. I was losing sight of her fast.

Her bare feet dug into the ground, pushing her body ahead of me as each step kicked dirt and grass up into the air. My wings made me swift, but there was no way I could catch up with her even with their help. Kathera was lean and agile and the curse had made her fast.

"Kathera!" Again, I called out, but this time, only to darkness. I'd lost sight of her already, even as my mind continued to throb with her crazed hunger. She was out of control and on the hunt. There was nothing I could do to stop her. I wanted to go after her, but something told me she wouldn't be in the mood for reasoning.

My coat had nearly been lost in the scuffle of her escape. I lifted it from the shore and gave it a hard shake to loosen the sandy remnants from the fabric, sweeping a hand down the back a few times to smooth the wrinkles. My wings re-tracted and folded into themselves and back into place on my back, snapping their top claws together into the inden-tion between my shoulder blades. I tossed the jacket over my back, shrugged my arms through the sleeves, and then buttoned the center button.

I headed back toward the city streets. As I walked, I could feel her moving through the night. The flashes of her con-sciousness were fragmented and inconsistent. She was confused and driven by desire. She was near and far at the same time—running, trying to get away from something or someone—probably me.

I had stopped killing years ago, but the transition had been difficult for a while. Surely I could train her to do the same, but at this point, she was rabid with the infection and I had no way of knowing how to get through to her.

All she wanted to do was kill. I knew the feeling well and it was an impossible temptation to ignore. Humans are so easy to find.

Flashes of blinding white light skittered through my brain and I cringed, wrapping my fingers around my head and growling in response to the sudden intrusion. A piercing scream filled the night air and I was quick to head in the direction of it, following the echo through the alleyways and straight to its source.

I found Kathera.

My arrival drew her attention away from the young girl within her grasp and her eyes flickered with contempt. I wasn't there to steal her prey, nor to pick a fight with her, but our bond was still too new for her to sense that.

Ve'tani had accepted and even praised me when I had started killing, and the blood from Kathera's victim had already begun bewitching my taste buds. My instincts were churning to get a piece for myself and my will was being tested.

The girl was no more than fifteen—still a child. I should have guessed that Kathera's first would have been an adolescent. The purity of their blood is apparent to our heightened senses. The younger you are, the cleaner your blood. Ve'tani had trained me well in the art of blood tapping and Kathera was following in our footsteps against my will.

It was screwing with my head—all of the blood. How was I supposed to control her when I couldn't even control my own wretched desires?

Kathera ignored me long enough to dig her fangs into the girl's throat and put an end to her cries for help. The struggle was brief. Her lips dripping with the young one's life, Kathera turned to me again and froze.

"Come..."

It was as if her eyes were speaking the words her mouth did not.

All of the blood... She wanted to share it with me.

My instincts begged me to take part in her madness.

I couldn't.

My silence made her furious and she clenched her teeth and hissed as I tried to approach.

"Stay away from me," she growled, finally speaking in words again.

"Kathera!" I reached out to her.

Her head cocked to the side and her eyes narrowed.

"I am *not* Kathera," she replied with a scoff. Her voice was thickly accented old Irish. She stood up from the corpse and straightened herself. "Stop following me."

That voice...

It was Kathryn.

The teenager's body was limp on the ground and Kathera nudged a stray arm with her foot so she could walk past.

"You can have what's left, if you wish," she snarled.

I was at an utter loss for words. I stretched my fingers toward her and stumbled over myself trying to form a sentence.

"Ka-Kathryn?"

It was all I could manage.

She had already turned her back on me, but she stopped in her tracks and I noticed her fingers twitch.

"If you cannot gain the courage to join me as what you are, then do not follow." Her voice resonated with unmistakable hatred.

"You have to stop. Kathryn, please!" I set off into a fast walk to get to her, but she noticed my movement and growled furiously.

"I am not yours to command!" She turned her head just enough to shoot me another sinister glance of piercing blue.

"Do you not remember me?" I said, raising my voice enough to cover the distance between us.

This time, she turned completely to face me.

Her lips were stained with blood and her shirt, again, soaked with fresh patches of deep red.

"I remember you," she said. Her tone was spiteful. "And I remember very well what a coward you are. You are weakened by your need for human blood and yet you avoid it. You are covered with the stench of the animals whose blood you choose in its place." Kathera's eyes narrowed again and she lowered her head slightly in confrontation. "Do you enjoy the struggle? Is it worth it, Matthaya? I can feel you inside my head—your thoughts pressing me to resist this hunger." She wiped the back of her hand across her lips and then rubbed it clean on her jeans. "I will not. Why not give in to it and join me in embracing the rage you are truly capable of?"

I couldn't gather the sense to reply.

For a moment, I regretted the decision I had made to become her Sire, but there was no way to change the past. I didn't know what to say. She wouldn't even listen to me. How could I possibly save her from the darkness that was smothering her mortal soul?

I cleared my throat and tried to fight the dark imagery Kathera was projecting into my mind. She was mad with horrible, blood-drenched visions of death and power and I had to shake them before I, too, fell victim to the hunger again.

Kathera turned her back to me once more. I'd hardly uttered another word before her hand rose flatly against the wind in a gesture of disregard.

"Save your breath for the pigs you worship," she said.

And before I could say anything else, she vanished into the darkness.

It amazed me how quickly she could move. I was nimble with my wings, but her speed on foot surpassed mine. I probably could have caught up with her had I *really* tried, but there was no use.

She needed help.

I needed help.

Was Kathera trapped inside her own mind? How could

my innocent Kathryn have been possessed by the darkness so quickly?

Ve'tani could answer these questions for me, but I didn't even know where to begin to find *her*.

Would she even help me?

To think that Ve'tani and I had been linked for hundreds of years and now, I couldn't detect the slightest sense of her presence. It was odd, awkward, and unnerving, now that Kathera's darkness swirled within me. I had hated Ve'tani for so long, but not even she had tainted my mind with such fervent impulses.

I had done horrible things in my first several years of the curse, but I had hoped Kathera would be different—that maybe she could have controlled it if I had willed her to.

I wandered alone in the night for several hours, accompanied only by the light of the moon and the horrible guilt that plagued me. I cringed at the strange rushes of color and sound as they pierced my mind, brought on periodically by splashes of blood being drawn by Kathera's hands.

She had killed another...

My lip quivered with the urge to call out for help.

I had to try.

"Ve'tani!"

My voice echoed through the shadows.

I called out again.

Silence.

Having had no reason to stay, she was probably long gone by now in search of a new companion who could satisfy her discerning tastes.

The soles of my shoes clicked against the sidewalk as I continued to walk through a dimly lit alleyway. Each victim filled my mouth with tastes I had not experienced in ages. I wanted to escape them, but there was no way to shut her out.

"Having second thoughts?" A scratchy voice came from above and I turned toward it.

I looked up toward the roof of a nearby garage and found Ve'tani perched near the edge, the hem of her robe dangling down from the gutter as she bent over to meet my gaze.

"Tsk, tsk, tsk, Matthaya." Ve'tani leapt off the roof and landed gracefully on the ground in front of me with a muted thump.

I was shocked she hadn't left yet, and even more surprised that she had responded to my pleas. I was almost—God forbid I say it—relieved to see her.

Almost.

"You came?"

She nodded cockily and grinned. "I came merely to observe," she replied with a nonchalant shrug. "It seems your little girlfriend is putting quite a dent in the population around here."

"How do I stop her?"

Ve'tani laughed.

As cold as ever.

"There is nothing you can do to bring her around," she said.

"What? There has to be a way." I clenched a fist. "Do not

lie to me, Ve'tani."

She crossed her arms. "You have to let her come back of her own accord. She has to find herself." Her head tipped to the side and she scowled at me. "And even if I could help... you betrayed me."

"You made me your slave!" I growled. "You stole me away from the life I had; you never asked me if I wanted this. If any-one was betrayed, it was her! Now she's trapped!"

"You're lucky you are a Sire," she sneered, glaring at me with her yellow-gold eyes. "Else, she would be dead right now! You *should* be thanking me."

"Damn you, Ve'tani!" I moved closer to her. "I'd kill you if—"

"If what, Matthaya?" Ve'tani hissed, her teeth bared, her lips saturated by a splash of bloody saliva. She licked her lower lip and then growled beneath her breath. "If you weren't so weak, Matthaya? If you weren't so... afraid? Go ahead and try!" she mocked, curling her fingers toward herself as her lips stretched into an excited grin. "You've forgotten some-thing, Matthaya: I made you what you are."

"And you'll pay for it." My fists tightened.

"*I* gave you your rage." She smirked. "*I* gave you your fire. You would be nothing without the power I gave you!"

"That's a lie, Ve'tani! This power means nothing to me. You ruined my life. You destroyed what I could have been."

"*Destroyed?* Harsh words." She let out an uncalled-for cackle and pointed matter-of-factly at me. "I saved you from the tiny speck of a worthless existence you would have had without me."

The edges of my folded wings scratched nervously at my shoulder blades and tingled with apprehension as I plotted my next move. With our connection finally severed, I wanted to end her right then and there.

"You never had a chance with that little Irish girl, any-way," she added.

"Don't you dare bring Kathryn into this!" I pulled off my coat and threw it to the ground, allowing my wings to break open unhindered. The joints snapping into place invigorated me, emphasizing my physical advantage over her.

She circled me, my steps mirrored hers in defiance, and my wings flexed.

"You can't kill me, Matthaya. I am much, much older than you. Do you think this is the first time one of my *creations* has turned against me?"

"What are you saying, Ve'tani? That I'm not the only one like this?" She stepped closer to me and I twitched, fighting the urge to take off her head with a swift crack of a wing, but her words piqued my interest.

A lanky hand attempted to trace along the top arch of my left wing, so I flapped it backward and out of her reach. "You may think a few centuries is a long time to live," she started, "but I've lived much longer. Years before I made you, I made another who was nearly as strong."

I didn't believe her.

"Where is he, then?"

"*She,*" she corrected, "is dead."

I gritted my teeth and bared my fangs with a snarl.

"I tore off *her* wings... and destroyed her. Just... like... that." She snapped her fingers and flicked her head to the side, throwing her shaggy blond tresses back.

"Why?" I asked. The brutal killer in me yearned to lash out and I imagined my nails pressing into her throat.

"Because she was more powerful than me and because she wanted to be the only one with that power. Don't think I won't do the same to you if you get in my way again. We are no longer bound by the formalities of our kind, Matthaya. My patience with you has worn thin."

I scanned our surroundings for an alternative way to get to her and listened closely to the ambient noises around us. Kathera's doings still flashed in and out of focus, provoking my old bloodlust to overcome me. I *had* to relax or I'd risk letting it possess me again.

Ve'tani sighed audibly and deliberately. "You disappointed me. I wanted you to be so much more." She turned her back.

I lunged for her.

My hands latched around her sides and my nails dug furiously into her ribs as I jerked her body toward me. Blood flowed down my fingers and she choked. It was the first time I had ever sensed fear in her.

"I will never be like you, Ve'tani!" I growled close to her ear, pulling her in and running my nails deeper into her flesh until they were stopped by rib bones. She groaned and shoved backward into me. Something rigid knocked into my chest.

It can't be.

I swerved my wing in front to keep her from escaping as I released one hand and brought it up against the curve of her back. The tips of my fingers traced over a hard protrusion in her lower shoulder blade. I moved to her other side and there, on her other shoulder blade, was another rough, jagged stump.

Ve'tani, too, had wings—or had had them at one time.

What could have been powerful enough to take them away from her?

While I ruminated on the thought, she pulled away and cowered—her hands embraced her shoulders as if she had been raped of her dignity.

"Ve'tani?" I'd never seen her so vulnerable, so naked with humility. "Why didn't you tell me?" I was more curious than angered.

She straightened up and cleared her throat, dusting a flattened hand anxiously down her cloak.

"We all have our secrets, Matthaya." She averted her eyes from me.

With a shrug and a grimace, which she tried to hide, she slunk off into the darkness.

Speechless and awestruck, I was hesitant to follow.

SHE HAS *to find herself?*

How long will it take?

My own period of darkness had lasted decades. Would I be strong enough to endure that much of Kathera's evil?

I knew she would quickly become a smart killer, but it wouldn't be long before the police realized the recent murders were all connected. The last thing I needed was someone snooping around my side of town and asking too many questions. I couldn't leave her to her own wickedness, though. I had to try something—anything!

To make things worse, I was barely able to sleep as she continued to stir long past dawn. She had somehow acquired a lack of sensitivity to the sun and that left more time for her to kill. I couldn't believe how much blood had been shed in just one week following her change.

Had I really done the same? I couldn't even remember.

Long periods of abstinence and physical struggle had made me capable of going days without blood. But now, this constant taste within me made it more and more difficult to adhere to my new ways. Every drop of blood from each new victim tempted me even as I slept. I awoke weary and famished.

As darkness finally came, I made my way back out into the streets. I had no choice but to confront her again—in whatever persona she chose to take.

"Kathryn!" It pained me to call out such a beautiful name so spitefully.

Her presence was strong and she wasn't far from Restless *Ink*. The shop had been closed since Derek's death, but she lingered near it.

Old habits die hard.

"Come out and face me, Kathryn!" I called again and waited.

It was quiet, but I felt a stirring deep inside. Now that we were linked, Kathera could not hide her emotions anymore.

"You do not have to yell for me to hear you, Matthaya." Her silhouette appeared faintly from out of the distance. It was quite different than before as her body was draped in soft wispy lengths of scarlet fabric and black lace. Layers of her dress moved with the wind as she stepped, and her bare feet were disturbingly silent against the concrete. The golden cross pendant glimmered near her collarbone. Lengths of her curled red locks flowed down over the curves of her breasts and the fair skin of her low neckline taunted me with visions of our past.

She was stunning.

And she now looked even more like Kathryn...

Her hair had been curled the same way. Her posture, an exact reflection. Even her accent and the way her lips formed her words were spot on.

However dark and twisted a manifestation of her she had become, there was no doubt that it was Kathryn my eyes gazed upon.

She approached me.

"Why have you come?" she asked, brushing a few fingers through my hair and over my ear. "Had a change of heart, perhaps?" Her naked shin teased my leg.

"You know why I am here." I tilted my face away from her hand.

"Yes. Your incessant brooding *is* difficult to ignore."

"You have to stop this."

"No."

A soft growl escaped my clenched teeth.

"Give me a reason," she added with a cold smirk.

As much as I had longed to have Kathryn back, I would have rather seen her dead than as the beast before me.

"Am I not reason enough for you to stop?" It was a stupid response, but the first one to come to mind.

She laughed.

Where was Kathera? Suppressed? Trapped inside herself? It wasn't fair to either of them like this. As much as I hated to admit it, I would have to find a way to rid Kathera of the vengeful spirit of my beloved Kathryn.

"And what of Kathera?"

She paused and examined me with a quick glance. "What of her? Why is she of concern to you anyway?" She was more than irritated by my question. "You pledged yourself to me and only me."

"I lied."

"What?" Her eyes grew wide and their glow ignited with her anger. "How could you?" She scowled. "What does she possess that I do not?"

It was hard to compare them, but I had to. Somehow.

It was impossible to think of Kathryn as anything less than perfect. She could be nothing less than an exquisite beauty—with the gentleness of an angel and the heavenly passion to match. And Kathera—she had been just as beautiful inside and out, even when I had pretended to ignore it.

Yes.

Yes, she had been.

"Gentleness," I started, recalling everything I had once loved in her. "Patience. Morality. Beauty and creativity, of course." Then I remembered. "Ah, creativity." I motioned to the storefront nearby and continued. "Kathera is an artist with talent beyond anything I have seen before. Her vision is vivid and real. She brings to life what others cannot. It was she who resurrected in me the love I once had for you. She made me remember how I once felt in your arms, when you wanted me with all of your heart and soul. She trusted me... like you once did."

"Traitor!" Kathera roared and took several steps back, almost stumbling toward the street.

I followed her and continued. "*You* are the traitor, Kathryn. You have betrayed me and have lied to yourself."

I could smell the faint scent of her blood as it laced the tips of her nails when they pierced her clenched fist.

"I have tasted Kathera's kiss and it was everything I *had* cherished in yours. She granted me new reason to live—new reason to anticipate and not dread each night. And unless you let go of the jealousy you harbor, I can no longer be part of you. I will never again become one with the darkness that commands you." I stretched out a hand toward her. "I will say it once more, Kathryn. Let me help you."

"It is not I who is in need of help," she sneered. "The power you despise has made me strong. I no longer need to fear. How can *you* deny such a gift?"

She was right. Immortality grants immense courage, and at the same time, deafens the senses to the cost. It had, at one time, been a comfort to know that I need not fear anything in the night, but that delusion had given way eventually and I had realized there was a horror I could never escape— myself.

"I could not at first," I confessed and she gleamed curiously at me. "I have overcome it now and I refuse to be controlled by it."

"And you want me to let go, as well?"

I nodded.

Kathera stepped closer, her dress drifting with a ghostly flutter as the breeze rushed past, her eyes fixated on mine. She came within a few inches of my face and stared into me as if she were searching for something deep within my soul. Her lashes lowered and she brought her face close to the side of mine, our cheeks almost meeting.

"No," she replied with a cold whisper and then backed away. "I've heard enough, Matthaya."

"But..." I could hardly believe Kathryn was turning her back on me.

Her head shook firmly in disagreement. "Leave me be." A flick of her hand made my stomach turn.

She was done negotiating.

I had no other choice but to let her go. All I could do was watch as my precious sun slipped through my grasp and back into the darkness. She was ignorant of my true intentions and unable to fathom the loyal passion I still had for her.

The past days spent alone after she had disappeared made me realize how badly I needed Kathera back in my life. I had felt such remorse for what had happened to Kathryn centuries ago that the guilt had become necessary to keep me going. I had only been fooling myself, when I had really needed to let her go and face the truth.

Kathryn and Kathera were very different people driven by the same cosmic force and bound to the same thread as me. Though they may have shared a soul, they had been shaped and molded by their centuries, each taking on her own unique self. As much as I wanted to imagine a life again with my Kathryn, I had to accept that Kathera had already written her own story, only weaving me into it because of the love she had retained from her life as Kathryn. She was beautiful, all the same, and even though I had lost the ability to feel the nuances of mortal attraction, I still found myself in love with her.

Now... all I wanted was to tell her what I felt.

All I wanted was Kathera.

23

KATHERA

"KATHERA?"

There it was again!

That damned name—Kathera!

Who was Kathera?

My head jerked toward the source of the voice—a middle-aged man in an unzipped, black leather jacket. He was in his forties, shaved bald, and of a heftier build. The reflection of his sunglasses beneath the streetlamp distorted my vision and I shielded my eyes with my hand from the halos of white light.

"Who are you?" I squinted and slunk back into the shadows to see him better.

"You know me," he said, "don't you? Don't you remember me? I heard the shop closed down and I was kinda worried about you after what happened to Derek an' all."

Derek? Who was Derek?

"I'm really sorry about everything, Kathera," he added softly. The man came closer.

I panicked.

The force of me tackling him to the ground knocked the air completely from his lungs and he strained beneath my weight to get a word out.

He coughed hard.

"What's wrong with you?" he groaned, his whole body pulsing with fear.

My nails pressed deep into his shoulders and I watched crimson ooze up around my fingers as he cried out in pain and struggled to free himself from my grasp.

I would kill him.

"Please." His voice was hoarse and shaky as he weakened. "Don't you remember?" He brought a hand across his chest and reached for his other shoulder. I growled and snapped my teeth at him, making him withdraw his hand quickly.

"Who is she?"

"Wh... what?" His consciousness fluttered in and out from the loss of blood.

Weak mortal.

I hadn't even bitten him... yet.

"Who is Kathera?" I bared my fangs and breathed the

words close to his face.

"Uh..." His eyes were dark and wild and he looked very confused. "She's..." He coughed again.

Something was wrong. I flattened my palms against his chest and listened. His heart missed a beat and he choked on his words. It was irregular and fervent, thumping at odd intervals. Then, it skipped again.

"Who is she?" I repeated, angry and impatient, lifting him a few inches up off the ground and then forcing him back down. I needed the answer before his heart gave out.

"She's..." His breaths were short and labored as he tried to look me in the eyes. The weight of my body crushing against his chest didn't make things any easier.

"She's... you," he wheezed with a wide-eyed gasp, and then his muscles released their tension. His clenched hands hit the ground and his heart stopped.

That was fast...

"Fool," I sneered. He'd had no idea what he'd been speaking about.

I stood and ran the tip of my index finger across my tongue.

Old blood. Disgusting.

My lips curled. It wasn't worth it.

I stood and turned to walk away.

Wait.

Something drew my attention. He had reached across himself for something—but what?

My head shook.

Surely it meant nothing.

Still...

I returned to the body and knelt down beside it. A firm shove with both hands rolled him onto his stomach and I pulled his jacket off from behind. Then, I rolled him onto his side and wrapped my fingers around the edge of his sleeve, sliding it up and folding it over his shoulder.

The fabric wrinkled up across his skin, revealing the details of a large image. Wings, fire, elaborate colors of silver and blue with bright orange flames decorated a large gargoyle-like figure of a thin woman with bright colored eyes and a conniving grin.

A demon? She was elegant and seductive—colorful and intricately drawn. She was almost familiar, but I could not remember where or how I could have seen such an image before. My fingers traced the edge of one of the demon's wings, pressing a crease into the man's skin.

A violent buzzing sound filled my ears. I fell back and covered them with the palms of my hands. The buzzing was repetitive. I moaned, hearing it over and over again. I was unable to focus on reality as my hands tingled with the soft sensation of a gentle buzz within them.

A vision of my fingers tracing the woman's wings across the man's shoulder clouded my mind. The colors were powerful and intense to me even in the darkness and I could see vividly what they had looked like the day they had been used.

What's happening to me?

Kathera?

I could hear the name again and again. Someone was using it to call me.

Who am I?

The man's body flopped back down onto his back while his sleeve remained rolled up. It was as if the demon girl was staring me in the face—taunting me with my lost memories and visions of someone I wasn't.

Or was?

What the hell?

Where am I?

BUZZ.

I tried to shake off the hysteria flooding my mind, but I couldn't get the noise to cease.

BUZZ.

I cried out to the darkness and held my head in my hands. "Stop!"

But the vibration continued.

"Please, stop!" My cries did nothing to dampen the sound.

To make things worse, *he* was back.

"Come to mock me while I'm down, have you?" I pressed my hands into my temples and closed my eyes.

Matthaya stayed at a distance and watched as my thoughts tortured me with images I could not remember.

That man—his face—it looked familiar now and a horrible guilt roiled in my stomach. I couldn't remember him well, but the accursed woman on his arm clawed at my conscience. She was a part of me and I hazily recalled her life being created with my hands.

I'm not an artist... am I?

Kathryn wasn't...

But this *Kathera*?

Was she?

Was *I*?

"Who am I?" The words formed at my lips even as I tried to keep them to myself. Taking his chance, I felt Matthaya quickly appear beside me.

"Come back to me, please," he said, coaxing me with a quiet voice.

He tried to take my hands into his own, but I hesitated to let him touch me. My knees scuffed against the concrete and smudges of blood appeared below them as I pulled away from Matthaya's grasp.

"Please," he said again, this time scooting directly in front of me and wrapping his fingers around my wrists. "Look at me!"

I shook my head and snarled, averting my eyes. The colors swirled inside me and I saw new images of creatures and monsters on the bodies of people I did not know. Their skin was beneath my fingers—their trust in my hands.

"Kathera!"

The demand in his voice drew my gaze to his and I went dead still.

"Kathera." He was quieter and more reassuring the second time as he pulled me close to his chest and released my wrists in order to embrace me.

Everything was blurry. I couldn't struggle anymore against

him; everything about the air was foreign and strange. It frightened me but... I knew he would protect me from it all.

And it felt nice to be protected.

But... the dress?

I was covered in blood-saturated lace—it was disgusting, but the sight of all the blood didn't scare me like I would have thought.

Why *didn't* it scare me?

"Come with me," Matthaya said. His voice was as soothing and patient as it had ever been.

I struggled to stand and stumbled against him. The buzzing had cleared from my head, but colorful drawings still danced in and out of my thoughts. I craned my neck around to take another look at my last victim.

"Don't." Matthaya tugged at my shoulders and pushed me forward. "It will only make it worse."

He was right.

But it was too late. The weight of regret had already sunk in.

The face was familiar now and I couldn't get it out of my mind. That tattoo—the demon girl—I remembered it.

I remembered *drawing it.*

"Matthaya... what have I done?"

"We all have our regrets, Kathera," he replied. His fingers trailed down my arm and he took my hand. "Let's go home."

Home?

Did I have a home?

We walked swiftly through the darkness of the back alleys and we came upon a doorstep I was sure I had seen before.

He unlatched the lock with the turn of a key and opened the door for me.

It was dark inside. A soft reddish glow bounced from the walls of the main room. The light was inviting and warm and I started to remember the place—his place.

The couch was still where it had been when I had last rested upon it. I took a seat again and curled my arms around myself, sinking into the soft cushions.

Matthaya left the room for a few minutes and then returned. He sat down beside me and looked as if he were searching for the right words to say. His thoughts, too, were grief-stricken and unsure. I could feel it in my blood.

He set a small pile of clothes beside me.

"If you want to change..." he began.

I was uncomfortable in the dress and grateful for his thoughtfulness. It wasn't like me to dress the way I had. I brushed my hands over my bare knees.

"Yes," I replied, looking down at the soft teal blouse and dark blue jeans he had offered. "Thank you, Matthaya."

I tried to smile, but it was awkward.

Memories were coming back to me, but I was lost in the contradictions contained in them all.

I knew I loved Matthaya. I just knew it—and remembered it clearly. I wanted to reach a hand to his face and touch his skin, but attempting to do so felt unnatural and difficult.

The action would have been so simple, and yet…

And then, I recalled how I had once kissed him long-ingly, but that, too, now seemed alien. What was wrong with me?

"Thank you, Matthaya," I repeated, this time, mustering the courage to touch his hand.

He leaned closer and pressed his lips lightly against my cheek.

"I know what you're going through, Kathera." His elegant green eyes looked sympathetically into mine. "Try not to think about it right now."

I felt the corset-style ties at my sides loosen as he wrapped his fingers around each of the threads and undid them care-fully.

"How did you get this on by yourself?" he asked with a faint chuckle, trying to lighten the mood.

The truth was, I didn't remember.

I shrugged.

He cleared his throat.

"I know it's not really who you are, Kathera, but you do look… beautiful."

A tiny smile tugged at the edge of my lips. I was too pre-occupied with other thoughts, though, for it to last more than a moment.

He untied the bow on my lower back and then unclipped the metal hooks that held it in place. He set the loose strand of ribbon down beside me.

"Will it come back to me?" I asked, hoping the emptiness I

was feeling inside would pass.

Matthaya glanced away toward the fire.

"Matthaya?"

He looked back to me and over my face for a moment. His hand came up to my shoulder and he fidgeted with the thin shoulder strap of my dress.

"Why won't you answer me?"

"It will take time to get accustomed to this new life," he said. "I want to help you." He brought his other hand to my other shoulder and cupped the back of my neck. "I want to be a part of you. But, this life has its limitations..."

24

MATTHAYA

I FOLDED the scarlet dress into a small bundle and tossed it into the fireplace. The lace quickly caught fire and shriveled up into tiny black cords that soon ignited and burned to dust with the rest of the fabric. It had been stunning and the fabric had been intricate and soft, but Kathera was better off without the memories it harbored.

I was done wanting something I couldn't have and glad to have Kathera back. Being together wouldn't stop us from feeling the natural emptiness that comes with the disease, but it would help ease some of the pain.

She slept for many days and I didn't interrupt her—I couldn't. She needed to recover and her body needed to rest or it would hunger again for the drug I would soon force her to renounce. Hibernation slowed the desire temporarily, but her consciousness stirred and she would eventually wake with a violent thirst raging inside.

Until then, I slept, too...

I awoke to the touch of fingers sliding down my temple to my cheek. I opened my eyes to the deep blue gaze of Kathera leaning over me with a subtle smile.

"Teach me," she said softly; her stare was earnest and loving as her lashes fluttered between blinks. "Teach me how to be..." she stopped and swallowed, "like you."

I sat up and placed my palm on her cheek. "You don't want to be like me," I said with a shake of my head. "And I don't *want* you to be like me, either." She closed her eyes. "But I will show you how to cope with what we are so that you will never have to return to what you *were*."

She nodded and acknowledged my reply with a tightened grasp on my hand. I lifted myself from the armchair and gestured for Kathera to wait where she was. I entered the next room and followed a slim hallway to the basement door. Once downstairs, I pulled open a large wooden storage case and slid a black bottle off one of the wire shelves. I shut the door and returned back up the stairs to where she was waiting patiently for me. The peaceful look on her face made it hard to believe she and I were one and the same.

I lifted a pair of fluted glasses from a wooden rack hanging in the kitchen and set them down on the marble countertop.

The clinking noise drew Kathera's attention and she walked curiously up beside me. I peeled a thick coating of wax effortlessly from the top of the bottle and jammed a long metal coil into the cork. I twisted it down until I was able to depress the handle and pry it from the bottle.

I poured the thick, deep-red liquid into both glasses, recorked the bottle, and then turned back around to face Kathera. Drinking it at near room temperature wasn't my preference, but her eyes were already fixated on the glass in my hand.

"It smells awful," she said with a downward curl of her lip.

"It is, at first," I admitted with a shrug. "You'll get used to it. Then again, it's more bearable when it's coming from a living animal and not a bottle."

"If you say so." She grimaced as she took the glass from my fingers. "What is it?"

"Pig," I answered, running a finger along the rim of the glass. They were the only other creatures whose blood could satisfy our cravings.

"It's better than human, I guess." She shrugged and glanced down at the glass as if she were still apprehensive about trying it.

She would soon learn that *nothing* could tide us over like *pure human blood*. The younger the victim, the better. But that was a fact I was hesitant to mention.

Leading by example, I brought the flute to my lips and took a sip. It washed down smoothly, leaving a taste in my mouth reminiscent of a fine metallic aroma with a thick, buttery undertone. Pig blood was heavier and thicker than human blood and the bottles I acquired had been purified and filtered to remove some of that thickness, making it more palatable to us. I'm not sure if any amount of filtering could have made it truly appetizing to a newly-taken, however.

Kathera took a drink from her glass and then closed her eyes in silence.

She wasn't revolted... nor was she satisfied by it.

"Well?" I asked, tilting my head.

She set the glass back down onto the counter.

One step and she was within inches of my face, her bright azure eyes meeting mine. She studied me for several moments and then took one of my hands into hers. I set my glass down and took her other hand, too.

"What are you thinking?" she asked in a whispery voice. "Right now, Matthaya? What are you thinking?"

Nothing...

Kathera's grasp tightened. She moved in closer and kissed me.

The warmth of her lips had been replaced by the synthetic feel of exceptionally cool skin.

Our lips parted and she asked her question again, differently.

"What are you feeling, now?" Her eyes searched my face for the answer.

"Remorse," I replied with an irritated grunt. I wanted to feel and taste her kiss as I had once. But I couldn't...

I was very much in love with Kathera now, even though the disease forbade it. It's one drawback of being what we are—one of the many. Hormone and endorphin production shuts down upon infection. Voluntarily or involuntarily, nearly everything humans do is driven by one or the other. From an embrace, to dark, primal sexual lust... it all dies in us.

I didn't miss what I had never really had, but my imagination taunted me every now and then. But to feel so emotionless toward Kathera's kiss angered me. I didn't want to react that way—to appear closed off. But it happened.

"I've been meaning to ask you something, Matthaya," she said, changing the subject at the sight of my discomfort.

"What happened... that night we were *together*?" She fidgeted with her hands and stepped back a few feet. She rested her palms on the counter just opposite me and leaned her weight against it. "Did it feel real to you?"

Of course it hadn't, but the truth would break her heart.

She frowned.

Too late. She had already picked up on my thoughts.

"Well, it felt real to me," she continued with a bashful shrug. "I only wish we could have experienced it together."

"It felt the way you *wanted* it to feel—the way you had hoped it would. But, that wasn't *real*."

"How do you know?" Her tone had a bitter edge to it.

"The look in your eyes. The smell of your breath. The purity in the taste of your blood. It wasn't *that* difficult to tell that it was your first *experience*." I took the nearby glass back into my fingers and had another sip. "Kathryn saved herself for me and... apparently, so did you."

"Did you?" Kathera stared longingly at me.

"Did I what?"

"Did you... *wait* for her?"

I think she knew the answer to that question but wanted a reply nonetheless.

"Honestly, I didn't have a choice," I replied with a dry chuckle. "Not that I *would* have done anything differently if I had, but when I was still human, I swore myself to only Kathryn. Now it's an impossibility altogether. Our kind do not require intercourse to procreate."

I tipped the foot of my glass up and swallowed what remained of the blood. Then, I stepped across the kitchen to join Kathera.

She lowered her head. "So, it was all just for me, wasn't it?"

Not all of it...

Her face came back up and her eyes narrowed. I swept my fingers across her jaw line.

"Savoring your blood was an erotic pleasure by itself," I replied, wrapping an arm around her waist and tugging her nearer. "Never have I experienced such luscious purity." I brushed a stray lock of hair over her shoulder and touched her neck lovingly. The bite mark had vanished long ago, but the memory of my sin remained embedded in my mind. "Draining it from your flesh, however, was a guilty and seductive pleasure that I will never forgive myself for."

Kathera finally lifted the glass back to her lips and drank

the rest.

"You gave me what I asked for, Matthaya," she said, calmly. "There is nothing to forgive."

25

KATHERA

I SHOULD have been happy. I should have been fulfilled.

Should have.

I'd gained all I'd wanted but at a heavy sacrifice. I had thought having Matthaya would be all I would need to be complete, and that his presence would end my sadness.

I had been wrong.

Inside me now was new sorrow that plagued me with utter emptiness and a feeling of worthlessness. He had tried to warn me. He had tried to convince me that even as it strengthened us in some ways, the curse enfeebled us in others, but I hadn't wanted to believe him. I had known I could overcome them—that *we* would overcome them.

Pig blood was sufficient to curb the hunger pangs, but it tasted disgustingly thick and metallic. I couldn't go back to killing humans, though, so I had to adjust. Matthaya told me it was addictive—human blood—but I was stronger than that. With him, I would be strong enough to fight it.

That's what he had told me, at least.

As I stared up at him standing beside me in the kitchen, I noticed the familiar misery in his expression. It was the same grief that had filled his eyes before, only now it was darker. There was guilt brewing in the shallow frown threatening his lips.

I caressed his cheek with the back of my hand. He closed his eyes.

"I love you, Matthaya."

His eyes opened and he smiled graciously. He was so beautiful to me and I wanted to love him like I had imagined I would. Those frivolous fantasies were out of the question. It's hard to understand how closely related our ability to show affection is to our ability to actually *feel it*.

"I know, Kathera," he replied. With an abrupt clearing of his throat, he turned to me and grasped my hand.

"I'm sorry I didn't say the words before all of this happened, but the thought *was* there, I swear it." He squeezed my fingers. "I love you, Kathera. I'll do *anything* for you."

He reached into his pocket and there was a soft jingle of metal. "Which is why I..." He pressed a small set of keys into my open palm.

I was shocked to see the familiar-looking key ring.

"Keys to the shop?" I asked.

"You don't have to do anything," he added quickly, his voice apologetic as if he had offended me somehow. "I thought, perhaps, you might want something from it. You spent a lot of your time there, after all. I'm sure you have memories you want to preserve." Matthaya's eyes searched mine for some gratitude and I knew he was desperately seeking approval.

I closed my fingers around the keys and thought about what he had said.

Yes, I did have many memories there: my art books, my drawings and sketches, not to mention the awards I had won for many of my pieces. Maybe there were some things there I wanted back, *if* I could stomach the emptiness of knowing that Derek wouldn't be there anymore.

"I've paid for a 10-year lease so there's no hurry to go back there if you're not—"

I interrupted him with a trio of fingertips touched to his lips.

"It's okay." I forced a grateful smile. "Thank you, Matthaya." I brought my clenched hand to my heart and closed my eyes in remembrance. "It means a lot to me that you thought of doing this." I glanced at him and saw the gloomy shadows of his eyes lighten. Witnessing the tiny spark of joy provoked me to throw my arms around his shoulders and embrace him tightly. He was, at first, surprised by my reaction, but then he pressed closer to me and I sensed an air of contentment spread through him.

His hair still felt soft in my fingers and his dark gray linen shirt was clean and crisp as always. It was nice to still remember how he had felt when I had first embraced him, although memories of those precious sensations were fading fast.

His arms released me and lowered back down to his sides. It was then that I noticed a yellow glint of light reflecting from his wrist. There was a pair of cufflinks at each of them—one silver and one gold. They had been deliberately placed that way, as the pairs were mismatched on both sleeves. I hadn't seen them before, but then, I had never seen him without his beloved coat either, which I had noticed earlier was hanging in the foyer.

"What are these?" I asked, lifting one of his wrists to eye level and examining the intricate metal work of the two very different cufflinks. The simplistic-looking gold one was diamond shaped, while the silver one was round and accented with tiny carved details that appeared to be Asian in origin.

"The gold ones were a gift," he answered. "From a friend, long ago. I bought the silver ones myself, back during one of my travels."

I had already forgotten he wasn't the same age as me.

I'm sure he had a million stories to tell me and I could only hope he would trust me with his every secret someday.

"I'd love to learn everything about you, Matthaya." I grinned and, oddly enough, he did the same.

"You will," he replied softly. His attention returned to the bottle on the opposite counter and he took a few steps to retrieve it. "I need to put this away." I gestured for him to go ahead, and he left the kitchen with the black bottle in hand.

While waiting for him to return, I decided to have a look around and see what else he had inside the house. It was a spacious place with several rooms on the first floor and a few on the second. Large hallways. Open floor plan. Vaulted ceilings. It was quite apparent he didn't like cramped spaces. To my disappointment, however, there were very few items around that seemed to be there for a reason. Abstractly colored dishes and vases were arranged here and there on shelves and tabletops, but none of them looked personal or his; they had likely come with the place when he had purchased it.

The walls were mostly bare, with few embellishments besides a couple of stock images in small picture frames hanging in odd places along the stairwell leading to the second floor.

One step after the other, the stairs were creaky and the layer of dust on the banister was an indication that they hadn't been used in years. There were three rooms upstairs: a small bathroom, a cheaply furnished guest room—not of his doing, as he had better taste than that—and a small library with several dozen books stacked up along the walls. Some new, some old. The incredible scent of aging paper filled the room.

The carpet was thick and plush on the second floor and felt more inviting to my bare feet than the hardwood finish on the main floor. Matthaya's room was downstairs, however, and he'd more than invited me to stay with him there.

But, upstairs, the carpet was wonderfully soft.

I jogged back down the staircase and a brief look toward

the patio windows revealed a soft, amber-haloed moon.

I smiled.

Harvest moons were rare and the sight of them had always made me feel good. The warm sun-kissed orange color was... *magical.*

Speaking of *magic...*

I wanted to make him happy. Somehow.

It seemed like once I had changed, he had forgotten every last subtlety of mortality. The consuming lack of warmth and emotion had now choked what little passion he had had left from his veins. There had to be a way to make him feel something again.

Then I remembered the kiss from earlier and how Matthaya had been awkward and uncomfortable—two things that shouldn't characterize an exchange between lovers. A kiss was supposed to be passionate and soothing, and each accompanying breath instinctual and reactive to the next.

A single breath alone was meaningful.

Habitual.

Now, breathing came only from will alone as it was no longer necessary to survive. Sighs and scoffs were forced and calculated. They had to be relearned, and the subtle nuance of a single breath was out of reach and distant—soon to be forgotten even by me.

I had a strong enough grasp on my memories to recall the intricacies of what he had long since forgotten. It might be a leap of faith, but I would try to help him remember what it meant to take an unnecessary breath...

Wrapping my mind around my idea, I walked down toward the large master bedroom at the end of the hall and entered quietly. It was the only room in the house pleasant in its own way. The colors were deep and welcoming, the fabrics intricate and soft, and the heavy carved-wood bed frame added a touch of grandeur.

Matthaya sat stretched out on the bed, his legs relaxed straight out before him, his back propped up against the elegant headboard, and a copy of a book by Hemingway cracked open between his hands. A whiff of sulfur tickled my nose. A recently-lit candle flickered on the dresser beside him, and the golden light refracted off his eyes when he glanced at me.

We didn't need to exchange words much anymore, now that our minds were linked. It felt right just to be near him. I stepped closer and he lowered the book into his lap. I climbed up onto the mattress and moved toward him. My fingers pinched the book by the cover, pulled it from his hands, and then laid it off to the side. His eyebrows furrowed at my actions and his lips moved as if they were deciding whether or not to question me.

I raised a knee up over his legs, inched closer to him, and then sat back against his knees. I took one of his hands and lifted it to my chest, placing it just above my sternum and pressing it there.

My hands took their places, one on each side of his face, and the delicate touch of my thumbs against his cheeks silenced him.

I closed my eyes.

I concentrated and remembered.

How it felt to love... and be loved.

How fulfilled it made me feel to sit with him each night near my mother's grave and do nothing more than talk of simple things.

The beauty of his eyes.

The sweet comfort of his company.

I tried hard to remember it all, but then the memories resurrected something else, too.

My lips tightened in an effort to disguise a muffled groan as visions of Derek invaded my thoughts and I fought to keep them from reaching Matthaya.

He didn't need to know about my mistakes.

I regretted it, but there had been times I had felt Matthaya when Derek had held me in his arms. And there had been other times when I had tasted Matthaya when Derek had kissed me. Maybe it had been a terrible thing to do, but I hadn't been able to help it at the time.

I took a deep breath and exhaled slowly... deliberately... audibly...

And another breath, filling my lungs with the warm atmosphere around us and willing every cell in my body to relive the passion I had poured into my dreams each night—longing only for Matthaya.

26
MATTHAYA

A BREATH poured from my lips involuntarily; I felt the rise and fall of Kathera's chest beneath my palm and gasped. I was overwhelmed—possessed by her thoughts and unable to resist the actions my body took.

I reacted to the intrusion of her thoughts and fought it for a moment—the control she gained over me—but then I stopped resisting. Why would I fight her? Why would I push her out when all I wanted was to let her in?

"Don't think," she said softly, her wonderfully smooth hands cupping my face between them. "Just remember what it felt like."

What *what* felt like?

Kathera's lashes came up and the blue of her eyes glimmered with fiery highlights from the nearby candle.

"You loved once before," she added. "Now remember how that made you feel."

I'd had a hard enough time "making up" a scenario for Kathera when I had taken her, but recalling what it had *really* felt like—recalling even the faintest impression of emotional love—seemed unlikely. I'd be naive to even try.

"I can't."

"You can," she said firmly, resituating herself so that she was sitting with her inner thighs pressed against the outsides of mine and was close enough to press her nose to me when she lowered her face. A whirlwind of thoughts rushed through me, each one carefully tailored and embellished within Kathera's subconscious.

A thumb migrated across my face to caress my lower lip. Her tilted face came close to mine and a cool breath teased my skin while her partly opened mouth remained a paper-thin distance away.

So close and yet we were barely touching...

"Breathe..." she whispered and followed the heated request with the pressing of a softly articulated kiss to my lips.

I did as I was told, taking in a slow breath through my nostrils as she instinctually did the same. My eyes became heavy with memories of my past and I closed them to keep the visions from escaping me.

A moment passed and our lips separated. I felt the impassioned breath seep from me like a cold puff on a winter day. She waited a moment, her fingers exploring the skin of my throat and neck, and then kissed me a second time.

"Breathe, Matthaya," she said, repeating the request just as softly and leading me with her own actions. This time, her hands latched onto mine and slid up, massaging a trail along the delicate inside flesh of my wrists.

The pattern was familiar. It came back to me, in scattered bits and pieces, but the feeling was there, awakening from its slumber. There was freshness and virility in it, pulling me into her kiss and reminding me how it was supposed to feel—how it once *had* felt.

Kathera's mind was crystal clear and contented. Each breath she convinced me to breathe made the next come faster, easier, and with less premeditation.

The smooth, supple skin of her waist lured my hands to wrap around her sides and I followed the gentle curves of her ribs up until her shirt bunched within my fingers. Her soft, fair skin felt right against my fingertips and the fine curves of her body beckoned for me to caress them as if she were mine.

Kathera worked to unbutton my shirt, slowly and meticulously, spending every moment with her eyes set firmly on mine.

It was as if my still heart was now racing.

Was she willing me to feel this way?

It didn't matter... not as long as my hands moved unconsciously along her sides. She separated the front of my shirt, leaning in to kiss the base of my neck as she folded my shirt down off my shoulders. The back of my head pressed against the headboard when she inched close enough for the tiny fibers of her clothing to tickle my chest. Then, she tipped her face down to kiss me again across my lips.

Though hesitant at first, I caught the edge of her shirt within my fingers and slid it up her sides again. This time, the gentle pressure I placed at her ribs persuaded her to lift her arms gracefully above her head while I tugged the remaining fabric over her face and placed it to the side of us.

Kathera lowered her arms and rested them at my waist. It was quiet as she remained still before me. I traced the ridge of her bare shoulders with my hands and drew her in to lay a selfless kiss at the center of her breastbone. Touching her naked skin was incredible and the subtle texture was perfection.

My fingernails trailed down the middle of her chest and she smiled—not the usual smile, but a small, daintily curving, beautiful and peaceful smile.

Kathera *wanted* me to touch her. She wanted me to put *all* of my reservations aside.

Her chest rose with another deep breath and her head fell back, her eyes closed. The pale lines of her throat teased my senses, her silhouette captivating me.

Even with only the candlelight illuminating her, I saw pink flushes of color accenting her skin. I traced a path up her sides, taking in each rise and fall of flesh and bone with adoration and respect. She was soft and natural, petite, and exquisite. The fine curves of her breasts enhanced her thin frame. I tenderly explored their shape, my palms cradling the delicate weight as if my hands had been precisely suited to caress her.

She reached both arms around my shoulders and brought me as close as she could until my cheek was near her heart. Her nails combed through my hair and feeling her nakedness completely against me made a plume of passion dance through my soul.

I thought I had lost everything when I had changed, but the simple magic that was pure love at work had me mesmerized. Just being held in her arms and knowing she and I were eternally one, granted me the illusion of a quickened pulse.

I needed her, always, and she needed me.

I wanted her forever.

Kathera...

Her embrace loosened and she smiled at me again, kissing me once more before moving over to my side. There, she walked a pair of fingers across my shoulder and sighed. I took a deliberate breath myself and returned a loving grin when I exhaled.

I felt happy.

I felt... *whole.*

Kathera took a pillow from the other side of the bed and fluffed it between her hands in a swift clapping motion. I scooted myself down and waited for her to place it behind me. My body lowered, my head sunk into the downy pillow, and one of my arms stretched straight out to the side to invite her in.

She reacted instantly, crawling closer and resting her head on my arm. And when she pressed her chest up against my side, nestled herself into me, and rolled her fingers up across my collarbone, I was provoked to take another breath. This one, much deeper and fuller than the previous one.

At the same time, I had a revelation.

Even if I couldn't express it the way I once had, I was still very much in love and we *truly did* have all the time in the world.

27

KATHERA

THE WATER *pressed against me, pushing and pulling. I was being tugged in every direction at the same time and could do nothing to resist. Words wouldn't form. My hands were numb, too weak to reach out to him.*

It was killing me...

I leapt from my sleep with a cry of fear and my gaze darted across the shadowy walls of the room. My fingers pressed into something cold and firm—it was him. His eyes were wide from the horrible terror of my scream and his arms remained open as I had pulled myself from them in my fright. He was still with me and, God, I was thankful for it.

"Kathera?" There was a quiver in his voice.

He knew what had happened. He could feel the darkness of the hellish nightmare still radiating from my mind.

I cupped my hands around my forearms and held myself tightly. Matthaya came up behind and wrapped his arms around mine, pulling me into his embrace. I felt the tip of his nose against the back of my head as he held me close and massaged his fingers along my arms.

"I love you, Kathera," he said again, his voice as sincere as ever, while his arms tightened their hold on me. "I'm sorry you have to go through this—that you have to face this hell... because of me. We'll make it stop." Anger and guilt filled him, but his love for me kept him in check. "I'll make it stop." The unusually husky pitch of his voice made his determination clear. It wasn't like him to let his feelings show, though I noticed that he had loosened up quite a bit since yesterday.

"It's not your fault," I said with a shake of my head, my gaze settling on nothing. "It was never your fault, Matthaya." All I could think about was the dream and how deep and real it had become. Splashes of fractured memories and visions had filled my nights before, but the vividness of this one had me trembling to the bone. It was even darker than the others and the struggle felt so real. For a moment in my sleep, I had felt as though I would die again if I did not wake soon enough. The brutality of it had rattled even Matthaya's steel nerves.

"Kathera?" He brushed my hair to the side and over my

shoulder and kissed me on the back of my neck. "Do you think..." He paused halfway through his thought.

"Yes?" I turned my face toward his. I felt so weak and drained from the nightmare that my limbs were heavy beneath me and I rested my weight against him.

"Maybe... going back to your drawings would help take your mind off things?"

It was such a simple suggestion. Drawing had always distracted me from the bad things in life. There was no telling if it would still have the same effect, but it was worth a try.

"Maybe," I replied with a nod. "Maybe."

I had to be inspired to draw, however, and with all the terrible pain whirling around inside, I would be asking a lot of myself.

"It's worth trying, Kathera," he whispered, his fingers pressing into my forearms. He kissed my shoulder. "*Anything* is worth trying."

℠ ℞

"Agh!" I shoved my palms against the table and I pushed it *hard*. It tipped over with a loud thud and the box of pens scattered across the floor. A few rolled one way and the rest another, a rainbow of shattered inspiration escaping my wrath in every direction.

I heard a light clacking of footsteps as he came jogging into the library.

"What happened?" Matthaya asked, his gaze chasing a few of the pens as they tumbled across the hardwood flooring. "What's wrong?" He stepped closer to the table and bent over to lift it back up to where it had been. He wiped his sleeved forearm across the wood.

"What is it, Kathera?"

I crossed my arms in my chair.

An eyebrow rose and Matthaya's lips curled into a partial grimace he tried to hide. He disappeared from sight for a moment as he bent down to pick the loose pens up from around the room.

I watched in silence as he patiently lifted color after color from the floor and rolled them into a level bunch in his hands, no pen sitting taller than another. He patted them even with his free hand and then retrieved the velvet box from a few feet away. He set the box down in front of me and placed the pens back inside, sliding them one-by-one into the tiny impressions along the inside of the box.

He had astounding patience.

He pulled out the chair beside me and sat down. His fingers traced the length of one of my crossed arms.

"Talk to me, Kathera," he said, his eyes piercing mine, imploring me to answer him no matter what I was feeling. "Please, my love." His expression softened against me as his fingers did the same.

"I can't do it anymore!" I said, stamping a foot down beneath the table. "I can't…"

"You can't do what?" he asked, as if he didn't already

know.

I felt so empty... so completely lost. It had never been so difficult and the struggle left me feeling pathetic.

"Draw..."

Matthaya's head dropped and he appeared to be mourning my artistic loss.

"It's exactly as I had feared it would be," he said, breaking the silence. "In all art, there is passion," he clarified, pressing the lid of the box closed. "And there is no passion in what we are." He slid the box of pens across the table and tipped it onto its side, letting his fingers drift across the soft velvet for a moment.

"But I *want* to do this," I said, closing my eyes to help clear my mind. "I want to get back into drawing. I want to work with others who want my art—who need me to share my visions with them." I reached past Matthaya for the box, and as my fingers stretched to grasp it, he stopped me with a flattened hand.

"Then you're going to need more than your own pure will to do this," he said, his eyes met mine and I had no choice but to concede.

My eyebrows furrowed and I tipped my face in question. He was full of riddles. Would I *ever* understand him?

He pushed the box from my reach and then gazed warmly back at me.

"Come with me," he said, turning over his hand and inviting me to take it. "I'll show you."

I smiled.

The simple act of his taking my hand—his gentle fingers cupping my own and his thumb caressing the back of my mine—put me at ease.

We walked downstairs from the library and down the hall until we entered our bedroom. Near the foot of the bed, Matthaya released my hand and fixed his eyes on a section of the flooring below us. He bent down, flipped the old rectangular rug over—folding it onto itself—and then whacked one of the floorboards with his palm. The board popped up on one corner and he wrapped his fingers around the edge so he could pry it up from the floor and set it aside. My curiosity had me eagerly peeking over his shoulder.

What secrets had he hidden just beneath my nose?

He stood and held a small blackish box tightly within his fingers.

"Sit down, Kathera." He motioned to the bed and I did as he had asked.

With poise, he knelt before me and lifted the box into view.

"I owe you many things, my love, and an explanation is surely one of them." His hands trembled as I took the box from them. It was cool, like metal. Tiny studs lined the four corners and a small, simple latch held it closed.

"Maybe this will help you understand me." He tried to smile. "Maybe... it will help you understand *us*."

I had no idea what he meant, or what the box held, but I knew it was nothing like what Derek had left for me the day he had been murdered.

Still, I was afraid.

Whatever was inside was light as feathers and hollow sounding. The box made no noise as I shuffled it between hands.

I wedged my thumbnail carefully up underneath the silver-colored latch and lifted it. The box lid opened. A tiny plume of black powdery dust drifted from my fingers. My nose wrinkled as I squinted in disbelief.

Ash?

Matthaya waited apprehensively, still on one knee, searching for a change in my expression.

"Look closer..." he said, nudging me gently.

My fingers sunk into the tiny ocean of gray and black. The ash was thick as sand. Sprinkled throughout, there were fragments of blackened pieces with barely legible ink letters written across them.

They had been actual letters... once.

"My God, Matthaya." I sifted a small handful through my fingers. "How many letters were in here?"

"Dozens. Probably more. It was how I coped with my feelings for you then." He stared intently at the box. "I couldn't let anyone see them, but I *had* to write them to you, even if it meant destroying them soon after."

I rubbed my fingertips together and marveled at what history I must have been touching. Matthaya was much deeper and more passionate than I could have imagined, but he had been forced to bottle it up inside throughout his entire love affair with Kathryn. He was devoted and faithful even though his stature in the household did not allow him to be.

A smile curled at the corner of my mouth and I reached out to caress his face. I gasped as I unwittingly painted a soft black smudge across his cheek. A faint chuckle escaped him, lightening the mood. I rested a little deeper into the mattress and made the smudge a bit lighter with a wipe of the back of my hand.

"There's more," he said, motioning again toward the box.

I shook the box delicately and the yellowed edge of a folded up note surfaced through the ash. I pinched it between my fingers and slid it from the box. It felt heavier than it should have been and there was a bulge in the center of the folds. It was so old and discolored that I feared unfolding it might damage it.

"May I?" I set the box aside and cupped the note protectively in my fingers.

"Please do." He nodded.

I used both hands to peel the folds apart. The first was the stiffest, requiring a gentle tug to separate the aged creases from one another. The second fold was easier, but my nerves caught up in my throat, as I feared tearing the letter. A few painstaking movements later, the last fold came into view. I could already make out a set of sentences exquisitely written in dark ink and the tiny bulge in the note was all I had left to reveal.

The final fold came undone and a heavy, gold ring slipped from out of the letter. A gorgeous green light shimmered across the bridge of my nose as I tilted the ring into view. It was deep antique gold, weighty and intricate. The sides of the thick band were covered in curves of elegantly carved dragons and six prongs securely held a large cushion-cut emerald in their grasp. Light glittered through the massive gemstone.

I closed my fingers around the ring.

"What is this?" I asked, feeling the cool, solid gold band press into my palm.

"Read the note and you'll understand," he said, touching my closed hand softly.

A nervous feeling coiled around my stomach as I returned my gaze to the delicately hand-written strokes of his penmanship. The faded calligraphy was still legible but aged and brownish in color.

"My light:

Forgive me for all that I have not said. There is reason behind my distance and I pray that for the sake of our love for one another, you can understand. I realize that this life has not granted us the freedom we long for, but I have found a way to change that.

It hurts me to let go of something so precious, but letting go of you would be like giving in to death himself. It is a sacrifice I have decided upon for the future of our romance as my heart cannot go on without you anymore.

I am sorry I did not share with you this secret before, but it is all I have left of who I was.

Now I am part of you, and with this, we can be free.

I will love you, always... like the sun."

The weight of his words made my heart sink. He had been so young when he had written the letter. It must have been very painful for him to keep it with him all these years.

But, what was he going to sacrifice?

And then, the coldness of the ring in my hand brought me back.

"Where did you get this?" I asked, unfolding my fingers.

"My..." He hesitated, mustering the courage to explain. "My mother..."

I gasped.

"My mother gave it to me the day I was taken away from her." Matthaya took the band from my palm. "She told me to protect it with my life. She told me it was part of who I was." He slid the ring onto his right ring finger and scowled at how loosely it fit. He moved it over to his middle finger and his lips thinned. "It was worth a fortune, even then. But it was all I had left of them—of me. And I hesitated to give it up."

He clenched his fingers.

"I could have changed things for us... I could have—"

"Matthaya." I embraced his hands with mine. "There is no use regretting the past. You can't change things now. Hating yourself over a decision you made centuries ago is pointless."

I pried his fingers from the fist they had formed and then thoughtfully polished the emerald stone with my thumb. "Be thankful you still have this. *This* is who you are. It's all we have now." My words replayed in my mind instantly and I re-peated myself. "It's all *we* have, Matthaya, of who *we* are." I smiled.

"I should have given the letter to you then," he scoffed, "but I was a coward. At least I could have left knowing I had told you the truth."

"Matthaya, I'm yours now," I said, folding the love letter back into its original shape. I tucked it carefully into the ashes and closed the box lid. He immediately went to remove the ring from his finger.

I stopped him.

"No." I set the box aside and pressed my fingers against his hand. "Keep it with you always. And stop apologizing for what you do have. I know how much you loved Kathryn then and I know how much you love me now. Stop grieving, my love."

He stood from the floor and took a seat beside me on the bed. His shy gaze came up to meet mine and his beautiful green eyes studied me intently. There must have been over a dozen soft shades of color within his eyes. They were enchanting—still.

I leaned forward to kiss his lips and our eyes closed in unison. It felt nice knowing his trust in me had grown.

"I can deal with this life," I whispered, planting a kiss against his cheek. "But I want you to help me."

He fidgeted briefly with his ring, and then nodded and took me into his arms.

"I'll stop grieving... if you do." A small breath of his tickled my ear.

I nuzzled my face against his chest and sunk deeper into

his embrace. His chin rested against the back of my head and the darkness within me began to fade. He was telling the truth.

He was... letting go of the past.

28

MATTHAYA

I SAT down at the desk and looked at the piece. It was something I hadn't seen before: a vivid, life-like expression framed by waves of glossy hair and baring a grin with exaggerated fangs. It was dark, lined heavily with thick black ink and the shadows were shaded roughly with jagged pen strokes. Her lines were clean and crisp and the coloring of the creature's crimson eyes was magnificent. She possessed so much talent with a pen.

"Well?" Kathera said in a small voice as she crept up behind me and rested her hands on my shoulders. Her half-cocked smile was hopeful and imploring.

I shuffled the drawing into a stack of others and then

fanned the entire set of pages out in front of me across the table. They were unique and new—every one of them—differing not only from one another in subject, but also in design and style from anything I had seen in her previous work. Though the colors she used were mostly shades of gray and red, there was a subtleness in the undertones which had been absent in her past work.

She was apprehensive about my opinion and her nerves perked up my senses. I knew how hard she had worked on her new drawings and it meant the world to her to know what I *really* thought. She wanted approval from me, but she wanted the truth, too, even if it broke her heart to hear it.

Truthfully, I liked them.

"I think they are beautiful," I said with a grin, spinning around in my seat to face her. Her hands lifted from me. "Well done, Kathera." I cupped the sides of her waist and tugged her closer. A smile of relief spread across her lips and she shuffled her feet a bit as I stood up and pulled her into me. She tucked her hair behind her ear—a telltale sign that she was pleased with my reply.

I had run my own fingers through her hair several times before. The dark, fiery-auburn strands were soft to the touch and framed her face perfectly. She was lovely and—in the good mood that she was *finally* in—breathtaking.

It had been many months since she had started drawing again and, at last, she had a portfolio that satisfied us both. I'd never criticized her work, but she was hard on herself, often tearing up drawings before they'd even been a moment in my sight. How very many days she must have spent huddled close to the fireplace set ablaze with "lost causes" and "soulless scraps," as she called them. They were all flawless in my eyes, just like she was.

My gaze met hers and her eyes narrowed.

"I don't know how I made it all these years without you there," I said honestly, "but I'm glad I have you now." I took her chin between my thumb and index finger and tipped her face upward. "I'll do anything for you, Kathera. *Anything*." I brushed my thumb across her lower lip.

"I know," she said. "And I think I'm ready to do this. Come with me?"

"Of course."

I had been hesitant to let her go anywhere without me after everything that had happened to us throughout the past year. During the time she had spent sharpening her skills and becoming reacquainted with her trade, the air had cleared of all the mysteries and murder scares that had happened the night everyone had gone missing.

Having both his daughter and wife vanish from his life, Kathera's father had chosen to move out of town. I had sensed her longing to try to ease his pain by showing him that she was, in fact, still alive, but I had firmly reminded her that it was not in our best interest.

Things were calm again. It was a good chance for her to get back to doing what it was she loved to do.

She fidgeted with the notch in my collar and bit her lip. "Do you think anyone from around town will remember me?"

"Perhaps." I shrugged. "But you are different now." I bared my fangs playfully and snapped them together with a smirk.

She laughed and I, too, smiled.

We had several things to do before we could re-open the shop: bills, paperwork, insurance, cleaning, only to name a few of the dozens of tasks that had to be done. I didn't know the first thing about any of it, really. Luckily, Derek had taught Kathera everything he knew about keeping a business alive and it helped us out tremendously.

I believed he would have given anything to make her happy, and teaching her everything he could may have been his way of making their future together possible. I admit, I had felt strange back when I had made the decision to buy the shop, but surely he would have wanted her to be happy—even it meant choosing to stay with me in the end.

It was hard, watching her take in all of the memories that were there at the shop—frozen in time. Nothing had been moved since the day she had disappeared.

Her fingers traced a thick line clean across the dusty front desk counter and then she wiped them off on her jeans. A few framed designs hung on the walls, as straight as the day she had left them, though I noticed she tried to straighten them further. Old habits?

She flipped the light switches on one-by-one to confirm they were all working, and then made her way to the back room.

There, she stopped and I felt a rift in her thoughts.

"What is it?" I came up beside her and looked the direction her eyes were locked. On top of the large drawing table was a thick sketchbook. The cover was made of soft, dark red, velvety fabric. It was Derek's...

The book was full of old sketches Derek had drawn and various tattoo ideas he and Kathera had collaborated on. Though she tried to hide it, I could tell Kathera secretly wanted to crack it open and stare into his imagination for a while. She probably thought it would somehow make her feel close to him again.

She missed him, even when she said she didn't. No, she hadn't really wanted to marry him and she had told me this, but it didn't stop her from feeling badly about losing him. Even I knew enough to know how much he had loved her and how, somewhere in the darkest corner of her heart, there would always be a place for him.

The past is the past, and we must move on. We have no choice.

"Kathera." I interrupted her thoughts by placing a hand onto the cover of the book. Her eyes met mine and she looked surprised.

"Yes?"

"Facing your past means coming to terms with the things you cannot change." I opened the cover and looked at the first drawing. She did the same. The page was filled with the heavy black lines of a dragon that Derek had drawn several years ago. "You have to accept our limitations... our strengths and our weaknesses, even if it means letting go." I closed the book and looked down at her solemn face. "We made a promise, Kathera. Remember?"

She nodded. "I know, but..."

"It hurts." I took her hands into mine. "It will. But you're stronger now. And so am I."

Kathera's gaze returned to the book and her hand skimmed over the cover affectionately. Her fingers lingered long enough to take in the softness of the velvet binding.

A frown threatened the edge of her lips for a fleeting moment, but she swallowed hard and sucked in the courage to fight it off. She wrapped both hands around the book and lifted it to her chest as if to embrace it briefly.

There was a stack of oversized paper sheets on the opposite side of the desk which she placed the book carefully on top of. Slowly, she folded each corner of the large sheet until the book had been neatly wrapped and protected by a layer of white. Taking up the book again, she bent down, slid a large drawer open, and then set the book down inside.

She pushed the drawer in and I felt her heart sink as the book disappeared.

I felt a sudden urge to break the awkward silence. "How long until we can open this place back up?"

She crinkled her lips to one side and raised an eyebrow. "I don't know," she answered. "I guess that depends on how long it takes to get everything cleaned and running."

I took a quick glance around the office and saw that most of the so-called mess consisted of dust and scattered paperwork. The place had been literally closed up at the drop of a hat and nothing had been moved since.

"A night or two at most," I said confidently.

"I could do it in a day," she added. "If I stayed, I could finish what we start tonight."

My stomach turned at the thought. I didn't want to leave her by herself. It was true that she could resist sunlight—Kathera had an immunity I wasn't lucky enough to have acquired—but that didn't make me feel any better about leaving her alone.

"I'll be okay," she said, tapping a finger against my shoulder. I didn't even realize I had lost myself in the thought.

I wasn't jealous of it, but the fact that the sun didn't sting her eyes as it did my skin was difficult to accept. For years, I had longed to escape the shadows of endless night, but my body had mutated in ways that only accentuated that darkness. I'd give up my wings any day to watch the sunrise again...

"Matthaya?"

I had gone silent again.

"I'm sorry," I said, shaking my head. "I was thinking."

"I promise you, I'll be fine. I can take care of myself." She grinned and crossed her arms.

She was right.

29

KATHERA

THINGS FINALLY fell into place.

I was exactly where I belonged—creating artwork, affecting people's lives, and sharing time with the one I loved.

It took awhile for Matthaya to get the hang of things. He's not exactly a "people person." Still, he did it for me. He buried his insecurities and opened up... for me.

As for me, it didn't take long to get back into the swing of things. I was drawing new ideas daily and tattooing nightly. I kept daylight hours to a minimum to keep Matthaya calm. It worked well for business.

We even discussed the option of hiring someone to help out, but eventually decided against it. After all, we made our own hours and chose our customers selectively. I didn't need help because I was doing it purely to keep myself active. Tripping over anyone else—especially a mortal—would just cause trouble and make Matthaya uncomfortable. We were happy right where we were.

At least, for a little while.

I don't know what triggered it, but soon after things had settled down... they struck me again.

The nightmares returned.

It was like cancer that had gone into remission and then returned without warning. As if dying *once* hadn't been enough, I had to relive my death as Kathryn even as I slept. I was disgusted with myself for being unable to stop them after everything Matthaya had done for me. I tried to hide them, but it was impossible. The bond had connected us so tightly that I could not censor a single thought from him.

He found out... and he found out quickly. He ignored it the first and second times, but not the third. He confronted me after work.

"It was the dream again. Wasn't it?" Matthaya said with a tightened jaw, making no attempt to hide the gruffness in his voice. "It doesn't make any sense," he growled. "There's no reason for it to haunt you still."

Maybe there was a reason, maybe there wasn't. Either way, I didn't know what was causing the flare-up of visions again, but I had to put an end to them. It was killing him inside to know that he couldn't stop the greatest pain of all from attacking me as I slept.

His expression softened and he excused himself from the room. He returned minutes later, bringing with him a pair of fluted glasses. He set them down on the table and poured a fine flame-red liquid into them. It smelled sweet and delicate, and it tasted more satisfying than the finest drink you could imagine.

It was precious, like ambrosia.

It was infant blood.

I had tasted it before, back when I had been killing for sport. It's not a taste you soon forget—or *ever forget*, for that matter. The nuances of its purity stick with you, taunting and tempting with each innocent glance a youth gives. We don't do well with children, for this reason.

It was a horrible irony, however, as Matthaya had a fondness for kids that I hadn't known about before. He and Kathryn had apparently once discussed someday having a family, but that possibility had died with their mortality.

Now, as I stared at the glass of innocence before me, I wondered where he could have gotten the blood. I even asked, but he knew well enough not to tell. After all, it didn't matter anymore, did it? The deed had been done. The life taken... or given. I shouldn't worry about the source when it weighed little next to the burden of guilt I carried because of my suicide.

Because of... Kathryn's suicide.

The final drop of blood trickled into my mouth and I licked my lips to remove every trace. "I have to go," I said. The precious young lifeblood now coursing through me made me antsy and anxious to get away from the confining walls of the shop.

With a quick puff, Matthaya blew out the candle on the table and trotted up beside me.

"What? Where are you going?"

"I need to clear my head," I replied, making the difficult decision to push him away for his own good.

"I'm coming with you." He followed me, failing to lock the shop door behind us as I left.

If being with Matthaya couldn't solve my nightmares, then maybe I needed to face them on my own. Maybe, I needed to get away from him for a little while.

I turned to him and put out a flattened hand to stop his approach.

"Let me go, Matthaya. Please."

He stopped in his tracks, appalled.

"Please, Kathera." His gentle eyes implored me to trust him—to let him ease my pain with the rapport between us.

No. Not this time.

"I'm sorry." I looked off toward the dark and empty, distant streets. "I need a little time to think. Alone."

My next step was unaccompanied by his. He knew better than to follow me when I had deliberately asked him not to. I was faster than him, and forcing himself on me would only make me push him away even more.

I wasn't exactly sure what I was going to search for out in the empty city darkness. There were few souls out at this hour and the few that were had not been the type of company

I'd keep. Streetlights dimly lit the barren pavement and only a few signs on the storefronts remained glowing along the road. Neon flashes caught my eye in the distance, but it was the part of town I did not want to be found in.

I looked both ways at an intersection and considered my options—to the left there was more street, going on seemingly forever, and to the right was the downtown business strip lined with towering company headquarters. I thought for only a moment before making my choice.

I craned my neck to look straight up at the massive series of a hundred or more glass-sided stories of the building before me. Like a shattered mirror, the building glistened, each pane of glass flickering with white moonlight. The window frames protruded from the building a few inches on each floor. They appeared to be sturdy and of a rough texture. Surely, I could have climbed up by hand, but a quick glance to the side revealed the fire escape ladder as a decent alternative. I wasn't really out to test the limits of my "immortality."

I took a deep breath, hoping to taste the origins of the breeze. Smooth. Salty. It was quiet on the roof of the skyscraper. The noise of the cars below was drowned out by the whistling wind.

I looked out over the ledge. The streetlights were flashing and the few cars that were out looked like tiny beetles scurrying through a maze of gray and yellow lines.

Everything up here was as I had expected—as if I had

known exactly how it all would look from a thousand feet above. The scene was familiar and it was as if I had done this once before in my life.

Had I?

Wait...

I remembered the second dream—the one I'd had when I was still human and staying with Derek. In it, I had been staring down off the tallest building in the city and... plotting my death. I remembered how easy I had thought it would be to just leap and fall. But then I had changed my mind and awoke from the vision with a new fear: myself.

Why did I have to pay for something I had never wanted to do? I struggled for many years of my life with the haunting memories of Kathryn killing herself—of *me* committing suicide.

Why was I *still* fighting it even after Matthaya had chosen me?

Were they connected?

I thought and thought about the two.

And the more I thought about it, the clearer things became. The puzzle pieces started coming together.

In each vision, I had been threatened by death and in only one nightmare had Matthaya actually appeared. I had reached out to him, but he hadn't reached back. I had called to him, but I had been helpless. Had he been unable to hear me? Or had he just not wanted to listen?

In the second vision, I had changed my mind, even though I had known what I had wanted to do was to escape who I was—to end it all with death. But, I had hesitated because I had wanted Matthaya to be there. I had needed him to help me. I had wanted him to take my hand and pull me from my watery grave *before* the night passed.

It never happened...

There was a shuffle in the distance. Two hands came up and over the ledge, feeling for a sturdy place to grasp. Then Matthaya vaulted onto the rooftop.

"How did you get up here so fast?" he asked, shaking the dust from his jacket and then straightening the wrinkles in his sleeves.

I shrugged. He always made things more difficult than they actually were.

"You followed me," I said as he neared.

"Kathera." He looked off into the distance as if distracted by something and fidgeted with the edges of his cuffs. "I've been thinking *a lot* about what's happened between us and there's something I need to say to you. It could put an end to all of this."

"What is it?"

"I've been thinking... about what we've been through and about what I can do to make you happy." He came closer and took my hand into his. His gaze locked with mine and his pupils grew dark and anxious. A faint spark of green light skittered through his irises as he spoke. "Deep down inside, I know there will always be a formality you will long for—something that will truly honor and justify the struggles we've faced. We need closure. The bond that we have now will never be enough for you, and it wasn't enough for Kathryn, either."

I felt his fingers tense up before he dropped to one knee in front of me.

"Matthaya?"

"Marry me," he said, making it sound more like a command than a request.

"But, how?"

"That isn't the question I'm asking you." His hands cupped mine and his grip softened with his tone. "Kathera, this may not be the life you've imagined, but I want to make the most of what we have. So I ask you this now—for all of the days we have been apart, for all of the nights we have been alone, and for every sunrise we have lost over the years... will you marry me?"

I couldn't believe my ears, though they were now hypersensitive and every word was unmistakably clear. I loved him, and my answer wouldn't be "no," but something felt out of place. Saying "yes" couldn't solve my problems. It wouldn't be that easy. The nagging feeling in my gut convinced me that it wouldn't put an end to the horrible bout of nightmares I continued to face.

I needed something else from him first. It would take more than a vow of loyalty to keep the terrors at bay. There was one more favor I *had* to ask of him. My soul yearned for closure and I had to silence it.

"I know what they mean—the nightmares," I said, backing away and sliding my fingers from his grasp.

"What?" Matthaya came to his feet.

"I understand what I have to do to make them stop." I took another step back and lifted one foot and then the other until I was standing on the ledge of the rooftop.

"I can't marry you... until you save me..."

30

MATTHAYA

BEFORE I could stop her, she lifted her arms out to the sides and fell.

I lunged for her, plummeting straight off the ledge of the building.

She gazed back as she fell ahead of me, her long ruby hair whipping wildly across her face as gravity dragged her down. Faster and faster. There was no fear in her eyes, but a silent cry for help echoed through my veins as she stretched her arms out to me.

She knew that I would come after her, even if I fell to my own death in the process. But she also knew me so much better than that.

Instinct kicked in before I had time to panic. A powerful split-second thrust of my wings sliced shreds of black fabric sheer off my back. The wings flapped open and snapped backward, immediately pressing close together to reduce wind resistance and close the gap between us as I dove after her. Kathera reached for me and I grabbed her forearms, pulling her in as swiftly and closely as I could before the concrete came into focus.

With a forceful crack against the air, I spread my wings out to slow our decent and we swerved off at an angle toward the ground. My wings wrapped tightly around us and then we crashed with a heavy thud, tumbling and sliding violently across several feet of blacktop before coming to a halt.

Everything went silent.

All I could hear was a dull ringing in my ears.

My head throbbed.

I should have broken every bone in my body from the impact. My back felt sticky and wet against the concrete street. My body was heavy, but I mustered the strength to unwrap my wings and release Kathera from my grasp. She was pressed closely against me still, her cheek against my chest and her hair plastered across my face like a web. She lifted herself from me and slowly came to her knees. Dizzy and disoriented, she brought a hand up to rub her forehead.

My body was stiff and I imagined the pain I would have experienced if I still had mortal nerves. I tipped my face to one side and then to the other to assess the damage. My left wing curled inwards slightly; the bony fingers were scratched and bloody, revealing small splashes of cartilage and shreds of peeling grayish skin. My other wing looked just as bad, but I was in one piece, more or less. Kathera appeared unharmed other than a few nicks along her elbows and forearms. Her hair was a disheveled mess.

I tried to sit up with her, but something stopped me. My right shoulder felt awkward and stagnant and an attempt to roll it back produced no response. It had been dislocated in the fall.

"Oh, Matthaya." Kathera gazed with widened eyes at my unresponsive limb and stretched her fingers out to touch the ridge of my shoulder. "Is there anything I can do?"

Many years ago, I had had a similar injury. It was no more pleasant then, either, but I had managed.

"I can handle this," I said, my other hand lifting in response. My badly scathed wings pressed into the concrete and raised me up to a sitting position. Kathera stood and backed away a few feet to give me space.

From there, the wing on my injured side bent back as if ready to return to its place near my spine, but instead snapped forward with a swift flap. Kathera cringed. The loud popping sound indicated that my arm had been set correctly.

My wings had a mind of their own sometimes, and the fluidity of their connection with the rest of my body amazed even me.

"Are you ok?" she uttered beneath her breath. She came closer and lent her arms to help me to my feet.

I was quite shaken; as my equilibrium reset, our

surroundings took a moment to come into focus.

"Your face," she said, tracing her fingers across my cheek and revealing the blood that stained them.

"I'll be fine," I replied with assurance, rotating my shoulder inwards and then back down, testing its condition. It would take time for everything to heal, but that wasn't a concern of mine anymore. "Kathera? Are you..."

She smiled at the sound of her name and brought her hands up to cup my face.

"Yes," she whispered with a nod. "Thank you." Her eyes traced the edge of my open wings.

I stretched my arms out behind me, flexed my hands, and felt the forearms of my wings crackle slightly as the fingers and pleats collapsed into each other. The limited mobility caused by my injuries made it difficult to fold my wings back into their place. It was possible I'd have to wait awhile for them to heal. I could handle a lot of trauma, but my body hadn't really evolved to withstand reckless dives off high-rise buildings.

I should have been angry, but the truth was, I knew why she had done it—she needed closure, even if it wasn't the kind I was offering.

And it had worked.

I instantly felt the burden of her fear and pain lifting. The horror that spawned from the doubts she had secretly held about me had been silenced. I had saved her from the one person she feared most—herself. And with Kathryn's insecurities put to rest, Kathera would be free.

"I'm sorry it had to happen this way," she said, smoothing

her hand over her hair and down the back of her neck. She pinched a stray lock from across her cheek and brought it behind her ear. "Things will be better from now on."

"Good," I said with a faint scoff, "because there is no way I'm doing that again." I rubbed my palm over a raw patch of skin on my shoulder.

Thank God I couldn't feel pain.

She chuckled, her eyes narrowed, and she revealed her teeth with an honest smile.

"I'll never ask you to." She grinned; her pointed incisors glimmered beneath the streetlights.

I cocked an eyebrow and shrugged. "You didn't exactly ask this time, either."

"Sorry..." She looked down sheepishly.

"But you know I would do it again if you needed me to." My fingers forked through her hair. "I didn't bring you this far to let a few bad dreams get in the way." I clawed at the base of her neck playfully and then tugged her closer.

Unprepared to move, she stumbled into me. She scrambled to grab what was left of my collar and I cupped my arms around her before she lost her balance. There was a tiny splash of blood across her forehead. It was likely mine.

"We should get cleaned up," I suggested, still feeling the wet blood on my back. A breeze rushed past and I flinched. The smell of our wounds was more an annoyance than a concern.

I twitched and her hands released me.

An abrupt snapping sound was my left wing folding up

and against the back of my ribcage while snapping into its place, flush between my shoulder blades. The right wing struggled to do the same and took a moment longer to collapse into place. The two of them clipped together below the base of my neck, and with the both of my wings healed, I immediately felt stronger.

31

KATHERA

WHETHER I would have tolerated the pain of it or whether it would have bothered me at all when I had been human, I'd never know, but the design was finished, and it was there to stay. I rolled my hand over and admired my workmanship: the fine lines and intertwining vines, the tiny diamond-shaped accents, and the way it belonged there—on my left ring finger.

Matthaya's left hand hovered over my own and then he lowered it to slide his fingers between mine, curling them in and grasping me tightly. I had done a good job making them identical and I was proud of my abilities. We shared the same design on the same hand. It was a ring that could endure forever. It would never break. It could never be lost, damaged, or stolen from us. And now I had something I truly *did* want to keep with me always.

"Are you happy?" he asked. His voice was wonderfully soothing.

"What do you mean?"

"Are you happy, Kathera?" His fingers tightened around mine. "With me?" The hauntingly beautiful green of his eyes reflected the fluorescent lights as he spoke. I was captivated by their color... as always.

"Was I happy?" he had asked.

Matthaya always needed to be sure he was doing the right thing, and I wondered how long it would take him to believe the truth. Although he hated himself for the sins he had once committed, it had been a necessary evil to become the man I had married. I have never regretted nor grieved over his actions toward me.

"Yes. I'm happy with you, Matthaya," I said. My other hand rose and I tangled the cross pendant around my knuckles. "I've *always* been happy with you."

I could have sworn I heard him sigh as a tiny smile of relief formed on one side of his mouth. He released my fingers and dragged his fingertips across my tattoo.

There was a faint jingle of bells against glass, followed by a reserved patter of footsteps and then complete silence. My head turned at the sound of the front door swinging closed.

I ignored them for a moment, but then the visitor's scent crashed into me like an avalanche and the familiarity of it left me paralyzed with fear.

Derek!?

I knew that smell and I knew it well.

But he was dead... Derek was dead. I had seen him die. I had watched Ve'tani tear him open. The scent was undeniably his, but something about it was... feminine. Subdued.

Matthaya, in the meantime, didn't react while he sat across from me, and I was relieved to know he hadn't recognized the scent just yet.

I gathered my senses, swallowed my apprehension, and then headed into the waiting room. There stood a small woman, no more than five-foot-two or three, maybe, and she was studying one of the framed pieces of artwork hanging on the wall. Her fingers rested against the glass and she gazed longingly at the drawing.

She looked to be in her fifties, her hair was brownish-blond with stray strands of white showing here and there, and her face appeared weathered and fatigued. She wore little make-up, had thin, faded-pink lips, and was dressed somewhat plainly in crisp, clean, neutral-colored clothing and a matching brown sweater.

"Can I help you?" I asked, poking my head out of the back and taking a step closer to the strange-smelling woman. She was surprised by my entrance and tore away from the image to look at me.

"Yes," she said with a crack in her voice. Her hands trembled, but she clasped her fingers together to try to hide it from me. "This is a nice shop you have." Her heartbeat quickened as she nervously glanced around the room as if in search of something.

"Thank you," I replied softly. She looked so timid that I was sure that any other tone would have sent her scurrying away.

"My..." She cleared her throat. "M-My name is Valerie Thompson. I'm..." She stammered as the words caught in her throat and she took a quivering breath.

She looked up at me as I came closer and I recognized the deep brown color of her eyes.

"I'm..." she tried again, still fighting to get out what she needed to say.

"I know who you are," I interrupted, saving her the trouble.

Derek's mother.

When I looked into her eyes, it was as if I could see him again. They were plainly inherited from her and it was eerie how alike they were in depth and color. It was uncanny.

"Please wait here," I requested, motioning for her to take a seat on the soft bench just to her left. She nodded and then slowly shuffled across the room to sit down. Her heart still beat like a frightened animal's and I struggled to keep the amplified pounding from driving me senseless.

"Who is it?" Matthaya was about to stand from his seat.

I was focused on the presence of Derek's mother and didn't reply.

"Kathera?" He pulled out his chair.

"No." I gestured for him to stay where he was and bent down to pull the lowest desk drawer open. It caught in the track and I jerked it hard.

"Do... do you need help?" Matthaya asked. "Kathera?"

The drawer popped open and slid off the hinge, taking part of the railing with it. I'd forgotten my strength.

Inside was the book I had covered in white paper; looking completely undisturbed from the moment I'd placed it there. I wrapped both hands around it and stood. Matthaya's brow furrowed, but he didn't ask me anything else.

I took a step closer to the waiting room and then stopped. My grip tightened on the book and I hesitated to move farther.

A brief peek out into the hallway confirmed that she was still there, waiting anxiously for my return. I turned and set the book down on the nearby table. I unwrapped it swiftly but gently and flipped it open. I knew what page I was looking for.

A quick tug and the page came out. I slid it from the book and set it face down on the desk. My ink signature still bled through the page and haunted me even from behind. I didn't have time to think about it as I rewrapped the book.

After a silent goodbye to its soft, red velvet cover, I walked back into the lobby. Derek's mother had lost herself in thought and I tried my best not to frighten her as I lowered the book down toward her lap.

"This was his," I whispered, opening my fingers slightly so she could take the book from them. "I want you to have it."

Her short, shallow breaths were laced with fear, so I took a seat beside her and passed the book off into her hands. She began unfolding the white paper, lowering one side and then the other side of the wrappings across her lap, until the contents were exposed. The red darkened as she caressed the velvet in one direction and then it lightened slightly as her hand stroked the other way.

She lifted the cover open and tipped her head to study the design on the first page. It was one of Derek's more reserved sketches—probably one of the first ones he had created for a client. Still, there was no denying the strength and ferocity in the line work of the beautiful Chinese fire dragon. The next page revealed a comparable beast, similar in color but with the shape of a more traditionally styled European dragon. Its eyes were accented by furrowing brows of green thorns, and a pair of silvery wings graced its back.

She turned the page again.

And again.

Her heartbeat calmed and an affectionate sigh wafted from her lips.

"Michael was always such a good artist. But I had no idea he could do all of this."

Michael? I was sure that's what she had called him. "I'm sorry. Did you say his name was Michael?"

"Yes." She glanced up at me with a confused look bending her lips.

"I always knew him as Derek," I said.

She gasped and brought her hands up to cup her mouth. The book clapped closed in her lap.

I touched her shoulder in comfort and leaned a little closer to her. "Are you okay? I'm sorry if I said something wrong, but—"

"Michael was his middle name," she clarified, her eyes sparkling with the threat of tears. She smiled. "Once he had started high school, he wouldn't let anyone call him by his first name anymore. It was like he had become someone else."

I had never even known that Derek had had a middle name. The fact that he had let me call him a name he hadn't even allowed his own mother to use made me grateful.

"Derek was a good man," I assured her, pressing my fingertips gently against her shoulder. I wanted to console her and tell her how much he had meant to me, but it felt awkward. Part of me wanted her to know the girl her son had asked to marry him, and the other part of me knew it was better off a secret. "As long as I knew him, he was kind and caring. You would have been proud of what he did to better himself."

"I am." Her voice broke with a sniffle and she wiped tears from her cheeks. "I am." Her body trembled and short breaths caught in her throat. I pushed discretion aside, pulled Valerie closer and embraced her. The feeling of her crumpled up against me, her tears saturating my shoulders and her hair tickling my neck, reminded me of not only him, but of my own mother. I imagined myself fighting back a well of tears in my own eyes, but they never came.

No heartbeat. No tears.

"Kathera?" Matthaya stepped out of the back room and took quiet steps toward us. He tilted his head, observed for a moment, and then his eyes grew wide and his jaw eased open. He, too, recognized the woman's scent.

Valerie's face lifted from my shoulder and she took a quick breath.

Matthaya sensed her anxiety, so he softened his entrance the only way he knew how.

"I'm Matthaya," he said, in a tone even gentler than his usual, coming closer and bending at the waist to better level with her worried gaze. He was trying very hard not to intimidate her and offered a hand out toward her with a sincere and inviting smile.

She seemed taken aback at first, a little surprised to see him there, but she soon shook his hand and introduced herself in return.

"Did you know him, too?" she asked. There was hope in her eyes.

"Yes." Matthaya nodded. "And I'm sorry for your loss, but you should rest soundly, knowing Derek did good things with the time he had."

Valerie coughed from her congestion and Matthaya reached across the front desk for a tissue.

"Thank you," she wheezed, taking the tissue from him and using it to wipe her eyes and nose. "I must seem like a basket case right now." She tried to laugh but couldn't.

"No." Matthaya shook his head. "Losing someone you love is *never* easy."

Her face rose up from the shadows to look him in the eye and her slumped shoulders straightened. There was something unusual about the way Matthaya's vivid green irises comforted Valerie with their empathy.

"You must be strong," he added. "You have to move on with your life. He would have wanted you to." A nudge of his fingers against the velvet book sent her eyes back down to its cover.

I slid a hand across her shoulder and patted her lightly on the back.

"You're always welcome here, Ms. Thompson."

And I meant it.

32

MATTHAYA

SHE STOOD from the bench and heaved a sigh. Her thin, pale fingers held the book protectively, hugging it close to her chest like the treasure it was to her. I walked her to the front door and held it open for her to exit the shop.

As she scuttled past, I felt the irony of the situation, and a quiver shot down my spine. The similarities of their scents made me uneasy and flooded my brain with memories of Derek's tragic end. His mother, however, held no foul opinions of me, nor did she know how much Derek had loved Kathera... and despised me.

"Matthaya?" Valerie paused a few feet from outside the door and turned. "Who was it?" she asked quietly. "The one you lost?"

It wasn't a question I had wanted to answer. And it wasn't a wound I felt like tearing open again, but her lonely brown eyes yearned for someone to relate to.

For the night, that someone was me.

"My mother."

"Oh, I'm sorry," she said, lowering her head in sympathy.

Kathera came up beside me and wrapped both of her hands around one of my arms.

"Thank you for everything," Valerie added, looking back up at us. A grin spread across her lips and she gestured to the book. "Thank you so very, *very* much."

"Have a good night," said Kathera.

Derek's mother returned to her car and drove down the street until she was nothing more than a tiny pair of red lights in the darkness, which soon faded away.

I felt pressure on my arm as Kathera lured me back into the shop. She locked the door behind us, flipped off the lights, and then pulled the shades down across the windows.

"That was a brave thing you did," she said, "facing your fears and swallowing your pride to make Derek's mother happy."

I hadn't really done it only for that reason.

"He meant a lot to you, Kathera," I reminded her. "Just because *we* didn't get along doesn't make me appreciate him any less for how much he cared about you. His mother deserved to know him for who he was *before* I came along."

"Yes, you're right." She headed into the back room and I

noticed her eyes dart briefly to the sheet of paper she had torn from the book. It was still face down, just as she'd left it. I'd had enough honor to know that she had turned it that way for a reason. Even if she had secrets still, I was willing to wait for them to be shared of her own accord.

After all, it wouldn't be the first thing she'd kept from me. A lot had happened after I'd left her alone with Derek. Some things she had told me and some she hadn't. But that's the process we all go through in our relationships. It is the disclosure of our weaknesses, our regrets, and our most coveted secrets that strengthen the trust formed by love.

Kathera switched on the radio and plopped down onto the brown suede couch that was pushed up against the wall. She liked sinking into that couch... and she liked music just as much. More so now that her ears had become especially tuned to its nuances.

We don't really think about it, but we hear a thousand sounds every day. Some of them stand out more than others. Music was one of the few things I'd never really been able to ignore. My overly sensitive hearing had made it difficult to tolerate at first—the bass, especially, had tingled my ears and irritated my senses, but I eventually learned to phase it out. I knew by now that she only listened when she wanted to clear her head of something else, and her comfort meant more to me than my own.

She bit her lip and stared off into the empty hall, tapping her fingernails repeatedly against the arm of the couch. I sat down beside her and nuzzled up against her shoulder.

"Are you alright?" I set my hand onto her thigh and walked my fingers down to her knee, massaging them against her leg along the way.

"Yes," she replied, still fixated on nothing.

She was thinking about her mother and missing her more than ever. Seeing Valerie had unearthed old memories, leaving us unsettled about our pasts.

I had been given up, had fallen in love with Kathryn, had been separated from her, and now I was with her in the form of Kathera. It was a type of closure, but I had never really known who *I* was. I had never really known who to miss in my life, and that emptiness had left me feeling transparent.

The tattoo ring around the base of my left ring finger was new and exciting for me. Now I had something and someone to make me visible again.

Ve'tani's chains had been broken by a love that had traversed centuries. But it had not been without the deepest sacrifice that I acquired that devotion. Kathera was pure of heart, and even with the hell of being tempted toward suicide conquered, she was still not without her own demons. Like cancer, they thrive on regret and sadness and will likely surface again in time. They will be a challenge I will face by her side, for we will always harbor our tragedies... and our darkness.

Thank you for reading!

If you enjoyed this story, please support the author's
writing journey by posting a review on Amazon
or social media. Share your thoughts with friends,
other readers, and book clubs.

More books at:
PANASTASIA.COM

What doesn't kill you makes you a hell of a lot stronger. A beast lurks in Kathera's mind, shredding her sanity until all that remains hangs by a fragile thread. While the line between fiction and reality blurs, a moral dilemma keeps her from fighting back. Can she find the answer without losing herself in the process, or will there be more blood on her hands?

With burdens too grave to bear, Kathera and Matthaya must grapple vengeful ghosts from their pasts and lay their demons to rest. But you can't bury your mistakes. Nor can you escape them…

Order *Grave Burden* Today!

Grab The Special Edition Hardcover Containing Exclusive Illustrations!

AVAILABLE AT MOST ONLINE RETAILERS
PLEASE INQUIRE AT YOUR LOCAL BOOKSTORE

Dark Diary Hardcover ISBN: 978-0-9974485-1-1

More from P. Anastasia:

Fates Aflame & Fates Awoken
Adventure that will lift your spirits and
romance to warm your heart

Magical journeys await you in this clean
epic sci-fi fantasy. With newfound powers
at hand and a dragon by her side, Lt.
Hawksford, star student of a prestigious
military academy, must face trial by fire.

Exile of the Sky God
"An effortlessly grand fantasy..." — Kirkus Reviews.

An adaptation of the lore behind the Sky God,
Horus, one of the most powerful gods in
ancient history. Embark on a mythical expedition
of self discovery with extraordinary revelations.

Fluorescence: The Complete Tetralogy
An infectious saga read across the world

Alice was a normal teenager until a dying race
of aliens chose her to preserve their bioluminescent
DNA. Fluorescence evolves from quiet
beginnings into a gripping tale exploring the
real-life dangers faced while harboring a
volatile secret.

The series includes:
Book 1: Fire Starter
Book 2: Contagious
Book 3: Fallout
Book 4: Lost Souls